About the Author

Meikko is a California born and raised writer and English teacher. She completed her MFA at Mills College in 2019 and contributed to the literary magazine *34th Parallel*. She loves to write characters who deal with conflicting desires, self-identity, and whatever else the world can throw at them. When she is not writing with her dog Cho at her feet, Meikko loves to tackle DIY projects, cook vegan recipes, binge read a juicy novel, and travel the world.

Situationship

Meikko Sheiree

Situationship

Olympia Publishers
London

www.olympiapublishers.com
OLYMPIA PAPERBACK EDITION

Copyright © Meikko Sheiree 2023

The right of Meikko Sheiree to be identified as author of
this work has been asserted in accordance with sections 77 and 78 of
the Copyright, Designs and Patents Act 1988.

All Rights Reserved

No reproduction, copy or transmission of this publication
may be made without written permission.
No paragraph of this publication may be reproduced,
copied or transmitted save with the written permission of the publisher,
or in accordance with the provisions
of the Copyright Act 1956 (as amended).

Any person who commits any unauthorised act in relation to
this publication may be liable to criminal
prosecution and civil claims for damage.

A CIP catalogue record for this title is
available from the British Library.

ISBN: 978-1-80439-606-3

This is a work of fiction.
Names, characters, places and incidents originate from the writer's
imagination. Any resemblance to actual persons, living or dead, is
purely coincidental.

First Published in 2023

**Olympia Publishers
Tallis House
2 Tallis Street
London
EC4Y 0AB**

Printed in Great Britain

Dedication

To mom: thank you for being my best friend.

Acknowledgements

A huge thank you to Oliver and Gwen for always encouraging me in the ever-humbling process that is being a writer. I appreciate you two more than you could ever know. Thank you to my Mills writing family, and my poet friends Mimi Tempestt and Darius Simpson, for being such inspiring and motivating figures in my life. You pushed me to grow in my presence as an artist and I will always be grateful for Mills bringing us together. Last and most definitely not least, thank you to my mother, Kolby, Sidney and Spencer for always being my number one in everything. You all have cheered me on to be anything that I want to be, and I am so honored to have the privilege of loving you. Thank you for always believing in me and never leaving me to do this alone.

Nayelli

"Hey mom." I drop my bags on the wooden steps inside my grandmother's entryway and embrace my mother before doing anything else. She smells of citrus soap and clean laundry and I find the familiar scent of her relaxing my too stiff shoulders away from my ears.

"It's so nice to see you pumpkin," she says, giving me a kiss on my cheek and grabbing one of the many bags of dirty clothes. Her midnight black curls are tied atop her head with a black bandana and she's wearing her black workout pants and old white tee that she reserves for around the house.

My mom walks down the narrow hallway to the guest room and I follow behind her. Setting my things near the door, she turns and gently cups my face.

"You look tired. Would you like some of my world-famous coffee?"

"Yes, please. I'm dying," I say and let my shoulders sag even further. I missed her so much.

"You got it." She steps around me and crosses the hall to the kitchen. I sit at the large round table in the even larger chair and watch her move around the kitchen.

"Where's grandma?" I ask, pulling my knees to my chest and tucking my toes into the cushion of the seat.

"She's at some event with your Aunt Stacey I think," she responds without looking away from the coffee machine.

Within minutes, she hands me a burnt-orange ceramic mug

that smells of hazelnut with traces of cocoa. I sniff deeply of the contents and my insides do a happy dance. She pours herself a cup and sits at the table to my right.

"So," she begins, blowing on her coffee before taking a sip, "you've decided to live my dream, huh?" Her brow arches over her mug.

"What do you mean?" I ask, my own brows knitting together.

"You're going to London! That's all I've ever wanted to do, you *had* to have known that. I've been talking about enjoying tea and biscuits in a cute, windowed cafe for years." She sighs into her coffee cup and stares into the distance, imagining every detail of the fantasy. "One day," she eventually says, "Anyhow, are you excited? You're leaving the day after tomorrow right? The twenty-third?"

"That's right," I grin wide. Butterflies tickle my insides at the mention of my big winter break trip. It's my first ever trip abroad, and I'm equal parts nerves and excitement.

Her sharp gaze narrows on me and she stares scrutinizingly at my face before saying, "You're gonna meet someone."

"Excuse me?" I almost lose my mouthful of coffee. Where in the hell did that come from?

"You heard me," my mom replies, doubling down. "You're going to meet a guy on your trip, I can feel it." Her smile is mischievous and every bit of the Cheshire Cat right now.

"Mmm," is all I respond. She's been predicting my love life for as long as I can remember, and although I know she only wants the best for me it can be a little much.

Like right now, when she's going on about how I'm overdue for an epic love since my last relationship ended so disastrously. I half listen, half stare into my mug as she continues on with how she has a feeling something and *someone* exciting is waiting for me once I get to London. Yeah, right. If there's one thing college has taught me about men, it's that there are more Johnny Bravo's trying to *Hey pretty mama* their way into your pants than there are Mr. Darcy's bursting at the seams with an all-consuming love for you. And the first just isn't all that exciting to me. Been there, and absolutely hated it.

My mom pauses her sentence, cuing into the fact that I haven't been listening for a while. "I know," she says, her voice perking up. "Since you're missing the holidays this year, how about we have a girl's day with just you and me? I'll do your hair and paint your toes and then we can go have dinner somewhere nice. How does that sound?"

Joy sparkles in her deep brown eyes and it is wonderfully infectious. "Sounds good to me," I say, meeting her smile with one of my own.

"All right then, just let me finish my coffee first because I'm going to need some *strength*." She attempts to run her fingers through my curls but they get stuck. "Jesus be with me," she mutters.

"Mom!" I exclaim, swatting her hand away.

"What?" she asks, shrugging her shoulders. "I'm gonna need all the help I can get."

While I gather the supplies, my mom scrubs the kitchen and bleaches the sink clean. Long gone are the days that I am able to lay on the counter and tilt my head back into the sink. So I stand — bending my neck down and leaning over the sink's ledge — risking a crook in my neck and early arthritis no doubt.

I keep the towel close to my eyes as my mom lathers and conditions my hair. Warm nostalgic memories from my childhood flood through and comfort me. Getting ready for special functions and occasions that called for doing my and my sister's hair were always so much fun to us. My mom spent her younger years as a hairstylist, and we always felt like we went through some kind of fairy princess transformation by the time she was done. But she made us feel that way over everything she did for us, that was just the magic that came with my mom.

She finishes the washing phase and grabs a chair that she sits next to the stove. I sit down while she digs in her large purple bag sitting atop the granite counter. From it, she pulls out a Yellow Bird hair dryer that she's had for the past ten years and begins phase two.

We don't say much, as the dryer is too loud for conversation and by the time she reaches for the hot comb she's too focused on finishing. From beginning to end, the process takes close to two hours. To call it a labor of love is an extreme understatement, especially since my straightened hair is close to touching my butt these days.

"Whew!" my mom says, putting her tools back into her bag. "All I can say is you're lucky I don't charge my children."

Pins and needles prickle my entire backside as I stand and stretch my legs. "I think my butt fell asleep."

"I wouldn't be surprised, I can't get through your hair as fast as I used to," she says, running her fingers through my hair once more. She grabs a piece and traces it down my back to where it stops at the tip of my lower back. "Girl, that's a damn shame," she laughs. "I used to have hair like this you know, until I got pregnant with you, that is. When you came along, you plucked me bald." She covers her mouth and theatrically shakes her head like she's about to cry.

"And you complain that I'm too dramatic?" I ask, arching my brow.

She chuckles at her own joke and taps me lightly on the hip. "Come on, let's get your toes out the way so we can get out of here."

We arrive at *Wasabi Off The Hook* an hour later and are seated immediately.

"What can I get you ladies tonight?" the waitress asks.

"I'll have the Cowboy and a water, please. And a plain iced tea." I close the menu and look at my mom.

"And what about you, ma'am?"

"Hmm," my mom says, deeply contemplating the menu. "What's your name?" She looks up and waits for a response.

"Alexandria," she answers, pointing to her name tag.

"Oh, that's such a pretty name. And it's so fitting, you are *gorgeous*."

"Aww, thank you." The girl blushes and fidgets with her all-black uniform, nervous at being put on the spot. I swear my mom can't go one day in public without striking up a conversation or complimenting a random stranger.

"No, I mean it. You look like you'd grace the cover of Vogue or somewhere like that." At this the girl laughs and shakes her head no. "Own it, girl. I'm sure you get that all the time. But anyways, I don't want to keep you waiting, I just had to let you know. So Alexandria, which roll is your favorite?"

"The same thing your daughter got, the Cowboy," she answers, smiling.

"We always get that." My mom looks down at the menu once more. "You can never go wrong with a favorite though; I'll have that as well. And some fireball."

"*Fireball*, mom?" I ask.

"Stay in a kids place and mind your business," she says, closing her menu.

Alexandria laughs and grabs our menus. "I'll be right back with those drinks ladies," she says and disappears to another table.

"It's pretty dead for it to be a Friday, huh?" my mom asks, surveying the restaurant.

"Yeah, it kind of is." I join her in looking around. I haven't been here since I left for college almost three years ago, but everything looks the same as it did in high school. The bamboo plants and burgundy walls are still accompanied by all black décor — booths, tables, chairs, napkins, chopsticks, the uniforms, you name it — and the sushi chefs behind the glass counter still yell "Wasab!" every time someone enters. Even after trying several of the "best" places in Santa Barbara, Wasabi is still my favorite sushi place by a mile.

Since there's not too many people, we get our food immediately. The mountain of seafood and tempura in front of me makes my mouth water. Dear god, did I mention how much I love sushi?

"This was a great idea," I say, beaming at my mom.

"It really was, pumpkin. Cheers." We clink glasses and dive in.

We eat and talk about everything.

"How many girls are you living with again?" my mom asks.

"Three, not including myself."

"I haven't heard you complain about them in a while. Does that mean things are getting better?"

Guilt and sadness flood my face, making my cheeks and neck far too warm for my turtleneck. I pull at the collar to air it out before meeting her gaze.

"It's worse," I mumble.

"Worse? How?" Her face is stern and in every bit of

protective mama bear mode.

"Well..." I glance around the room at everything but her face. I set my chopsticks down, not interested in my tempura any more. "There's been a little bit of a situation. I'm handling it, but it's becoming way more dramatic than it needs to be."

"What situation? And with who?" she says, setting her own chopsticks down and tucking her hand underneath her chin.

"Around two weeks ago, I noticed there was some money missing from my account. I called the bank to see what was going on and there was an extra rent check to our landlord that had been signed by Sofia, the one I share a room with."

"What?" she shrieks, her tone full of disbelief. "The bank processed one of *your* checks signed by someone else?"

"Apparently."

"Well, did you report it as fraud?"

"No, I texted Sofia and told her about it. I figured it might've been an accident." I shrug and take a sip of water.

"Trust me, that was no accident. It wouldn't even make sense."

"I know," I shrug again, "but I was trying to give her the benefit of the doubt. But things have been weird ever since. She asked me if the check bounced, I said no. Then she said she mixed our checkbooks up when she was cleaning and that she'd send the money right away. But now it's been weeks and her story keeps changing and she still hasn't paid me back."

"Hm," my mother leans back against the firm black booth, her eyes shrinking down to calculating slits. "I'll handle this."

"How?" I ask, leaning back against my own chair.

"Just trust me, I got it. Give me her number and I'll take care of the rest."

I do as she asks and shortly after the night resumes its lighter cadence. Our conversation shifts to more mundane things like how my grandma and papa can't seem to get their shit together even after almost fifty years; and how proud of me she is for doing what she never did — go to college and on track to finish — even though it may seem like I'm having a shitty time right now.

Her last admission makes me feel warm and soothed in a way only she can. Coming home to spend time with my mom feels like recharging my battery. She gives me just enough juice and motivational talks to keep going through all of the shit. I honestly don't know how I would survive this hellscape without her. It's also why I don't have it in me to tell her to stop talking to me about my dating life. It would hurt her feelings and I can't bring myself to do that after all she's done for me.

"Thank you," I tell her, squeezing her forearm.

"For what?" she pauses around her bite of sushi.

"Being my mom. I… feel a lot better."

"You make it easy being your mom, pumpkin," she responds, squeezing my arm back. "I am so inspired by you. You'll come out of this stronger than ever. And you may not see it now, but you'll look back on this time and laugh. I could tell how down you were when you showed up, stop letting those people get to you. They don't deserve your energy."

"You're right," I agree, and sip on my water thinking about all that she's said.

"Hey Nayelli. Hi Ms G."

At the sound of the familiar voice, I choke on my drink. It burns my esophagus on its way down and I fight back the urge to cough. I peek across the table at my mom and see murder in her eyes.

No, murder might be too kind. In her eyes I see mutilation

and torture — and the medieval kind at that.

I take it upon myself to respond since it's obvious my mom has no intentions of speaking.

"Uh, hey Will. What are you doing here?" I ask, keeping my voice calm and controlled — or at least as calm and controlled as one can when running into their cheating high school ex.

"Oh, you know," he responds, shrugging, "same thing as you guys."

"Awesome, well you enjoy the rest of your evening." I dismiss him quickly with a forced smile, but it comes off as a grimace. The way he acts as if nothing has passed between us is astounding. Especially since I'm pretty sure he's put it together by now that I've blocked him on all socials.

"Yeah, you too. I'll see you around," he says with another smile, and vanishes back to whatever dark corner he emerged from.

"Did you *see* him?" my mother asks.

"I was trying very hard not to," I respond, resuming a slow slip of water.

"I mean the *nerve*! To just walk up to you like he didn't disrespect you — publicly, might I add — in every way imaginable! He's lucky I don't feel like going to jail tonight. And why in the *hell* is he wearing gummy bear earrings? He's on drugs, Nayelli! I know drug users when I see them!"

"*Mom,*" I whisper, hoping she'll catch a hint.

"What!" she yells, obviously still worked up.

"People will *hear* you," I whisper again. "You're causing a scene!"

"Nayelli, who cares? I'll shout from the top of the bar if I want to. Will has got the *wrong* one. I do not play when it comes to my kids."

I flag down the nearest waitress. "Excuse me, can we get our check please? Thank you." The best option is to leave before things escalate further, as there is no hope in calming my mom down while she and Will are still in the same vicinity.

Once back at the house my mom walks straight to her room, complaining of a need to rest after letting an idiot like Will run her blood pressure up.

I head to the guest room to change into a pair of joggers and a cropped tee before plopping on the living room couch. The chocolate leather sighs in unison with me as I sink deep into its cushions. What a damn night.

The TV across the room blares a local newscaster's announcement of tonight's topics for the ten o'clock news. Mostly death, fear, and depressing events that I have no control over. I hate watching the news, always have. But it's all my grandma ever watches — well, that and her soaps. My mom says that she's convinced my grandmother thinks she's the real-life Vicky Newman, and honestly I have to agree.

Slippered footsteps shuffle down the hallway towards the kitchen. "Oh, I thought that was you," my grandma says, crossing into the kitchen. "Hey Elli," she smiles.

"Hey, grandma. How are you doing?" I twist my body on the couch so I'm facing the kitchen. She's wearing one of her notorious matching PJ sets. This one is a lavender wide-strap tank with coordinating lavender and sage plaid pants.

"Oh, just the same old stuff. You know how it goes." A deep sigh escapes her as she sits down at the table. It's no secret that my sixty-five year-old grandmother is tired. Tired of running her daycare, tired of being the matriarch of the family that gives more than she receives, tired of her husband that only ever cares about himself. The whole point of my mom moving in was to help ease her responsibilities, but it doesn't seem to make much of a difference to my grandmother's fatigued spirit.

"Where's Papa?" I ask. I haven't seen him once since I got here, even though that might be my own fault since I avoid him as much as possible. We don't have a relationship outside of *hi* and *bye* due to equal parts of him blurting something offensive when he sees me and the fact that his breath stinks. Once when I was eight he took out a measuring tape during family dinner, put it around my arm, then laughed and said my arms were bigger than his and that I should probably slow down on the food.

I guess you could say some wounds never heal.

"Gone to bed, *thankfully*." My grandma laughs.

I sometimes wonder if it's the time spent with one another that keeps them under the same roof. They haven't shared a room or a kiss in over ten years, yet they still hold on to the titles of husband and wife. I don't visit my grandparents often, but every time I do I pray like hell I'm never cursed with the same fate.

"Nayelli?" My grandma's voice breaks through my internal reverie.

"Hmm?"

"Would you mind helping me roll my hair?" she asks, patting her decades old canvas bag full of pink and green hair rollers.

"Sure," I nod, prying my body from between the cushions and joining her at the table.

I grab the small black comb and begin parting my grandmother's hair in the way she taught me how to all those years ago. Whether it's one of her daughters or granddaughters, my grandma always has someone else rolling her hair at night. It makes me chuckle because I wonder what she does when no one is available.

"Are you enjoying yourself in Santa Barbara, Elli?"

I pause and think seriously about her question. "No," I reply, and continue rolling her honey blonde hair into place. "Did Nia give you highlights?" I ask, the new light blonde streaks are subtle but noticeable. My grandma has been going to the same stylist for as long as I can remember and she always makes her look vibrant and gorgeous and much younger than her sixty-odd years.

"Yeah, do you like it? She told me she was going to take me a little lighter because it would look good with my complexion," she explains, patting the unrolled side of her hair.

"I love it, it's perfect. You look hot grandma," I say, smiling. And it's true, the color brings out the golden undertones of her tawny skin.

"Oh, stop it girl." She laughs to herself like a young child. Compliments are the way to my grandmother's heart. And according to my mom, they always have been. "So tell me, why are you not liking it there?"

"Umm," I take a deep breath to think. "The list is too long, if I'm being honest. But I guess the main thing is that every single person I've met there just seems… fake. Always pretending to be someone else — someone decent — when I meet them and then I find out later that they're god-awfully horrible human beings. Some of the worst people I've ever met, actually. And it just seems to be like that across the whole entire town." College is different from high school — in a lot of ways, obviously — but at least in high school either someone liked me or they didn't. No one spent time getting to know me or being my friend just to turn around and hurt me once my guard was down. It's why I keep mostly to myself in SB. I don't think I can take being let down by anyone else there.

"Mm," my grandma responds after a long moment. "You're almost done there though, right? You graduate soon?"

"One more year," I say, my tone deflating at the prospect of over three hundred and sixty-five more days in that place.

"Oh, well then you're fine!" she says. Unless you are dying, things never seem that bad to my grandma.

"I guess," I grumble. I finish with the last roller and give her a pat on the shoulder. "All done."

"Thank you, Elli. I really appreciate it,' she says, smiling at me in thanks. She stands, grabbing her hair things, then gives me a hug. She's almost six feet tall, so she has to bend down to give my five-foot-four self a hug. "Goodnight babe, I love you. I'll see you in the morning, okay? I'm really glad you came, it's so nice to see your pretty face," she says, holding me in her arms.

"I love you too. See you in the morning, goodnight grandma." I give her a kiss on the cheek and she ends our embrace. She reminds me to lock up before I go to bed then leaves down the hallway back to her room.

My phone buzzes on the table.

It's a message from Will on Facebook. *Dear god.* The one thing I forgot to block him on.

I know you have me blocked on just about everything but can we talk? Please?

About?

It was really nice running into you tonight…

Bye, Will.

No, no. I mean it. I just meant it's been a minute.

Can I come over?

Nothing weird, just wanna talk.

Fine.

I know my mother would think I'm ridiculous if I told her what

I'm up to. She'd say it was a trap of some kind or that he didn't deserve a chance to talk to me or that he could rot in hell.

And she would be right.

However, I know that I am over him and have been for a while, so I don't really care what he has to say in regard to our relationship. But the way we ended — from finding out he had another girlfriend through an Instagram post of them together, to him pretending like I was a stranger after we broke up — left me with a lot of questions. The very least he can do is give me answers for my peace of mind. That, and closure on one of the most devastating periods of my life.

I throw on my sneakers, tie my hair into a loose ponytail underneath my black baseball cap, and quietly grab my phone off the table. After turning off all the lights, I tiptoe quietly across the wooden floors and out the front door. We'd have to meet out front, so no one can hear us. And as long as I was back inside in a reasonable amount of time, no one would be the wiser.

His dark mustang flips a U-turn at the end of the cul-de-sac then pulls neatly next to the curb of my grandmother's house.

I expected memories of our three year relationship to flood me when I saw him again, but all I can feel is an overwhelming need to be anywhere else. Why did I think this would be a good idea?

The heavy door slams and a tall lanky body emerges from the driver's side. With each approaching step, the realization that I never want to see him again drives home. Until now, we've always run into one another in the midst of a crowd. But his presence, now isolated, makes me sick. All I can think about is how we grew up together and instead of breaking up with me, he humiliated me — in front of everyone I cared about. Things hadn't been going well for us, we talked about breaking up the night before I found out. But instead of agreeing that we should end things, he took his girlfriend to the state championship game in our hometown. A game our entire town attended, including my family. I think my cousin still has the photos of them cuddling in the bleachers together.

"Hey," he says, taking a seat on the curb next to me. His face is tucked away in his hoodie so I am only able to make out his sharp nose and the gleam of his slanted eyes. Bits of his inky black hair poke through, flopping onto his forehead. His scent floats in a cloud around me, sweat with a little must that is in no way pleasing. It's hard to wrap my mind around ever being attracted to him.

I stay silent, too many things fighting to fly out of my mouth first. I never got the chance to be angry — to yell or scream or ask *how could you?* He robbed me of that when he pretended I didn't exist after I found out about his second girlfriend.

But do I want to do that now?

"Hey," I answer, and leave it at that. He had been trying to get into contact with me for months before I blocked him. Why do I want to talk now? What would be different *now*?

"How are things going with the girls?" he asks, probably to break the awkward silence.

"I think they hate me," I answer automatically.

"Well I could've told you that."

"Wait, but how would you — Oh." My current roommates are the same girls who lived on his floor freshman year. Their friend group was tight. Being his girlfriend, I was the outsider. Not him. How could I not see this before? "You guys talked shit about me behind my back."

"Well... yeah." He shrugs his shoulders as if it means nothing. As if I mean nothing.

"I see," I say, trying to conceal my rage. I did myself the largest disservice by ever allowing this man into my life. He only ever meant me harm. I can see that clearly now. "What did you want to talk about?" I ask, my patience for this conversation beyond gone.

"I don't know really, I just — well when I caught up with the girls, they mentioned you aren't seeing anyone these days." He studies my face but I keep my eyes trained on the asphalt beneath my feet.

"Okay?"

"I guess I'm bringing this up because I still think about you Nayelli."

At this, my head snaps up to meet his eyes. Is this man out of his *mind*? "I don't care."

"But we were talking, at least for a little bit. I thought maybe you didn't hate me any more and we'd be okay."

"Mm," I shrug. He's right, during my sophomore year I allowed us to talk again out of my own insecurities that were left behind after our break up. I even stupidly — mostly drunkenly — had ex-sex with him a few times. I hid the pain, and pretended like I was fine. I thought that if we were at least friends, maybe I wouldn't feel so humiliated and alone. I would seem cool and like I didn't give a fuck. If we were friends, I wouldn't have to feel like the whole room was judging me when our mutual friends invited us to the same party. But being "friends" and having sex with him felt so wrong, I couldn't shake it. After breaking things off, and then blocking him, I realized that it was my damaged self-esteem seeking validation and not a genuine desire to be anything with him.

"That's all you have to say?" he asks incredulously.

"Why are you here? What is it you want from me, Will?" I ask, exasperated. "Because I can guarantee there's nothing else I can give you." Suddenly, I don't need answers to my questions any more. All along I thought if I could just know *why* he treated me like such a huge piece of shit, maybe comprehend his logic, I could find peace and move on. Or why out of the blue one day he decided to waltz back into my life like all was forgiven. He blindsided me and it never made any sense. I could never do someone the way he did me.

But none of that matters. Because when it comes down to it, he's just a shitty ass person. No need to go all Dr. Phil on him and figure out why. The sooner I remove him from my life permanently, the better off I will continue to be.

"I could ask you the same thing," he says after a while. "Why did you agree to meet with me if you didn't *want* to see me? You know, I'm actually really touched that you did. I knew you still cared about me. The girls made it seem like you didn't care about me at all, but here you are. With me," he smirks.

It takes everything within me not to reach my hand back to Timbuktu and slap that disgusting grin off his face. "Leave. Now," I force out through my teeth.

"Why?" he asks, surprise plastered on his ugly face.

I jump up from the curb and point to his car for added emphasis. "William, I fucking *meant* what the fuck I just said. Leave and never contact me again!"

"You know what," he stands up from the curb, his six foot-one body now looking down on me with malice. "It isn't *fair* Nayelli!" he yells back.

"*What* isn't fair, Will?"

"I know you. I know how you are. Whatever you end up setting your mind to do with your life, you will do it well and you will make a name for yourself. And when that day comes, I *deserve* to be there! I deserve to reap all the rewards that come with your new fancy ass lifestyle because I was with you when you didn't have shit."

"Oh my god," I mutter under my breath. My mom was right, this kid is on fucking drugs.

"I'm serious!" he says, still yelling. He crosses his arms in front of his chest and his eyes condense down to slits. "I was there from the beginning. You weren't always the girl that could *afford* to hop out the country for her birthday. But I supported you through all those hard times you and your family had. And now look at you: a fully immersed Santa Barbara girl with her nice clothes and car and expensive trips out the country. It's not hard to see that you will do well in life. And when that day comes, you owe me. You owe me for supporting you."

My jaw drops in disbelief. I don't want to believe that he's referring to the high school jobs my sister and I had because my mom needed help with bills after losing her job, but I know he is. Because at the time, he was my best friend. I told him everything — like how we were close to being evicted or having our electricity shut off. He was always the person I cried to when the world became too much.

And now he decides to throw it in my fucking face. Over some imaginary high-profile life that I don't even have yet. He was right about one thing: we're doing much better since then; but isn't that what you should want for someone you watched struggle? According to Will, however, financial stability apparently meant you were all of a sudden on a path to become the next Kim K. What does one even *do* with a French Studies degree?

"Are you done?" I ask, schooling my expression into one of boredom.

"For now," he spits.

"Well, remember this and remember it well. The day you fix

your mouth to say anything else to me is the day I cut out your tongue." I push to get past and shoulder-check him in the process.

"This isn't over, Nayelli!" he yells to my back.

I flip him the bird but don't give him the satisfaction of turning around. If I never see his face again, it would still be too soon.

The next morning, I rise early to have coffee with my mom. My foot taps restlessly against the tile and the moment she sits down, I spill my guts about the night before.

"Whew," she says, then blows on her coffee before enjoying a sip. Her jet-black loose curls are piled in a messy bun and she's still wearing her pajamas — a black cotton button down set.

I hang my head, feeling like I've let her down somehow. She gently cups my chin and lifts my face to meet her gaze, then drops her hand.

"You know why he said those things, right?" my mom asks.

"No," I answer, my lip poking out in a pout.

"He sees in you what everyone else does. Nayelli, you have an energy about you that is intoxicating. Whether it be friends or lovers, people can't help but be drawn to you and love you. That's just the type of person you are. And you *will* go very far in life. You have that *je ne sais quoi* written all over you. I've always known that, but of course I have, I'm your mom. It's not crazy that other people see it too, but some people will see that in you and despise you because they don't see it in themselves. They get jealous. And honestly, that's probably exactly what happened with him and that awful thieving roommate of yours."

"I guess," is all I say because who wants to hype up their own compliment train?

"There's no guessing about it. There's a lot about you to admire and be jealous of. You're stunning, educated, a soon-to-be world traveler, and carry a happy peace about you — I could go on."

I get up to grab more coffee, just to have something to do. I both love and hate when she gives me a compliment shower like this. On one hand it makes me feel amazing and validated, but on the other hand I feel so shy having this much attention and praise put on me.

"Answer me this," she says, adjusting her body towards the counter where I'm filling up my cup with more coffee. "Were your roommates nice to you before your weight loss?"

I think back to freshman and sophomore year before the "big drop". "Actually, yeah. They were extremely nice. It's why I felt okay moving in with them."

"Okay, so they were nice to you during that time. You move in with them, get serious about your fitness and lose — ?"

"Thirty," I supply, sitting back down.

"Thank you. You lose thirty pounds and all of a sudden they hate your guts. What's the common denominator there?" she asks.

"Wow, I never thought of it that way." As always, the lady makes a lot of sense.

"Of course you didn't. Because you would never treat anyone how they've treated you, especially not because of those shallow reasons. But baby," she reaches across the table and grabs my hand. "Please hear me when I say this. Those girls you live with, Will, and anyone else who has hurt you — you have to let them go. You'll wind up trapped in misery, always searching for yourself in others, and it will consume you. *You* get to say who and what Nayelli is. *You* are the one who gets to live your life out loud if you want to. No one can take that away from you. But it's up to you to decide to be done with that mess and take your life back."

I look down at our warm entwined hands, then into her face.

"You're right, mom." She almost always is. Even Bri, who tended to be the nicest of the three, asked to borrow my clothes often but didn't want me wearing hers because she didn't want me to stretch out her tops. Who says that to someone? But it doesn't matter, it's past time to stop making excuses for their behavior. "I'm done. I want a new start to my life. I want to leave all that chaos behind." It takes everything to talk around the lump in my throat and not cry.

She takes a long look into my eyes and says, "Then do it baby. Live your life how *you* want to. And live it well."

James

The side of my face tingles, the short hairs of my beard are raised in alarm. My eyes, still stinging with sleep, focus in the dark and register the woman staring at me in bed.

"Shit! Damnit! Jesus Christ!" My heart thunders under my palm that is now clutching my chest. I should have known better than to trust a woman willing to travel an hour across London the night before Christmas.

"Great! You're up!" A crooked grin plays across her mousy features.

"Will you keep your voice down? You'll wake my whole family!" I rise up next to her.

"*You're* the one that's bloody yelling! Not me." She ends her declaration and folds her arms across her thin chest.

"Because you were performing an exorcism with your eyes!"

"I did no such thing!"

"Okay, okay. Everybody calm down, yeah?" I raise my palms openly towards her, my brain exhausted. This lady is fucking mental. Who wakes up someone by staring at them? "Look. It doesn't matter who was peacefully trying to sleep and who was casting spells with their eyes during the aforementioned sleep. Is everything okay? It's," I check the time on my cell by the nightstand, "five in the morning. Are you bloody *joking*?"

"Well that's the point, I need to get going. I still have some presents to wrap."

The moon shines brightly through the window, illuminating her pearlescent skin as she climbs across my body to the edge of the bed. I silently stare as she begins to put her clothes on, her smooth back interrupted by the indents of her spine and ribs.

"You drove, right?" I ask, followed by a gigantic sigh that releases some of my irritation.

"Yes, I'm parked out front." She stands, fully clothed; her short brown hair now stuck to her scalp and her sparkling green eyes more crazy than appealing when we met a few hours ago.

"Great. Shall we then?" I throw on my crumpled trackies and exit the room behind her.

We walk down the staircase in silence. Approaching the last few steps, my foot steps onto air instead of something solid and a loud crack echoes throughout the ground level of the house. My breath rushes out of my body at the impact and I snap my eyes shut against the sharp tracks of pain that shoot across my bum.

"What happened?" Her hands are flitting about me, not quite sure where or how to help.

"Fucking motherfuck! Christ!" I count my breaths in hopes that the pain will start to dull. It doesn't. *Keep it together. You're tough mate. It's okay. Just breathe.*

"James?"

"Yeah, yeah. All good."

"Here, let me help you up," her thin arms reach down but I wave my hands to stop her.

"Honestly, I'm okay. Go ahead and go, I know you have things to do. I'm right behind you to lock the door." I smile and attempt to sit up.

"Okay," she replies hesitantly. "Well, I guess I'll message you on Tinder then? For next time?"

"Mhmm."

"Lovely. Happy Christmas James!"

"Same to you Sarah."

"It's Jen!" she corrects loudly before slamming the door. Another sigh escapes between my lips. I gingerly rise into a standing position. There is no way my parents are still asleep. *Fuck.* I should really do a better screening of my matches.

After gingerly returning up the stairs and to my bed, I struggle for two hours, staring at my phone and swiping through faces until even that bores me. I finally quit trying to rest and give my blankets two sharp kicks to remove them off me. Sitting up, my body is consumed with restlessness and exhaustion from running off interrupted sleep.

Goosebumps engulf my skin as my feet pad lightly against the chilly wooden floor. I round the corner and the even colder bathroom tiles fuel my agitation further. "Fucking socially ignorant... rude as fuck..."

I grab ahold of the porcelain sink's edges and let out one giant huff. And then another. My eyes connect with the wall's mirror, thoroughly criticizing my appearance. Lips too bright and too pink from kissing. Eyes creased and baggy. Black facial hair threatening to take over the bottom half of my face like a goddamn neanderthal. *Aye. You've seen better days, mate.*

I turn on the tap for hot water but know that it will take a while before anything warm pours out. The sound of rushing water fills the silent room and my hands return to their former position on the sink. Like every other morning, I take this time to study the sticky note taped to the mirror. The once bright yellow is faded down to a soft beige with one of the taped corners beginning to ruffle away from the mirror. The sharpied words on the note are worn down in color too but still legible. Part of me can't bring myself to re-write or re-tape it — fearing it might lose some of its magic if I do.

I complete the morning ritual by reading out loud the four rules I set in place nearly a year ago.
1. Be famous (can apply to acting or music).
2. Never live with your parents again.
3. No drugs until you are successful.
4. No serious relationships (ever?).

I repeat them again and again like a mantra until the believability of the words resonate within me. A few moments pass like this until steam begins to rise from the faucet and curl around the mirror. I cut the words short, finally satisfied, and begin to get ready for Christmas Day with my family.

After quietly getting dressed, and in further preparations for the day, I make a trip down to the neighborhood Starbucks.

Grabbing my cup off the cafe table, I spin it until the sharpied *James* is in view. The purple hibiscus liquid swirls, then comes to a stop with specks of blackberry floating to the top of the ice. Tapping my fingers against the brown leather couch, I look around the upstairs dining area. I've been the only customer for the last forty-five minutes. Granted, it is Christmas, but I thought I could at least people-watch some ritualistic blokes who wouldn't miss a day of having a coffee and reading the paper at the shop. I tilt the watch on my wrist into view, it shows 9:37 a.m. Maybe I'm just too early.

Whatever. I'm sure my family is done by now with the annual Christmas "wake and bake". Mum and Dad could never take more than three hits without getting too stoned. My younger brother Alex, on the other hand, can definitely handle an entire joint on his own. Although, I highly doubt that he would do that on Christmas. We do have to be functional today after all.

Taking in one last sweeping glance, I feel a pang of disappointment and loneliness that shapes my mouth into a frown. People watching is one of my favorite forms of idle entertainment. I mean, what is more thrilling than making up stories for the different strangers that pass you?

Across from the cafe sits a closed bank, another empty coffee shop, and the closed Wimbledon station in the distance. Even the chatty birds seem to be on holiday.

It's clear this place is going to remain an absolute bore, so I sip the remaining contents of my cup, discard it into the rubbish bin, and jog downstairs to the exit.

Upon reaching the door, I pause, handle in hand, and mentally prepare to go back into the bitter cold.

"Holy fuck," curses from my mouth. The wind gets the best of me, chilling me straight through my two shirts, jumper, jacket, and coat. I try to close the door behind me but the wind is impossible, making my scarf fly every which way. Eventually, I wrestle it closed and turn to leave only to find that I've closed my scarf in the door and nearly choke myself unconscious.

"You all right man?" a deep voice asks, helping untangle my scarf.

"Yeah," I reply once I'm free, but it comes out too high from the lack of oxygen so I clear my throat and try again. "Yeah, I'm good. Nice save there mate, cheers." I slap the short, grey-haired man on the back too hard, then straighten my clothes.

He's probably throwing me an odd glance, but I don't hang around to find out. I yell, "Happy Christmas!" over my shoulder, then make my way down Wimbledon Hill Road.

After a minute of walking, I search around in my pockets but apparently forgot my earphones at home. *Damnit.*

On the next street corner, *Bar and One's* black and gold sign gleams in the morning's light. The door is open, but I don't break stride. Last year I spent it there and have since learned my lesson about drinking too early on a holiday morning.

I slip on my gloves from my coat pockets and bury my face deeper against the godforsaken chill. The roads are sickeningly quiet, allowing my thoughts too much of a podium. I struggle to tamper down one in particular, but the more I fight it, the louder it becomes. So I give in and allow myself to ruminate over how many more Christmas mornings I might end up spending alone.

Most days I keep myself too distracted to care but I have always known that there's an unfilled emptiness inside the very depths of me yearning to be normal, to be like everyone else, to be able to smoke an occasional joint with my family and not spiral down a path of self-sabotage and destruction.

The town's backdrop of rolling green hills catch my eye, framing most of the neighborhood and effectively ending my mini mental crisis. It's my favorite part about growing up in Wimbledon, especially when I walk to the top of the steeper roads. Since secondary school, I would find different walking paths that gave me the bird's eye view and look down below at the world beneath my feet. Something about it made me feel powerful and in control and — I don't know. The feeling is hard to explain, but everything is just so small and insignificant from up there. The trees, the churches, the primary school not too far down, the people going on about their lives. But the busy world below doesn't matter because when I'm at the peak of the highest hill everything pauses, the world slows down. From the top of a Wimbledon hill, it's as if I rule all that I survey and nothing and no one can reach me.

But today I am not perusing the hills, I am walking down the flat streets that will take me to my parents' home.

Christ, I never imagined myself twenty-six and still dependent upon my parents to catch me when I fall. Or to fall so many times.

Get a grip, I chastise myself. Christmas is not the day or time to wallow in the shortcomings of my life. There will be plenty of time to beat myself up another day, as I am never short on reasons. For now, at least, I need to focus on the good. It's just another few months before my Netflix gig airs, and that's something to be fucking proud of. I'm headed in the right direction and have made so much progress. Two years ago, I was too distracted by my breakup and too high off whatever was available to even sing any more, let alone audition for acting gigs. And look at me now, self-diagnosed with depression but sober as a nun — and with the upcoming gigs I have lined up, almost fully back on my feet. Christmas will come and go before I know it, I just gotta find some fucking chill.

I round the last corner to the street of my childhood home and release a pinned-up breath that's been wanting to escape for a while now.

It's just one bloody day.

*

Later that evening, my legs are stretched before me with my stomach slightly protruding from my mother's Christmas roast. I rest my arm against the back of the couch, licking my thumb that still has a bit of the meat's juice flavored in herbs and salt. *Damn.* That was a good roast. But then again, all my mother's cooking is out of this world — one of the many perks of moving back in with my parents.

My younger brother, Alex, is occupying the other end of the

couch while my older brother Daniel and his wife sit on the dark wood floor next to the pile of presents, no tree. My parents are still somewhere upstairs rummaging through their closet for the last of the presents to place with the others. We have to wait for every single gift to be in the room before opening even one — it's tradition.

My eyes narrow in on the orange and yellow flicker from the fireplace, remembering that earlier this year they gifted my older brother Daniel with a down payment for a house. *Hmm*. If my present isn't at least half as great as money for a house, I will be sure to make a scene. Although, last Christmas they did buy me the thousand-pound synthesizer that I wanted. I guess beggars can't choose the least shit gift, or however that saying goes.

Festive lights drape across the white walls, giving the room a soft, warm glow. Daniel is laughing and kissing his wife by the brick fireplace. Their brown and blonde heads bob up and down as their mouths and hands go back and forth, telling secrets to each other and totally ignoring Alex and me. I can't put my finger on why, but there's just something about being an observer to this affection that makes me want to gag. I shift my attention to my younger brother — all two plus meters of him sprawled out on the couch — rubbing his belly and sighing in utter bliss. I kick his shin and he responds with a mouthed *What the fuck?* No one should be that content from food alone. It's annoying. Especially since he's just as single as I am. Aren't single people supposed to be depressed during the holidays or something?

Nevertheless, part of me still feels blessed — not that I believe in blessings, I gave up on the idea of God a long time ago. But I know that I am more fortunate than others, and it is almost enough to make me forget everything else.

Almost.

I lean further into my side of the couch and pull out my phone.

Swipe. Swipe. Swipe. Swipe.

Nice face. Nice shape. Good god! That one made me twitch.

"James, you all right?"

My fingers pause in their rhythmic stroking and my heart skips one of its beats. *Shit.* I hurry to exit the app but it's too late, Alex is already invading my personal space before I have enough time to close it.

"Stuck on that too, eh?" His mouth is curved in the most knowing grin. "Just don't get catfished... or murdered. And make sure she buys you dinner. Some women only want one thing and you're no cheap lay mate." Alex's face is about to burst with suppressed laughter.

"Murdered?" my father asks. He returns with his arms full like he's holding barrels, my mother trailing shortly behind him.

"Fuck *off*," I whisper-threaten Alex and give him a light shove to the chest.

"No, no Dad. Alex didn't say murdered."

"Well then, what did he say?"

My eyes dart around the room for assistance but nothing helps. "Umm, he said *Herbert*. *Herbert* might want to meet up for drinks tomorrow and Alex was asking if I'd like to go." A bad lie is less embarrassing than explaining to my forty-year married parents why I'm on a dating app. Which would then turn into a dreadfully painful conversation about what exactly went wrong with my last, and only, girlfriend. Earlier this morning with — Jen? — was a close enough call as it is.

"Who is Herbert?" asks Alex, his smile threatening to split at the seams.

Oh, for fuck's sake. I spring to my feet at Alex's sabotage.

"Drinks anyone? Yes? No? Great, I'm gonna go grab a whiskey," I spit out the words and exit the room before anyone has the chance to answer me.

One of my most believable exits? Probably not. But I hope that I can at least stall with my drink long enough for my family to change the topic of conversation to something else.

I turn the corner from the living room and pass quickly through the dining room to the kitchen. The bottle of Jameson is still on the tile counter from dinner, so I grab a glass tumbler from the cabinet and fill it with coke, ice, and more than enough whiskey. The brown liquid courses down to my stomach, soothing and warming me from the inside out.

Christ. Almost a year has passed and yet Christmas is still hard without her. I managed to go the whole morning without really thinking about it, but watching Daniel and his wife dealt the landing punch to my stomach. Leaning over the counter, I grip its edges for support, trying to control the feeling of drowning in my own mistakes. I know that our breakup was for the best. That we became toxic to one another. But at the same time, I can't help but feel like it's just another thing I've failed at.

Emily was such a ball of joy with curly hair that was almost too big for her body. Last Christmas, we spent it together here at my parents' home. We whispered by the fire, laughing and making plans for the New Year. Little did we know, we were sitting in the eye of an ever-gathering storm.

I should go back into the room with the others. My dark thoughts trouble me most when I'm alone and there's no use in beating myself up over the past.

I practice the calming method my old therapist taught me years back. My breath filters first through my nose, then through my mouth, then finally, a roll of the neck and a quick shake of the hands to release the negativity. "Accept the things you cannot change," I mock in the nasally voice of Dr. Shepard.

I top up my drink and head back to the living room. At least the holiday is halfway over.

*

As the night comes to a thankfully uneventful close, I'm finally able to retire my rugged old body to my room. Once I'm finally alone, however, I'm consumed by a restlessness to do something other than lay down.

Is it pathetic to watch a movie by yourself on Christmas evening?

I opt for picking up my guitar by my bed and strum out a few C chords. My heart isn't quite in it, so I put it back. Then, in perfect response to my boredom, my phone pings from the nightstand. I've gotten a new match on Tinder. Perfect.

The flame glows and pulses as it loads the app and my eyes concentrate on it — curious as to which profile I have matched with.

My thumb strokes through her pictures over twenty times, studying them. I wonder if she actually looks like this in person or if some squat man in Birmingham stole these photos and created a profile. That happened to my mate Chris once, bless his soul. He was able to laugh it off, but it still has me scarred.

Nayelli's bio says that she is on holiday from her Uni in California, with the ocean sunsets and beach bikini photos to match.

I look once more through her profile and decide... *Fuck it.* She looks way too amazing to not at least say hello. Besides, I

can always have her FaceTime me later to be sure.
With a grin on my face and excitement in my fingertips, I type out a message to the girl from California named Nayelli — and pray like hell that she replies to my message sooner rather than later.

Nayelli

An alarm cycles through Apple's opening ringtone for the fifth time. I wish someone would shut it off so I can sleep just a few minutes more, but they don't. Another round of the annoying tune begins to play and I realize that it is my phone and I am that someone. I crack my right eye open just enough to find my phone, but not too much as to let full consciousness flood in and wake me.

"Happy Christmas Harry!"

I groan and roll onto my back, un-wedging my face from between Olivia's desk and rolling chair. Sunlight floods in and singes my eyeballs. I narrow my gaze to slits, trying to see where the fake British accent is coming from.

Olivia is perched above me on her twin bed, her golden-brown hair hanging around her pale face. She is obviously expecting more movement from me than just the opening of my eyes. "It's already past noon! Wake up, so we can explore London!"

I roll the computer chair away from me and sit up, willing my brain to wake up my body. A sharp pain races down my neck and concentrates in my shoulders.

"Nayelli. You have managed to move all of three inches. Things might be closing soon because of Christmas. We have to hurry!" she explains.

"Okay, okay!" My vision is still unfocused. I rub specks of sleep from my eyes, savoring the precious seconds before I have to get ready.

After checking her phone, Olivia bounces off her bed, steps over my body, and looks back at me while holding the door open to the en-suite bathroom. "You have until I'm done showering to be up and moving, okay?"

"I got it."

"I'm serious Nayelli!" she yells, closing the door behind her.

With Olivia gone, I take a moment to lean against her desk and just breathe. I fill my lungs until they are completely full, hold it until it almost burns, then slowly let go of the air.

Tired doesn't even begin to cover how I feel right now. On top of flying into London late last night, I was given a small scrap of a blanket — if you can even call it that — to battle a twenty-eight degree night.

It probably didn't help that instead of sleeping I spent countless hours on that app.

I told myself that I would only swipe through faces until I became tired, but those faces just so happened to be awake as well, and naturally, wanted to talk. It sparked a thrill that coursed through my body and sunk deep into my bones, making me high off its possibilities. I wanted more. More swiping, more connections, more conversations.

I'm not sure what time it was when I finally collapsed from exhaustion, but the day was beginning to break and the tone of muted blue light sifted through the beige drapes of Olivia's dorm window.

Now that I'm awake, last night's revelation slams into me all over again and the muscles around my mouth stretch into the widest grin I've ever had.

"No one knows me here," I whisper to the empty room. I can do whatever the hell I want. I am a woman without a past here, I can let go. But more than that, it's way past *time* to let go.

My cell rings, cutting through my thoughts. I pick it up from the green freckled carpet and answer.

"Hello?"

"Finally!" my mom yells. "Did you forget how to use a phone? This is my fifth time trying to call you." Her tone is jesting, yet concerned.

I check the time and subtract eight hours for California's time difference. "Mom, it's four a.m. there. What are you still doing up?" I ask, wrapping my arm underneath my chest.

"It wasn't four a.m. when I first called. You just never picked up," she pauses but I don't speak, knowing she has more to say. "*Anyways.* You were the one who was supposed to call and let me know you made it safely. I was worried when I didn't hear from you."

Crap. I pull my arm around me a little tighter. "I got in late and forgot, my bad. But I'm almost twenty-one, mom. I'm being the appropriate amount of safe and cautious, you can relax." I bite my bottom lip, bracing for her backlash of do's and don'ts when traveling alone. She almost made me miss my flight, prepping me with her list.

"Nayelli, you are my *baby*. You may be almost twenty-one, but you're still my baby. Can't a mother be concerned that her child is six thousand miles away from her for the first time?"

Her admission makes my mouth spread into the smallest of smiles. If no one else loves me, at least I know my mom does. "You're right. I'm sorry." It's a wonder she ever let me go to college in Santa Barbara.

"Well, what are you doing today? Are you having fun? Have you met anyone? A *man?* Tell me everything!"

A laugh escapes before I reply. "I've been here for all of

twelve hours Mom. There's nothing to tell yet. But I have to get ready. I love you, I'll talk to you later."

"I love you too. And don't forget to call later," she warns.

"I won't, bye Mom."

My head turns toward the soft click of the bathroom door. Olivia pokes her Carmen Miranda wrapped head through the crack, scrutinizing my appearance. "Ready?" she asks.

"Yup." I answer in my newfound excitement. "Let's get this day started!"

Following a too hot shower where I scrub the sins of long distance travel from my skin and give my hair a brief check, I step out the bathroom refreshed, revived, and ready to take on the city.

Olivia and I exit the black iron gate of the campus and step into the wintry late afternoon. A multifaceted array of emerald, jade, and sage fill my peripherals as I take in my first daylight view of London. I've never seen this large of a city be able to maintain such a fine balance within nature. I glance back at her dorm to get a better look. It's obviously newly built, taking up modern space in a rustic family neighborhood. The cluster of dorms are all several stories tall with pastel colors and open windows trimmed in thick steel. The dorms almost seem out of place amongst the rest of the street.

I make a point of taking slow and purposeful strides to absorb the rest of the scenery, but quickly realize there isn't much more to see other than trees, cars parked on the wrong side of the street, and tri-colored brick homes. Not a single soul is out for me to harass like a typical tourist.

"Sooooo," I begin, scanning the surrounding area of more brick buildings that make up this part of town, "tell me everything. How is it living here? Miss being my roommate yet?"

I wonder to myself if the rest of London is like this, or if it's just this neighborhood.

"Living here has really taught me to value home," she starts solemnly, "I never thought I could miss my mom so much. I just want to go back to SoCal already."

Her admission is filled with a rawness that tugs at the strings of my heart and overrides the importance of my observations. This is not the spunky, quirky, fun-loving Olivia that I lived with last year. This is supposed to be the girl who threw a weekly *Wine Wednesday* when we were only twenty for Pete's sake. How could she not be having the time of her life? I would kill to have the chance to study abroad here. But unfortunately, I received a D in microbiology last year and ended all hopes of meeting the GPA requirement to study abroad this term. Lost in my own reveries, I forget to press more about her melancholy state.

"There it is, Fox On The Hill!" She points at a two-story building sitting literally on top of a steep grassy hill. "The tube stops running today, so we'll have to stay in my dorm's neighborhood. We can grab breakfast here at the pub, then walk to find a store for dinner groceries," she instructs on our way up the slope.

By the time we make it inside, my chest burns and I want to wheeze. It takes everything within me not to put my hands on my knees and catch my breath. Olivia strides gracefully past me with her long, lean limbs, stopping in front of the bar counter.

"Welcome!" the barkeep greets. His face is warm with velvety brown eyes that match everything else about him. His black bow tie and white starched shirt makes me laugh a little. He looks so old fashioned and cute. "You girls all right?"

I look to Olivia and wrinkle my brows in silent communication. Does it look like we're *not* all right? Maybe he can hear how labored my breaths are. Or saw me struggle up the stairs.

"Yes, thank you," Olivia replies, unphased. "Can we get a booth for two?"

"Sure, sure. Americans, are you? Are you here on holiday?"

"She is, I'm studying at King's College for the year." Olivia gestures over her shoulder with her thumb.

The man nods at her, "That's lovely. Well I do hope you enjoy your visit." He exits the back of the bar through his secret swinging door and walks us over to a wooden booth.

I begin to wonder if wood and brick were all that was on hand when this country was shaping up.

After being seated and Olivia ordering for the both of us, she dives right into my personal life — wanting to catch up on the gossip of my deplorable circumstances back in Santa Barbara.

"Those girls you live with! My god!" she exclaims without preamble. "I don't know how you do it. I would be so fucking miserable if I were you."

Her statement makes me feel all the worse because I actually am me, no *if* about it. "I am miserable," I grumble.

"How did you end up with them again?"

"Because you left to study abroad, and they offered. They were so nice to me freshman year, how was I supposed to know they secretly hated my guts?"

"True," she nods, "but it's still so crazy to hear about how catty they are with you. And that one — I can't remember her name — even stole money from you. Did you ever get it back? Have they done anything else?"

"Ugh," I rest my forehead on top of my hands, "yeah, finally. My mom called her and threatened her with a misdemeanor if she didn't give me the money back immediately. But nothing else to report. Thankfully, winter break started before any more damage could ensue."

There is no tiptoeing around the facts, my junior year has not been kind to me. Mainly because my housemates are the imps of Satan. Well, all except for my roommate Bri. I'd more so describe her as a lost sheep following the wrong herd. But Sofia — the one who, "accidentally mixed up our checkbooks to pay her portion of the rent and then asked if the check bounced" — is definitely head imp.

We met because the girls lived on the same floor of my then-boyfriend our freshman year. He became friends with them, and by extension of our relationship, they became friends with me. Will and I went our separate ways before the year was up, but I still saw the girls from time to time — which is how I ended up with the proposal to move in with them for junior year. From what I knew of them, they liked to party but were fun and easy going. That's the kicker when living with someone, though. You share each other's space twenty-four seven — aka — there's nowhere to hide your crazy.

"What about your ex?" Olivia asks. Before I'm able to answer, the barkeep shows up with our food.

"All right loves, two plates of bacon, eggs, and toast; and two ciders. Enjoy," he smiles at the both of us and leaves.

I reach for the cider first, bubbling over at the novelty of having alcohol with my breakfast. I feel hip, trendy, bold— and may I dare say a tad bit wild, even. "So weird! This is normal," I exclaim, taking a sip of the tart, yet crisp Stella Cidre with a beaming child-like grin on my face.

Olivia chuckles at my naivety. "*You're* weird. This is common in Europe. It was like this when my family went to Germany last summer."

"Mm," is all I respond. I've never left the country before, I wouldn't know. I poke my fork at the odd piece of pinkish meat on my plate. "And this is bacon? Are you sure?"

"Yes, now stop poking it and eat it." Leave it to Olivia to be bossy, nothing's changed there I see.

I spear it, take a bite, and let the thick salty meat move around the palate of my mouth. "Not bad," I eventually say, my words sounding unsure to my own ears.

"American bacon is far better," Olivia says, cutting through the bullshit.

"Cheers to that! I was just trying to be nice." We raise our glasses.

"You have to look me in the eyes before you clink," she warns, "it's bad luck not to."

"Right, right. Sorry." Olivia and her damn superstitions, I almost forgot. "What else are we cheersing? I'll let you decide."

"Cheers to a new year with better male candidates!" she proclaims.

"What, are we going on *The Bachelorette* or something?"

"Just cheers me, damnit!"

"Fine," I mutter, and cheers to a year filled with better men.

We finish our brunch and walk around the neighborhood a bit. Olivia informs me that there isn't much more to see this far out of the city center but it's nice to have some movement all the same. We make a wide arc around her neighborhood, googling and walking to any market that might be open but continuously come up empty handed. After the fourth failure, and what felt like the ten thousandth mile to my feet, we ultimately give up and return back to the dorms.

"I can't believe every shop within a three-mile radius is closed!" Olivia says for the tenth time over her third glass of wine.

Apparently, London takes Christmas more seriously than California. Normally there's at least a grocery store open until the early evening, but everything short of one corner *Off License* store is closed. Naturally, we made an executive decision to buy a bottle of gin and several bottles of wine before coming back to her dorm.

"How's the pasta coming along?" Olivia asks from the living area couch. The common space is in the shape of a long "L" with the couches and dining table in one corner, and a small kitchen on the other.

I am in charge of dinner and Olivia is, of course, in charge of drinking. Given the fact that I've watched her burn macaroni noodles, it's definitely safer this way.

"It's done!" I yell from the kitchen. "Pour me a glass of wine and I'll bring our plates."

We slouch into the living area's green faux-leather couch after our overdose on carbs. The couch — and the carbs for that matter — feel stiff, yet comforting all the same. Two bottles of wine have been split between the both of us and somewhere in between one of Olivia's complaints about how terrible everything is in London, we switch over to gin.

"Do you remember Hailey?" Olivia asks, cutting the silence.

"Yeah, why?" She was one of Olivia's friends that would come to the Wine Wednesday gatherings. She seemed nice enough, but we never had the chance to speak much.

"Well," she starts, leaning across the couch to pour herself another drink from the coffee table. "She's studying abroad in Madrid and apparently broke up with her boyfriend. Something about the distance putting a strain on their relationship or whatever."

"Okay?" I mimic her actions and pour myself another as well.

"And since then has hooked up with like *four* guys." She emphasizes the number four like it's a dirty French curse word.

My brow arches over my glass and I pause before taking another sip. "And again, *okay*?"

"That's so many! She's *literally* quadrupled her count. And it hasn't even been that long since the breakup. I mean, I get it; be free and explore your options or whatever but there's no need to be a hoe while you're doing it. Like have some respect for yourself, you know?"

"Mm," is all I respond. I can't believe she called her own friend a hoe. What was Hailey supposed to do, commit herself to a nunnery because things didn't work out with her first boyfriend? Talk about dramatic. But I don't know Hailey or their friendship well enough to comment so I keep my remarks to myself.

Olivia leans back into the couch, arms crossed with a smug expression on her face and glass still in hand. My noncommittal response is obviously not what she is looking for.

I wait to see if she has anything else to say, but she doesn't make any effort to redirect the conversation or her unexpected pissy mood, so I let the silence stretch on and grab my phone.

Time passes with some kind of show playing in the background on the flatscreen. We haven't seen each other in over six months, yet the conversation isn't flowing very consistently. Then again, all of my hand-eye coordination is devoted to the pictures on my phone in front of me. I don't even register that Olivia is peeking over my shoulder. "You're on Tinder *too*?" she yells and her voice echoes off the empty living room walls. I swiftly tuck my phone underneath my leg.

"Yeah, what about it?" I feel my cheeks, neck, and back get hot.

"Well, since you obviously know how it works, maybe you can help me with an issue I'm having," Olivia says. Her dark eyes, heavily rimmed in eyeliner, light up with the glow of an untold tale. I don't make another sound, giving her my undivided attention. She pauses dramatically and after what seems like the longest minute of my life — she begins.

"A little while after getting here, I decided that I wanted to go on a date with a British man. *Obviously* the easiest way to make that happen is through a dating app, so I downloaded Tinder. But honestly, at first, it was so freaking discouraging because I only matched with like ten guys!"

Geez. Either she's the pickiest woman on Earth or British Tinder men *reaaalllyyy* aren't feeling her. I don't even think about saying either out loud, in case it's the latter of the two.

"But then," continues Olivia, "I matched with this super crazy hot model guy." Her mouth is turned up into a bit of a smirk and I can't quite read if this story is about to take a positive or negative turn.

"He took me out a couple of times and was super sweet. He even paid for everything. Then, after our successful second date, I just so happened to be reading this Cosmo magazine that said you should wait until the third date to have sex with a guy, so I thought, 'Okay Olivia, put on your big girl panties because next time it's going down in the bedroom.'"

"You *what*?" I screech. "No, no Olivia. Please don't tell me you were taking sexual readiness cues from a damn *magazine*?" Olivia acts as if she doesn't hear me and chugs right along with the rest of her story.

"*Anyways*," she starts again, "we go out on our third date and he invites me back to his apartment, so of course, I went. The date and the sex went so well — or at least I thought it did — but I haven't heard from him since. And that was well over a week ago. Then, the worst part of all, I thought that it would be a good idea to text him Merry Christmas today just to maybe get a conversation going and he's said nothing. *Nothing.* He doesn't even have a 'Merry Christmas to you too' for a girl that he just slept with." By her last sentence, her face is in a full-on pout.

Still, I can tell she's trying to put up a brave front and not cry. I reach for her right shoulder and give it a light rub followed by a soft squeeze to her hand. Part of me wishes that I could have been here to prevent the devastation that Olivia so openly wears on her face. Then again, she didn't listen to me the last time she found herself in a situation such as this one. My heart hurts for my friend, she's always been so fragile and trusting when it comes to men.

"Hey, fuck him. That's just him being a classic dickface of a guy," I console.

"But why?" Olivia asks, amber eyes wide and liquid and completely earnest.

I rack my brain for an answer but don't have much of one. Flashes of our sophomore year come to me all at once. Olivia pursued some lame jerk who gave her only crumbs of his attention and affection. That entire rollercoaster of a year with him I begged her to choose herself and let him go, to make sure that whatever she did to *please* not lose her virginity to him. She did anyway and then he dumped her shortly after. Now here we are with guy number two. "I'm not really sure, but don't take it personal, okay? If he only used you for sex then he's the one who's a douche bag and it does not mean that you're lacking in any way. Remember that." All this time I thought she was living it up and having the time of her life in London. Why didn't she mention this during one of our phone calls?

"Yeah, I guess," she says, pouring herself another shot, and I can tell that she doesn't really believe me.

James

Wool gloves, hot tea, and four layers still aren't enough for this fucking frigid day.

"Shit weather we're having today, isn't it?" I ask, leaning over to the bundled old gentleman in an expensive black coat and leather shoes sitting next to me. He gives me a sharp look out of the corner of his beady eyes, then shimmies slightly to put more space between us. At this, a small chuckle escapes my mouth. *Fucking Londoners, I tell you.*

I can hear my brother Alex asking me, *Come on James, are you really going to complain about the cold every single day? You were born here for Christ's sake.* And to that, my answer is always the same: the day this weather stops being god-awfully miserable all the time is the day I'll stop complaining about it.

The tube's sign for train times says two minutes. While I wait for my red and blue ride to pull up and take me to Waterloo station, and since old Mr. Grumpy Grump obviously doesn't want to chat it up, I pop in my earbuds and search through my phone for the perfect song to soundtrack my commute.

After a tight race between James Blake's *Wilhelm Scream* and Jai Paul's *BTSTU*, I decide it's the kind of morning that needs that latter of the two choices.

Once I make it to the music shop, the rest of my morning passes by in a blur. Having a routine of doing the same exact thing on the same exact day has a way of doing that.

Before I know it, it's my lunch break and I thank the universe for tiny mercies. A wicked throb has been working its way into my head for the better part of the last hour, so I use my free time to plop on the basement sofa and close my eyes.

"Hey, James. You okay?" my coworker Eddie asks, descending down the stairs to the basement of our music shop.

"Yeah, mate. Wonderful," I lie. The soft ache currently rooted in my temples indicates I overdid it on whiskey last night. "Why are we open today anyway? Who's really going to come buy instruments the day *after* Christmas? We've hardly had a customer all day." I shift my weight to lean my head back and the old, beaten leather couch groans underneath me.

"It's our mandatory Boxing Day sale. You know that."

Eddie responds, standing directly in front of me — all short and ginger and always-angry looking. There's only one piece of furniture in the cemented space, and I happen to be taking up all of it with my body. "Besides," he continues, arms crossed over his narrow chest, "you're scheduled to give guitar lessons today, aren't you?"

Ah, fuck me. My lesson is supposed to start in the next five minutes. "Fine. I'll be upstairs soon," I respond and close my eyes.

Eddie leaves up the stairs to the upper level of the shop, and I take a minute before following. I look around at all of the hanging instruments: guitars, keyboards, saxophones — you name it. Each one is tetrised to cover every inch of the wall of the small basement. Eight years almost exactly since I've been at this music shop, and not much has changed. I can't tell if I find that extremely comforting or sad.

After taking in one last sweep of the room, I bound up the stairs to bring my client down here for lessons.

"Okay, now watch my fingers one more time. The G major

chord looks like this," I explain as I flex four of my fingers into position, demonstrating the modern G. I set my guitar down against the chair next to me and prop my hands on my knees, hoping that this time he'll get it a wee bit more.

The kid, Lucas, scrunches his blonde freckled face beneath his gold-rimmed glasses. His chest puffs up like a peacock, displaying letters that spell "ACDC" on his T-shirt more fully. His red tongue darts out of his pudgy twelve-year-old face in concentration, his fingers set into position on his medium-sized Yamaha. Lucas then raises his right hand far higher than what I taught him to do and bangs down across the strings, the resulting sound one of terror. It's like his strings decided to get into a street fight with a tomcat.

The noise finally stops reverberating around my brain and I peak over at his face, beaming with a smile of triumph and pride. "Like that, yeah?"

"Splendid," I reply. The corners of my mouth are tight from holding in my honesty, but I hold onto rule number one of music lessons: always encourage. "Let's practice our finger placements and strumming on the foam guitar, shall we?" I strip the guitar out of his hands and lean it next to mine. The pulse in my head from earlier resurfaces and sharpens against my forehead, Lucas' sharp guttural twang still ringing through my head.

My hangover can't take this.

I make eyes with the clock on the shop's basement wall. Only fifteen minutes have passed since we started our lessons.

Fucking hell.

*

I lock the shop's front door and place the keys in my backpack.

Instead of heading home, this evening I have a date with a self-proclaimed model named Svea. We have decided to meet at a bar in Soho not too far from my shop. I waste no time in weaving through the stone-faced sea of five o'clock foot traffic. A man — or woman — jabs me in the ribs with their elbow without apologizing or breaking their stride. I shake my head. Two rude people in one day, not bad for a weekday in London.

Cutting through a dark puddled alleyway, I finally approach the glass-front corner pub. It has lamps above the awning of the building highlighting gold lettering that says *Dog and Duck Wines and Spirits*. I don't think I knew of its existence before today, but it's where Svea wants to meet. I open the glass door and walk to the back where Svea messaged she is waiting for me.

Crossing the red and white checkered floor underneath antique-looking chandeliers, I say a quick prayer. *Please don't let her be a catfish.*

It hasn't happened to me yet, but that doesn't mean it can't; and just that thought alone keeps me paranoid about these first time meet ups. "Svea?" I ask hesitantly to a head of long blonde hair.

Svea stands up and turns to greet me, a smile softening up the sharp angles of her facial features. *Wow.* Her tall, lithe frame and ample breasts add splendidly to the adorable dimples resting in her gorgeous face. She hugs me and we both have a seat opposite each other inside the burgundy leather booth.

"Can I get you a drink?" A drink usually takes the edge off the awkwardness that is bound to appear on a first date.

"A vodka cranberry please," she replies without hesitation, her Swedish accent thick and stroking against each syllable.

She must be thinking the same thing.

I walk to the bar and send up another prayer — now that I

know she isn't a catfish — in hopes that she isn't an absolute lunatic.

I return to the table with our drinks in hand. Svea thanks me promptly and launches straight into an inquisition of my life's story.

"Are you really an actor? Or do you just say that to attract the girls?"

Every time Svea asks me a question, she leans onto the table between us, effectively pushing her breasts out of her V-neck jumper and into full view.

I train my eyes on hers. "Uh, no. I mean yes. Yes, I really am an actor. One of the shows I'm in is on Netflix right now, actually, and another one is set to premiere rather soon." She licks her red lips and my thoughts scatter into pieces across the wooden table. "What about you? Do you do anything besides modeling? Or is that your main focus?"

I use the pause after my question to take a long drink from the honey-colored liquid in my tumbler while her dimples and cleavage animate her brief account of getting into the business.

"Well, it's my main focus *now*. It started out as just something to do on the weekends. Then one day, I got asked to do a photo shoot that I knew would make a difference for me, but it conflicted with my work schedule at the time. It made me realize that I could really make a name and career for myself if I took it seriously. So I quit my job as an office assistant and have been pursuing modeling ever since. As far as I know, it's been the best decision I could have made for myself." Her pinky circles the cranberry and vodka glass as she explains this.

"That's amazing. I could never imagine quitting my job at the music shop to focus only on acting or music, it's sort of become a part of me. How did you know everything would work out?" Now I'm the one leaning across the table. My fingers lightly stretch open and close against the table as I listen.

"I didn't. But half the battle in jobs like yours and mine is believing that somehow if you love it enough, it will all work out," she says simply and her icy blue eyes gleam with a confidence that I find myself longing for. "You obviously are good at what you do if you're on two Netflix shows. Just put full faith in yourself and really *do* it. You'll be robbing yourself of your full potential if you don't."

"Hmm... I guess you're right," I say just to say something. Life is never that straightforward and easy.

"To be fair," Svea adds, "I did have a guide to help me make the big transition. Their kind words and sweet energy made me feel confident enough to believe in myself and take the big leap."

"Guide? Like an agent?"

"Ha, no," she chuckles and tosses her hair back with her hand, "Although, I do have an agent too. But I was referring to my fairy guide."

My forehead creases in lack of comprehension. I tilt my empty glass towards me and stare into it as if the answer is swimming in the melted ice. "Did you just say...?" I can't bring myself to repeat the last words.

"Fairy guide, yes. That's what I said. They've been with me — helping and guiding me — ever since I was a little girl."

My gaze suddenly zooms out to the entire pub, and I check to see if a passerby might have heard this. But no, the room is mainly empty outside of a few blokes who have their asses glued to the stool at the front. *Jesus Christ.* No one is going to bloody believe this.

"And have you ever *seen* one of these fairy people?"

"Well, yes and no. That's not really how it works, you see."

Her fingers begin pantomiming a history of fairies to me, as if their gestures will somehow make her words more believable.

"Okay, let me get this sorted. They're some kind of little bee-sized energy things — that you can kind of see, but not really — doing magic to make people's lives better?" Does she hear herself?

"Correct," Svea responds, deadpan.

"How do you know it's a fairy, then? Maybe they're just magical bees."

"Because that's what they *told* me they are," she says as if explaining why you need a cup to hold liquid.

"Wait. They *talk* to you?"

"Ah, well, it's more like little whispers — tiny little voices that I can hear in my head." And I can tell by her serious stare that she really does hear them.

Holy mother of fuck. She hears people in her mind.

I want to keep listening to what she's saying, really, I do. Someone, in this day and time, who can sustain a belief in something as ludicrous as fairies is worth hearing out. Well, now that I'm thinking about it, I guess it's not that crazy. People believe in Jesus. And he's kind of like a religious fairy, isn't he?

I spend the next few minutes trying very hard to concentrate and grasp the evidence that she is doing her best to convince me of — but I can't help but to dip in and out of what she's saying — my thoughts swimming in absolute incredulity at her complete devotion and belief in this.

"Cobwebs are how some of them travel... lying down in the grass and I'll feel the strokes of their fingertips in my hair... You're just not paying attention to their presence. But they're all around you."

She finishes, and I steeple my hands in front of my face to

hide my expression. "Interesting," I nod, then check my watch. "So it's getting a little bit late…" I start.

She looks down suddenly at the gold watch on her thin wrist. "Oh, I guess you're right. Well, I don't have much going on tomorrow. We could continue this conversation back at my place? I think I have a bottle of gin there."

"I," I pause in my answer. This could be a colossal mistake. Like she performs spells and rituals over the men she brings home, type of mistake.

Svea leans across the table with her chest again, and lightly runs the pads of her fingers across the back of my left hand. The hair running along my forearm and even the hair on my chest stand at attention at her touch and a slight zing zaps through me.

I don't take the time to sort through whether the reaction is one of fear or excitement. All I know is, the next words out of my mouth are, "Sure. I'd love to."

*

"You know how much I love you. You are the best, smartest, and handsomest brother," I whisper into the phone.

"What do you want James?" Alex grumbles at me.

"Well, since you asked, I need a lift. Right now," I look around the dark living room, making sure it's still only me. For safe measures, I huddle a little deeper behind the ficus positioned in the corner of the room.

"Are you serious, mate? It's a bit late, isn't it? Why didn't you think to mention this earlier? Instead of waking me up in the middle of the bloody fucking night, hmm?"

"You see—" He cuts me off.

"I asked you if you were all right and guess what you said?

You sent me a text saying everything was all good. Calling me at three in the morning is *not* all good James!"

"Okay, but if you knew what I've had to endure you'd be a little more understand — wait, shh." I stop mid-sentence and scan the room. I could've sworn I heard the floorboards creak, but after holding my breath for a whole minute, I determine that it's just my nerves. "Look, I'll owe you big time. I would've Ubered but it's far too expensive from here." I fully sit down in the corner behind the ficus, my body's exhaustion suddenly catching up to me.

"Where are you?"

"Enfield." The word comes out unintelligibly.

"You're gonna have to speak up." I can hear his smirk through the phone.

I roll my eyes and let out a strong-winded huff. "*Enfield*," I pronounce slowly.

"No."

"No?" *Shit.* I lower my voice before repeating, "No? What do you *mean* no?"

"I am sick and tired of your reckless decisions. I'm tired of you and your women. James, you make me *tired*. If you really need to get home right now, pay the money for a cab."

"But—"

"And don't even think about blowing up my phone with calls because I'm turning it off. Goodnight."

"But—" The phone call ends. "Damnit."

Nayelli

My heart thrums a fierce rhythm at the back of my throat. *You can do this Nayelli. Just follow the directions and you'll be fine.* Check into the hotel. Meet Olivia at Hyde Park. Simple.

My eyes are — and have been — glued to my pre-downloaded directions, only allowing me to notice the lack of grass and abundance of asphalt and cement beneath me. I'm almost to my hotel but I use the last few moments of my walk to just... exist.

There are only six thousand miles between me and my college town in California, but this might as well be a whole new world. I have no idea what I expected London to be, but it wasn't this.

The early dusk is beginning to blanket the tall buildings in dark obscurity, but the vivid charm of the streets remain. I have to crane my neck to get the full effect of the buildings that have faded down over time to a ruddy brown. Everything on this street just looks so old — as if contemporary life exists only indoors, while the exterior remains embedded in centuries of history. After walking through Olivia's neighborhood with more of the same structures, it's clear that most of the city is fashioned in this way.

Until I saw it for myself, I was incapable of conjuring up all the intricacies that make this place such a massive metropolis. Navigating from my hotel has allowed me to take note of the massive museums, the coffee shops on every corner, the shopping villages amongst the neighborhoods, and the quaint pubs that populate the entire city like stars in the night.

I still have so much to see, but my mind is already made up: I'm in love. Although, I will say, the local food is quite terrible. You would think that the place literally known for "chips" would also know about its best friend: ranch.

After a sharp left and a half *kilometer* down Bloomsbury Street, I am assaulted by the cold winds of London. My black wool coat is failing me so miserably, but at this point, it comes as no surprise. In a short amount of time I have learned that your phone plan doesn't automatically work in other countries, American clothes are obviously not made for English winters, and the dollar conversion rate is so bad I'm basically being robbed. The lack of research and preparation for exploring a new country is definitely coming back to bite me in the ass.

Nevertheless, there's nothing I can do about it now. I count the adjacent buildings on the narrow street, all squished together like the end of a monopoly game until I find the one I'm looking for: Bloomsbury Palace Hotel.

I lug my suitcase across the threshold and scan the entryway for help. The reception area is small and carpeted in an ugly brown. Once spotted, the front desk woman wastes no time in checking me in and taking me to my room on the first floor just a few steps down the hall. She shows me how the lights work, points to a pamphlet that includes their Wi-Fi, hands me my key card, and disappears in a blue-uniformed flash.

All I can say is: the pictures on the internet lied.

The angles that the photographer took of this room are magical — in the dark arts kind of way. How in the world did they make this room look comfortable?

To describe the room as small would be a gross

understatement: a narrow walkway leads from the door directly to the bed, with the bed jigsawed between three of the four walls — leaving absolutely no spare room except for the square foot of space in front of the night table. The bathroom located near the entrance, although modern, is tiny too; it has barely enough space to be functional — enough room to stand to brush your teeth in front of the sink, sit down on the porcelain toilet, or step inside of the granite shower — nothing more, nothing less.

The space gives me tremendous Alice in Wonderland vibes and I feel as if I have consumed the enlarging properties of the "Eat Me" cake. I am barely of average height for an American woman and yet almost entirely too big for this room. *Freaking Olivia.* She's the one who recommended I change my hotel room from the city's eastern outskirts of Wembley to the center of London because it is "closer to what we'll be doing and will balance out price wise." But at such short notice, this was the most affordable room I could find.

I give the cramped hotel room one more overview. It is my first taste of London without Olivia, and so far it seems completely underwhelming. All white linen for the bedding, thick tan drapes that frame the expansive window, a small dark oak night table with one lamp, a tray filled with tea fixings, and — last but not least — an extremely well-designed bathroom covered in granite and steel. Oddly enough, the bathroom is the only piece that reminds me even remotely of something from home.

I grab the white card the receptionist left behind and follow the instructions for the Wi-Fi. Connecting without issue, my phone chimes with missed iMessages and notifications.

I settle atop the twin bed and open a Facebook message that's from… Will. My ex.
Happy Birthday Nayelli!

Ugh. It's not my fucking birthday. Asshole. I struggle to find some kind of peace within myself while my stomach threatens to fill with hate like lava and explode with years of hurt and anger. We dated for almost four years. He knows when my damn birthday is. The petty side of me wants to give Will a piece of my mind, but I remind myself that he isn't worth it. I promised myself that this time I would leave that chapter of my life behind for good. So, I do something I should've done over a year ago and block Will on every social platform I have and double check that his phone number is still blocked too.

After the deed is done, I give my wrists a little twist and roll my neck in hopes of relief. Taking a long breath, I let out all of my pinned-up frustration in one big sigh. My whole point of coming to London for winter break was to get away from SoCal, not be reminded of the shit show of a life I have back there.

Checking the time, I set my phone down on the nightstand next to the bed. *Damn.* I need to get going. I walk over to the full-length mirror by the door to make sure I am making the right outfit choice for tonight. I pivot onto the ball of my right foot and then my left, trying to see how I look from all possible angles. Even though I'm thirty pounds lighter since the start of the school year, I still feel as if I am a guest visitor being hosted in this body. Being surrounded by skinny girls my whole life, I've developed the habit of neurotically making sure that my clothes are one hundred and ten percent flattering to my shape and body. The girl in the mirror lets out another huge sigh. I really should learn to just enjoy myself. I make a mental note of that and tuck it away for later.

Staring back at me in the mirror is my curvy shape accentuated by my fitted jeans and sweater. *Okay, very cute.* After checking the round curve of my ass in these particular jeans one more time, I tell myself to get a grip because let's face it, this is as good as it's going to get. My reflection gives me a small encouraging smile and I finally, with a sense of urgency, grab my coat and purse and rush out the door to meet back up with Olivia.

*

I've messed up. I've messed up big time.

Anxiety creeps its way down my stomach and forms a knot tugging at my insides. I check my phone. Again. I was supposed to have met Olivia almost two hours ago at Winter Wonderland but — thanks to my lack of phone service and Wi-Fi — I'm lost. Common sense should have told me to ask the locals, but the fear of being lost in a random neighborhood is overriding my senses.

"I could've sworn I had it right," I mumble to myself. "Get off the tube at Hyde Park, make a left exiting the station..."

I inchworm my way from shop front to shop front in search of free Wi-Fi, with no luck — all of them asking for too much money. I pause, frustrated in my endeavor, and look up. The soft blue sky rolls thick with cumulus clouds and pockets of peach sunset that backdrops the huge structures. My breath catches at the back of my throat. It's so beautiful. I know that no matter where you are in the world, the sun has to rise and set every single day but I still take the time to stop in the middle of the sidewalk and capture the memory with my phone.

Another hour passes and I am highly convinced that Olivia has probably left me. My steps briefly pause in front of each shop, still in search of Wi-Fi. All the while, the wind carries brief hints of garlic and baking bread and other delicious food from the restaurants clustered in front of me. My stomach rumbles aggressively. *Ugh.* I don't even remember the last time I ate today.

My feet shuffle a few more steps and my eyes catch on the sweetest words I've seen in the last three hours: *The Cloud*. I tuck myself against the shop boasting the free Wi-Fi signal and reorient myself to Winter Wonderland, followed by a quick message to Olivia apologizing profusely and letting her know that I'll be there in fifteen minutes.

"Where have you *been*?" Olivia shouts at the carnival-looking entrance. High above us, yellow light bulbs spell out "Winter Wonderland" against a painted wooden sign.

"I got lost, okay?"

"Really! For three hours?" She places her hands on her hips, her eyes — appearing almost black by the surrounding night — narrow to slits.

"Well excuse me for not knowing how to navigate London without a phone. It really wasn't my fault! You could've met me at the station, you know." You would think she would be a little more understanding. I'm sure she's gotten lost once or twice when she first moved here.

Her stare is cold and her weight shifts to her other foot before she replies. "We have to go." She walks out of the festival entrance and into the dark and creepy park.

"But I just got here!" I yell after her. Not much is lit except for a single cement pathway that exits out of the park, with leering black trees lining each side. I quickly jog to catch her, not wanting to be left alone and lost here at night.

"We have to meet my friend at the comedy club, remember? We don't want to be late and miss it," she says without looking in my direction, her long jean legs moving a mile a minute.

She's obviously pissed but I don't say a word about it, too thankful that I have been released from navigating duties. I follow closely behind as she sharply weaves us through crowds and across zebra sidewalks as we find our way back to Hyde Park station.

Eventually, we silently make it to the dark corner pocket of a comedy club in Leicester Square. We are led to a small room downstairs with black painted walls, a wooden stage, a few spotlights, and a small bar set up at the back. The one hundred matching black folding chairs are all filled, but I see a small hand wave to us from one of the nearby rows.

Within seconds of sitting, my forehead breaks into a full-on sweat beneath my beanie from all the high speed walking to get here. I can smell the tell-tale sign of my curls fighting back against the flat iron I used this morning. *Damnit.* I take both my peacoat and hat off in hopes of cooling down.

"You remember Nayelli, right Jasmine?" Olivia says by way of introduction to her friend.

"Yeah, of course. Nice to see you again," she smiles kindly at me and her green eyes sparkle against her olive face.

Jasmine used to come over to the apartment that Olivia and I shared, dancing on the stripper pole in our living room during Olivia's infamous "Wine Wednesday" parties. Olivia informs me that she's passing through before studying abroad in Bordeaux.

"I'll be right back," I announce, "I'm going to go grab something to drink."

"Oh! Just get something for all of us, and then we'll take turns getting rounds," Olivia instructs as I walk away.

My feet pause and my eyes squint slightly at the floor, remembering her saying the same exact line on the first night that I got here. Only, before Olivia was able to buy a round she claimed to be done drinking for the night and ready to go home.

"Sure," I respond without turning around.

By the end of the night, the dry humor of the comedians

mixes well with the sweet burn of the pink wine from the bar and I am able to completely let go of Olivia's negativity.

We exit the comedy club in good spirits. Still high off laughter and my wine buzz, I hardly notice the cold any more.

"This was such a good idea! I loved it! What a great first night out," I say to Olivia.

"Yeah, it was fun. I just can't believe Jasmine though," Olivia grumbles.

I feel the dip in my high-on-life feeling just from her tone of voice, but still do her the courtesy of asking, "What did she do?"

"Well I'm just pissed that we all came here together, and Jasmine literally spent the *entire* night talking to those guys that sat next to us. Like not once did she think to say 'Hey, let me introduce you to my friends.' Or, 'Hey, maybe my friends would like to drink with us too,' But no, instead she got free drinks for only herself, flirted with them, and acted like we weren't even there!" Olivia's cheeks begin to brighten by the end of her rant.

"Hey, hey it's okay," I soothe. "Those guys were really feeling her and she was just enjoying herself. Tonight wasn't our night to be chatted up, it was Jasmine's. Let her have her moment," I explain in hopes of consoling her. I'm not sure why guys hitting on Jasmine and not her have her panties up her ass, but I also don't get the chance to ask. Jasmine rejoins us after saying goodnight to her new friends and we head off.

We reach the station and I'm bubbling over with so much happiness that I can barely tap my Oyster card to get through the turnstiles. No school, no drama, just out on the town having fun and doing my own thing. The simplicity of my vacation life makes me giddy.

Downstairs at the tracks, I try to keep my cool as a rat passes by. Part of the experience I guess. My mouth turns down at my instinctual hate for rats, but I just as soon forget about it and take a seat on the bench next to the girls to wait for the next train.

On the ride back, Jasmine is still telling us about her company for the night. "Dude they were *so* cool! They were asking me different things about myself and somehow we started talking about my gluten allergy, and that led to shots of tequila." Out of the corner of my eye I can tell that Olivia is doing her best to feign interest in her recount.

"For tomorrow, are you still meeting me in the morning for a walk around the winter market before dinner and the club?" I ask, standing up and grabbing my purse. My stop is next.

"Yeah, of course. It is your birthday after all," Olivia answers with a small smile. She is trying her best not to be a Debbie-Downer and I can only hope that by tomorrow she'll shake it off. Call me selfish, but I only have a week left of being here and I want to make the most of every day. You only turn twenty-one once after all, and I don't want to spend my birthday trip sitting in Olivia's dorm complaining about men. Besides, deep down I know that she'll be okay. She just needs a little more time to get over her fuck boy experience.

"Okay! See you tomorrow Olivia, and nice hanging out with you again Jasmine," I say as I step off the train and onto the platform.

"Text us when you've made it safely to your room! And I'll be gone tomorrow, so HAPPY BIRTHDAY!" Jasmine yells before the doors close, and then I am left alone to navigate the streets of central London once more. I put on my Dora the Explorer attitude like a real woman and figure out how to orient myself underneath the streetlamp glow. In the dimly lit night, I spot the corner street sign and send up a little prayer that for once I'm going in the right direction.

James

By the time I walk through my parent's foyer, it is some time past eight in the morning. Without pausing to look in the living or dining room to see if anyone is up, I trudge my ragged body to the stairs.

"Good morning, Dear," I hear my mother call from the dining room table.

She is still in view from the stairs, so I turn to the left and put on my best face. "Morning, Mum."

I resume my steps. "Would you like some breakfast?" she asks.

"No, it's all right. I think I'm gonna have a nap."

"Are you sure you don't want anything? I made too much this morning."

"Yeah, James. Are you sure?" It's Alex's voice that repeats the question.

A mountain of frustration with my brother boils to life. "Yeah," I squeeze out through gritted teeth. "I'm *fine*."

"Okay, great. Just wanted to make sure you're all right. You know me, being considerate and all that."

"You're lucky I'm tired." I narrow my eyes at the sight of him smugly eating toast at the table.

"You're tired? But didn't you just get home? What were you out doing?" My mother's eyes look up from her tea to watch me answer the question.

I hold my fists at my sides and clamp my mouth shut. "I shall see you all after my nap," I announce, then bound quickly up the stairs.

The rest of the day is most unkind to me. It's as if a tiny little man has crawled into my head and started smashing up my brain to bits. I am in absolute pieces. I haven't had the strength to move out of bed since seeing my mum and Alex this morning.

A light knock raps on the other side of my door.

"Yes?" I yell at the door, still not having the desire to get up or move.

"You're *still* in bed?" I can hear the judgment, and I'm not in the mood.

"Here to be even more of an ass, Alex? Because if so, kindly revisit me tomorrow during business hours."

"About that," Alex says, sitting down at the desk across from me. "We should talk."

His tone sounds a bit serious, so I roll over under the blankets to look at him. "Is that my Jimi Hendrix T-shirt?"

Alex's sandy brown head dips down to look at his shirt. He shrugs, not caring. "Stop trying to distract me, I'm being serious right now. What the hell happened last night?" He leans forward and rests his forearms on his legs, a move our dad always did when we were in trouble and he wanted us to explain ourselves. But he's being dramatic and overreacting, like always.

"Oh, so *now* you care?" I sit up and match his body's position, only I am wearing nothing but my sweatpants so I wrap my covers over me to fight off the cold air in the room. It makes me feel like a large Russian Matryoshka doll.

Alex arches his left eyebrow at me, refusing to say anything else until I explain myself.

"Fine," I huff. And to the best of my ability, I explain the existence of fairies as told to me by Svea.

"You're joking," Alex leans back from the edge of his seat, pushing his Clark Kent glasses up the narrow bridge of his long, straight nose. "And you thought it would be smart to go home with her?" He sucks his teeth at me. "You're a lot denser than I thought."

"Oh, shut up. That's not even the worst part."

"There's *more*? Something *worse* happened than your date turning out to be completely mental?" Alex steeples his hands in front of his mouth before pointing his two index fingers at me. "Well then, out with it. And don't spare a single detail."

I roll my eyes before beginning. "She had... things. Decorating her house." A chill runs through me and I pull my blanket even tighter around myself. "Like, little wooden statues of tribute. To the fairies. There was something like a Wiccan circle, too. And after we walked in, she got in the middle of the circle, lit the candles, and prayed to the little things for guidance on if she should sleep with me or not."

"HO-LY *shit*! And you *stayed*!" His hands slide down his face in frustration. "James Benjamin Marcus, I am quite disappointed with you." He shakes his head at me incredulously. After a long pause, he asks, "Well? Don't leave me hanging. What did they say? Did the wood thingy's let you shag or not?"

I drop my head a bit... "We did. Not worth it. She wanted to do another ritual afterward, *with* me, but I stalled in the bathroom long enough to miss it. Then I waited until she fell asleep and snuck out to the living room to call you."

He nods in acknowledgment. "Well, I hope this taught you to—"

"To never trust you again? Yeah, mate. Not calling you for shit next time."

"Well, yes, that. But also, slow your fucking *roll* man." He throws an object from the desk at me.

"Hey, what was that for? So what? It was one bad isolated instance."

"Oh, isolated, aye? Then what would you call that banshee waking up the whole house on Christmas morning, hmm?"

"I don't know what you mean." Alex locks eyes with me, but I refuse to flinch. There's no way I'm letting him have the upper hand about this.

After what feels like an eternity, he stands. "I really worry about you, James," he says, exiting the room quietly.

I really don't understand why he feels the need to worry. I'm fine.

Nayelli

Crisp grey light begins to dance through the taupe drapes. I roll over and balance the pillow on top of my head, wanting to cram in at least another hour of sleep.

"Oh my god!" Realization dawns and I wrestle out the covers. It's 8 a.m. on the dot, which means it's midnight back home. My phone rings and I snatch it to my ear, already knowing who it is.

"Happy birrtthhdaaayyy toooo yoooouuuu," my mother sings. She then follows the traditional version with my childhood church's rendition of the birthday song. Finally, after two rounds ending with, "One more time!" she says, "What am I going to do? My oldest baby is twenty-one years old!" She begins to fake cry.

"Moooommmm. You're so dramatic," I laugh, "But thank you for the birthday wish. You're the first one."

"You're very welcome princess. Even though technically it's not your birthday yet since you were born on December 29th at 5:02 p.m.." She tells me this every year. You would think she would just start calling at 5:02 p.m., but no. Without fail, she calls at midnight and then complains. "What time is it over there? What are you going to do to celebrate?" she asks.

"It's barely eight. Olivia and I are going to—" before I can finish the sentence, my phone vibrates. "Hold on, I think this is her now."

My mood deflates slightly at the text. "Never mind," I say to my mother. "Olivia said she's too tired, so we're not doing anything until dinner."

"Are you scared?" she asks pointedly.

"Scared? Of what?" My brows stitch together. I plop down onto the bed and stare at the ceiling, not knowing what to do next.

"Of being alone in the city."

"No, not really." Where is she going with this?

"Then put on your big girl panties and enjoy your day baby girl. You only get one twenty-first birthday. Have breakfast at a cute cafe, get your nails done, go shopping. Do whatever it is that will make you happy on your special day. But whatever you do, don't waste half your birthday doing nothing in a foreign country — all because your friend is tired. Or, at least, I wouldn't if I were you."

You know, the lady makes a lot of sense. "You're right, Mom."

"I know I am. Now go get dressed and put a smile on that pretty face of yours and have the best time," she instructs.

I smile on my side of the phone. "I love you, Mom."

"I love you too, call me later."

I slide up the bed and lean against the headboard. One of the Tinder guy's may have mentioned something about checking out a place called Angel Market, so I scroll through my messages to find our conversation, hoping that he — or one of the others — will be awake and willing to help me plan out my day in the city.

Unsurprisingly so, my mother and the Tinder men have given me the loveliest suggestions and I end up having the most perfect morning I could ever wish for. After a mimosa toast to myself at a French cafe, a pedicure at a hole in the wall nail shop, and a mini shopping spree at the Primark and Topshop on Oxford Street, I head back to my hotel to drop off my bags before going out again.

The Tinder guy told me that the market is right around the corner from Angel train station and I find it without a single problem.

Hell yeah.

The words "Chapel Market" are boasted across an iron banner between Marks & Spencer and some other store that's being covered up by a stand for mobile accessories. The sun is playing peek-a-boo behind the buildings, but the clouds are thin and the sky mainly blue. A wonderful thing on an English winter day, or so the men on the app have told me. I snap a picture before looking left, like the crosswalk instructs me to, and stroll across the street to the market's entrance.

The entire street is blocked off for the occasion. Tall brick houses are stacked on top of eclectic shop fronts that are stacked behind endless stands and booths. The crowd of people in the street are thick and static, some yelling in thick accents, most of them bundled and unidentifiable. I can't tell who's buying and who's selling. An overwhelming rush of intrigue washes over me, it's all so much.

From cell phone accessories to winter coats, suitcases, fish, a myriad of fruits and veggies — this place has it all. It reminds me of the old strip mall in my hometown, mixed with the downtown Santa Barbara Farmers Market.

A middle stand boasting a rainbow assortment of produce catches my eye, and I scan the rows until I find what I'm looking for.

"'Ello Love, you all right?" The merchant greets me as I pick up a box of strawberries. His bright smile causes his face to crease deeply, displaying his older age.

"Yes, I'm fine. Thank you," I reply, still comparing boxes to make sure I have the prettiest batch of berries. I note to myself how it still catches me off guard with the way they throw around "love" and "sweetheart." I think my uber driver even called me love on my drive from the airport.

"You like strawberries quite a bit, yeah?" he asks watching me, no doubt wondering why I've been picking up boxes and putting them down for a solid ten minutes straight.

"You could say that," my grin is mischievous. Strawberries are my most favorite thing *ever*. Always have been. My mom even used to call me her little strawberry lady. But there's no way I'm sharing that with him.

"Where's your accent from? America? Are you from America?" He's obviously amused. He crosses his arms across his chest and waits for my reply.

"Yup. Visiting from California." I put the strawberries down. I can't concentrate while he's talking to me.

"California? Get out of here! Are you lost then? What in the hell are you doing in England in the middle of winter?" he chuckles deeply, and I can tell this isn't his first time saying that. It must be his running joke with Californians.

"Just visiting my friend from college, or I mean, *uni*."

"Well then, Miss California. I do hope that you are enjoying your time here in London. And the strawberries are three baskets for ten pounds."

"Three for ten? Amazing!" I grab the three boxes I was debating between and hand them to him to bag for me.

Heading back out of the market, my legs feel light and airy. Who knew a day alone in this place could feel so… invigorating? I could not have had a better start to my birthday. Even so, a small spark of dread ignites deep down in my chest. It's almost time for me to meet Olivia at her place before dinner, and based on her weird mood lately, who knows how that could go?

A sigh unwillingly escapes my lips, but I shake my head in hopes of clearing away the negativity. It's like my mom said, I'm in a foreign country. That's already a bonus, especially considering the fact that I spent last year's birthday watching *Fences* with my mom and grandmother.

"It's my birthday. My day will be fantastic," I say aloud in hopes that it will make it true.

James

As I blow off the day in bed, Alex words sit with me. Bothered and frustrated about his implications, and in an attempt to prove him wrong, I sit my blanketed body at my computer desk and power up my Mac. While waiting, I check my phone and notice a new WhatsApp message from the girl Nayelli.

Elli.27, 4:38 p.m.
Still want to meet up with me?
5:05 p.m.
Absolutely. Are you up to anything this evening?
Elli.27, 5:07 p.m.
Headed out to dinner actually.
5:08 p.m.
Got time for a quick chat?
Elli.27, 5:08 p.m.
Aren't we chatting right now lol
5:09 p.m.
Yeah, but I mean a call on here so that I can see you.
Elli.27, 5:12 p.m.
Oh, no way. I'm too shy. We're already meeting up tomorrow.
Why do you need to call me?
5:12 p.m.
Just want to check if you're a catfish.
Elli.27, 5:15PM
You can find that out tomorrow... if we meet.

5:17 p.m.
You don't even want to see if I'm a catfish?
It'll be super quick. The quickest of quick.
Elli.27, 5:18 p.m.
Fine. But I really do have to go soon.

Oh my days, this is really about to happen. My heart kickstarts and thumps a little harder against my chest than normal. As I've mentioned, the first time meeting my matches makes me a little nervous due to my catfish paranoia. She could look absolutely nothing like her pictures because they aren't her pictures. Or they could be her photos but photoshopped. The possibilities of what people hide in situations like these are endless. My friend Dave never went on an app date again after his catfish experience. It was *that* bad.

Only a few minutes pass, but it feels like forever before her call pops up on my screen.

"Hi, there! What? What's this? Where are you?" I ask, confused. All I can see is the ceiling.

"Sorry, sorry." Her voice is soft and light, with the smallest hint of sultry. "Here I am." Her American accent is also not blaringly thick and obnoxious. A welcome surprise since I've heard the complete opposite about the people from Boston. Or maybe it was New York? The camera shuffles around on unidentifiable things before settling on her smiling face. "Hello, James."

"Wow," I manage to choke out, "I see why you're so popular."

"Popular? What do you mean?" She sets her laptop down on what I assume is a bed but remains standing, walking about and grabbing things around the room.

Nayelli's top is black and see through where it counts. The mesh part of the top starts at her overly generous cleavage and tapers down to her belly button. My eyes scan down her fit waist and across her luscious hips. The way the black jeans cling to the curves of her body makes the center of my palms itch. She's going out looking like that? With who?

"James?" she asks, taking a seat on the bed and bringing her face into close view — and Christ, what a beautiful face it is.

"Right. I, um, just meant that you look nice."

"Oh! Thank you, I'm glad you think so," she scans her outfit and then beams the brightest grin back at me. Even her teeth are perfect.

"You're very welcome. So where are you going?" My mind is completely shattered. I can't stop staring at this girl. Her lips are full and kissable, her dark eyes sharp and roguish in a delayed gratification kind of way. Her thick, dark hair rests in soft waves around her like a halo. Her bare skin looks so soft and glowy. My god, I want to explore every last inch. What day did I suggest we grab a drink again?

"I'm grabbing dinner with my friend. This is her room, actually. But I thought I'd give you a quick call while she grabbed some wine from the kitchen. Oh, no," she responds to her cell phone, wrinkling her forehead at it.

"What is it?"

"My friend poured me a glass and said I'm taking too long. Bye James, I'll text you later!" And in the same blur of movement that she greeted me with, she leaves.

"Wow," I say again.

Feeling like my day's luck is turning around, I shoot Nayelli a message to confirm an actual date and time for our meet up.

I spin around twice in my computer chair, excited. It's like the universe knew my exact type and then delivered her to me on vacation. "Fuck," I whisper in excitement.

This is going to be so much fun.

Nayelli

"How does it feel to be twenty-one?" Olivia asks from across the table of the Italian restaurant *Trattoria Mondello*.

She chose it for us because it's close to my hotel, but the linguine and clams are to die for and the wine is so freaking delicious. Twirling more pasta around my fork, I give a slight shrug of my shoulder before answering her.

"Not much different I guess. I think it will feel more like a milestone once I'm back in America. No one cares about being twenty-one here, their drinking age is eighteen." Silence falls on the small, candle-lit table. Feeling an urge to fill the void, I rattle off the first thing that comes to mind. "Will text me."

"Ew! Seriously Nayelli? You don't have him blocked?" Olivia's eyes snap up with judgment and disappointment.

I've seen the look before. Mainly when Will came to our apartment a few times because I had the dumbest idea that we could be "friends." To me, he was like a safe bet. In hindsight, however, screwing the ex that cheated on you is a whole lot worse than putting yourself out there or being rejected. At least now I know better.

"Calm down, I blocked him after he messaged me," I say around another bite of pasta.

"You should've blocked him after he *cheated on you*." Olivia always feels the need to bring this up like hearts run on common sense. Old habits die hard, even toxic ones.

"I know, I know. But he's blocked now, so let's move on."

"Well, have you thought about any more activities that you want to do while you're here?" she asks.

"Don't you have a few things in mind from living here? I thought you were supposed to be my personal tour guide or something." Maybe she doesn't remember the plan because so far she is sucking at her guide duties.

"Give me your phone," she says, ignoring my last question.

"Why?" I ask. What could she possibly need it for? She never asks for my phone.

"Because I want to look at your Tinder men. Now give it here," Olivia says with a smirk and her palm outstretched to me.

I hand over the phone but keep my gaze locked on her every movement. Where is she going with this?

"Five hundred men? You matched with *over* five hundred men! How in the hell did you do that?" she yells.

"To be fair," I lower my voice in hope that she'll do the same, "some of them are from California. You know how intense the UC finals week gets... I used it as a distraction from studying." I focus on the white linen underneath my silverware instead of her judgmental face.

Olivia leans back in her chair and squares her shoulders at me from across the table. "Well then," she begins softly, "why don't you ask one of your *five hundred* men what you should do with the rest of your time here?"

"Geez Olivia! Can you not yell that?" I scan the intimate restaurant to see if anyone is eavesdropping, then give my gaze back to Olivia. What's gotten into her?

"What's wrong with me saying that? It's true," she says, twisting her mouth upward like the Grinch. She's obviously taking her issues with the model fuckboy out on everyone else.

Ugh, but I swear to Bob, I am *two* seconds away from

continuing this trip on my own. Between coming off finals week, fighting through the seventh circle of hell (my housemates), and the eight-hour time difference, my head is pulsing with sharp twangs — and Olivia's attitude isn't making it any better. I rub my temples with the pads of my fingers before speaking.

"*Because*," I roll my eyes as hard as I can and then look at my dim-witted friend, "someone who overhears me having five hundred men with no context might think that I'm a lady of the night or something." Why do I even have to explain this?

My last sentence settles on the table between us and after a short pause, we share a laugh, effectively lightening the mood.

"Well, are you going to meet up with any of them?" Her voice is back to its usual easy cadence.

"No," I pick up my wine glass and look into the shallow red abyss as I answer. The familiar tingly sensation in my stomach signals a buzz is coming on.

"Why not?" she asks.

"I've never met up with anyone from the app before, only had little conversations. The idea of it all makes me too nervous. Also, I didn't come all the way to London to *date*. I'm here to spend time with *you*. I mean, I am also here to recruit a foreign sugar daddy to pay my way through college, but that's beside the point," I wink at her and finish the last of my glass. I think I've had more drinks in the last three days than in my last three years of college, but hey, I'm on vacation and plan to take advantage. Plus, my tolerance is way higher here. Maybe it's the jet lag. Either that or I've been drinking nothing but shitty alcohol back home.

"Oh my god," she laughs. "You have to go out with at least *one* of them."

"Well there is this one guy who wants to take me out on

Saturday but I plan on flaking. He could be a total creep. A sexy hot creepy man, but a creep nonetheless." Just the *thought* of meeting this gorgeously photogenic man in person and he either turning out to be a serial killer or a total bore that I have to pull teeth to make conversation with is bad enough. I don't need to see that drama play out in real life.

"Do you even hear yourself? You're overthinking it. And being overly dramatic. Let me see what he looks like," she says and offers her hand out yet again for my phone.

I pull up his profile. She scrutinizes him silently, but I don't need her approval. I already know he's attractive — dark hair with deep waves, full lips, large brown eyes that I could get lost in, and a solid body that looks as if he is on the taller side — all confirmed by our brief FaceTime session earlier tonight. Then, as if that isn't enough, in his bio it says that he sings, is an established actor, and plays the guitar (which is captured in one of his photos). Looking at this man makes me feel as if my ovaries might explode.

"You should go," is all she says, handing back my phone.

"Are you sure?" I ask, trying to read her face but it's blank.

"Yeah, I don't see why not. Tonight's Friday, right? We already made plans to go to the club tonight to celebrate your birthday, and then my family flies in tomorrow — Saturday. I won't be doing anything but waiting around for them, it's perfect."

"All right, I guess. But remember that if something goes wrong, this was *your* idea." I send the guy a quick message confirming our date then slide my phone back into my purse. I sit back in my wooden chair and can't help the grin that erupts across my face. I'm really about to do this! I'm going on a date with a sexy British man.

Just as quickly, the giddiness transforms into a spike of mild panic. Yeah, he's hot. But he's still a man that I met online… who can turn out to be completely crazy…

Geez, am I really about to go through with this? I flag down the waiter and order another glass of wine.

The club we go to after dinner is sweaty and humid with randomly spaced pinatas on the walls. Dia de Los Muertos masks and mariachi sombreros fill in the leftover colorful space, really tying together the latin club vibes. We dance and sing our asses off and once again my curls fight me, trying to resemble a blow-dried sheep instead of the sleek and straight style I started the night with.

Olivia points and screams at the top of her lungs pop hits of 2010 and for a moment, it's like we're back in our small second-story apartment in Santa Barbara.

The third week after moving in, she talked me into buying a stripper pole for the living room. We almost gave our mothers a stroke when they came to visit their daughters in their first college apartment.

"A stripper pole? *Really* Nayelli?" my mom said upon entering the apartment. For some reason, stripper poles and morally conservative mothers just didn't mix well. She dealt with it by shaking her head in judgment and scrutinizing me with stern eyes. But eventually, she let it go since I was, "technically an adult now."

"Gonna go get some water from the bar!" Olivia yells over the music, bringing my attention back to the club.

"Ok!"

In her absence, I check my phone. Waiting for me is another WhatsApp from James.

Jayyy333, 10:35 p.m.

Where are you and your friend partying?
11:17 p.m.
Torteria.
Jayyy333, 11:18 p.m.
Where in the heck balls is that?
11:23 p.m.
Leicester Square.
Jayyy333, 11:24 p.m.
Oh! You mean Tonteria!
That's not too far from my house, you should come over.
11:29 p.m.
I just googled your address and it says
that you are 30 minutes away.
So that will be a hell no for tonight.
Besides, we're supposed to meet up on Saturday anyway...
that's only tomorrow.
I don't see the point in me coming tonight.
Jayyy333, 11:32 p.m.
Oh, come on! That's like the length of one Simpson's episode.
Just take a cab, watch the episode,
and you'll be here before you know it.
11:35 p.m.
Why is it so important that I come tonight?
What did you want to do?
Jayyy333, 11:37 p.m.
I can show you my collection of rocks.
11:40 p.m.
In that case I'm not coming.
Jayyy333, 11:42 p.m.
Look, I promise that I will be a complete gentleman.

We can do whatever you want, I'll leave that completely up to you.

You're just already next to my neighborhood. Might as well.

I read over his messages again, trying to figure out what his game is. Part of me doesn't understand the immediacy. What's the rush? We literally have a date planned for tomorrow. On the other hand, I have a blossoming curiosity that can't wait to be fed. Is he just as quirky in person? Will he like me? Will I be too nervous and forget how to speak? Is he actually tall or just takes photos at the right angles? And what is it about me — someone he's only seen photos of and for two seconds on FaceTime — that is driving him to rush our first meeting?

After hesitating for a few moments more, my curiosity gets the best of me and I let James know that I'll be on my way soon.

"Hey," Olivia says, parting the sea of club-goers and walking back up to me. "I'm pretty tired, and it's getting late. I'm gonna head back to my dorm. Wanna walk out together?"

"Sure, I'll call my Uber."

James

The doorbell rings and I race down the steps, trying to grab the door before she has the chance to ring it again and wake my parents. Or worse — Alex.

Swinging the door open, I put on my most welcoming smile and give Nayelli a cheerful hello. One look at her and my excitement for the evening reignites below the band of my trousers.

She steps in quietly, covered from neck to toe in a black trench coat and tan heels. Her eyes lazily scan the room, yet she says nothing. The silence begins to make me anxious so I fire off questions to break the stillness.

"How are you? Was the ride okay? Would you like something to eat? Or maybe something to drink?" I just want her to say something, anything. Do I look better in my photos and she's disappointed?

"I'm fine, James. Thank you," she replies softly. Then more silence.

"What about some wine?" I try again, hoping I can get some conversation flowing. Is she nervous? I sure am. A drink should help with that, right? Then again, wasn't she drinking at the club?

"*Please*," she says with a surprising amount of enthusiasm.

Good, okay, good. Perhaps she doesn't hate me after all. My body races towards the kitchen without her, feeling the need to make this evening as smooth as possible, willing to give her whatever she needs to feel comfortable. And not to mention, reassure her I'm not *that* guy from Tinder.

"Join me in here, will you?" I call to her once the drinks are ready.

She walks in barefoot with red nail polish on her toes, still bundled in her black coat. Taking her wine glass, she immediately brings it to her lips — her eyes staying on mine the whole time. My focus fills with her lush lips around the glass, then snaps back up to her gaze. There's no way she could know what that move is doing to me. *Dear god.*

I'm dying inside, my insides torn between wanting to kiss her but also not wanting to rush things and scare her away.

"Food? Did you say you wanted food?" I ask, distracting myself.

"No," she laughs into her glass, "no food."

"Are you sure? I have some delicious chicken that's already made."

"Yes, I'm sure, James. I had a burrito at the club. Why do you keep trying to feed me?"

"I guess it's the Jewish mum in me."

She laughs again, the dim light sparkling off her white teeth, then takes another deep drink of wine. "Why aren't you drinking your wine?" she asks matter of fact.

"I hate wine." I only poured the cup so she wouldn't feel alone. She stares at me for a long moment, waiting to see if I'll take a sip. Hurrying a rushed sip of the disgusting drink, I try to keep a straight face and ask, "Would you like a tour of the house?"

"Sure," she answers.

"Wonderful. Right here where we're standing, as you probably already know, is the kitchen. The door behind me is the back garden." It's too dark to actually see anything, so I move on. Walking from the kitchen, we pass through the dining room.

I point out that it's our dining room — then we cross back out into the foyer. "And last but not least, the sitting room on your right just there." Jesus, house tours are so boring. How in the world do people make a career out of this? "How about we go upstairs now? I can show you my room?"

Nayelli nods her head but doesn't say anything. I thought she was so enthusiastic about the wine because she wanted to calm her nerves but even with it, she still hasn't said much. Then again, she hasn't made up an excuse to leave either.

Pausing outside of my closed door, I point to the room directly across from mine. "That's my younger brother Alex's room," I whisper, then point to the stair banister on my left. "The second level contains my parent's room."

Again, she nods but doesn't say anything. My mind wanders in the direction of judgment — she's silently judging me, isn't she? That's why she hasn't spoken all evening, she's disappointed with the man in real life.

I look down. I'm wearing a white T-shirt with a dinosaur on it and living in my parent's home for fuck's sake.

We're still standing in the hallway, my hand on the doorknob. I mentally slap myself, I need to pull it together. Now is not the time for outfit regrets. And more importantly, when did I start caring about a stranger's opinion?

After opening the door and turning on the light, she walks in after me, looking around at everything.

"Let me take your coat," I offer.

She nods and I slide it down her bare shoulders.

Trying to swallow at the vision of her, my Adam's apple almost chokes me. A sleeveless one-piece bodysuit molds to her hourglass figure like an etch-a-sketch, her voluptuous breasts spilling out the top. Her dark brown hair hangs softly in loose waves past her breasts, just like on our FaceTime call.

"Umm," I try to think. "Would you like me to show you how to create some beats? I have a synthesizer my parents got me last Christmas." As long as I keep us preoccupied, I won't do something stupid and ruin my chances with her before she's ready — *if* she's ever ready.

Her smile is slow in arching across her face. "Yeah, I won't be any good though."

"Oh, pssht. I'm sure you're a natural."

Turns out she is god-awfully horrible at the synth, but her horribleness is admirable in that she doesn't give up.

Hours slip past as we talk and drink with a random iTunes playlist playing in the background. She loves the MCU just as much as I do, apparently her father got her into it when she was a kid. And after confirming that she indeed knows the origin stories of my favorite Marvel characters and isn't bluffing just to impress me, I become genuinely intrigued in picking this woman's brain. Granted, I think there's nothing sexier than a British accent, but I'm loving hearing her speak. Any topic I bring up, she has some sort of well informed — although sometimes eccentric — opinion about it. I realize I might've misjudged her. Or, at the very least, been very limiting in my perception of her. Based on her photos, I had pegged her as the type that's shallow and boring — maybe even not that bright — but at the very least an attractive fuck.

Are all beautiful women dense? No, of course not. But have I run into my fair share that more often proves the stereotype than not? You bet.

Nayelli is sitting on my bed with her legs tucked beneath her, passionately explaining her conspiracy theory of an octopus' intelligence not having its proper recognition.

At least it isn't fairies.

Sitting across from her at my computer desk, I lean forward and rest my forearms on my thighs. "I mean, are you kidding me?" she continues, "They decorate their ocean homes! Why would you ever want to eat something that is skilled in interior design?"

She has a bit of a point. I'm not even sure how we started talking about this. I think she might've asked me if I like to eat seafood, and well, here we are.

"I'm sure you've heard of the one that escaped from the aquarium in California, right?"

Why she thinks an octopus escaping would make international news, I'm not quite sure. And from what I've asked, she's not a vegan or vegetarian and has never considered a PETA membership, so I'm not understanding the fascination. Still, it's a sweet contrast to her quiet nods earlier. It's kind of adorable seeing her all worked up and researched about a damn sea creature that has absolutely nothing to do with her. I simply reply, "No," keeping my smile stifled so as not to offend her.

"Well then," she begins, and I notice both empty wine glasses next to her on the nightstand, "you're about to have your mind *blown*."

When in the hell did she manage to take my glass *and* finish it? It must have been when I went to the bathroom after introducing her to her first *Adventure Time* episode.

"So," she starts up again, "there's two octopus — octopuses? — octopi? — escape stories, but I'll start with the mastermind. This one in particular escaped from his tank, slithered down the hallway that leads to the drains, and then squeezed through the drain pipes until he eventually dumped out into the ocean. He is currently out free at sea, living his best life."

"Bullshit."

"I'm *serious*. I told you, it made the news! And they had the *nerve* to call it a 'lucky accident'."

"I still don't believe it," I say, just to be contrarian. She then goes on to detail another octopus that would sneak out his tank every night to steal a fish from his neighboring tank, then hop back into his own as if nothing happened. I realize she talks a lot with her hands when she's excited.

"All I'm saying is, if there wasn't that whole land/sea factor, octopus would definitely whoop our ass and take our spot at the top of the food chain." She finishes her spiel, hands on hips, satisfied with her argument.

I can't help but laugh. This chick is unbelievable. If I were asked how I thought this evening would go, I would have never in a million years factored in this conversation. I look up from laughing and she's beaming, happy with herself for making me laugh so hard.

"I'm just saying. The more you live, the more you know." She shrugs her shoulder, still smiling at me.

"Right. Well then, now that we have that sorted, what would you like to do?" I ask.

"Umm, we could watch another episode of *Adventure Time*?"

Oh wow, she actually liked it. And for some reason, that makes me happy. Or maybe it's just the unexpected good vibes flowing between us. "Sure, I'll put it on." I swivel around in my computer chair towards the desk and pull up the next episode from my iTunes library.

Nayelli joins me at the desk, her hand lightly touching my shoulder, watching what I'm doing. Without thinking too hard — or else I might chicken out — I reach my hand to cradle just behind her thigh.

She stops moving, her lips part. It's the first time we've touched this whole evening. I turn to face her fully and lean towards her, slowly, leaving room for her to walk away or say no if this isn't what she wants.

She does neither of these things.

Instead, Nayelli trains her eyes on my mouth and tilts her head slightly for better access. Our lips finally meet and the kiss is lush, warm, and inviting.

"Wow," is all that I can manage to say after we part. "What a kiss. You have absolutely incredible lips."

"Thank you," she answers, and it takes everything to not moan at the sudden rasp in her voice. Or the sparkle of hunger that shines brightly inside her deep brown eyes.

My mind is mush. Words exchange between us but I'm not aware of what they are, only aware of my desire to have her. She moves to step away and I instinctively catch her by the waist, not wanting this tether between us to sever. She balances herself with her hands on my shoulder, her breasts now properly in my face.

A moment passes and I force my eagerness to settle. We stare at each other in this position for lord knows how long. Nayelli looks down upon me with my neck tilted back to look up into her face from my chair. Her gaze grows even heavier, her breaths come faster. Her soft hands move to lightly stroke the stubble on my face. I reach around to find the zipper to her outfit, stopping with it in my grasp before proceeding.

She nods and I continue my pursuit. An electric charge runs through me, intensifying my need to both see and feel what lies beneath.

It's like Christmas all over again.

The clothing drops down to her ankles, and she breaks away

from me to step out of them. Waiting with her hands at her sides, I take my time absorbing every inch of her from head to toe. Nayelli is not very tall but in her short amount of space manages to fit so much. I have yet to come across a woman with curves as defined as hers who wasn't on Instagram. Or Beyonce.

My mouth goes dry looking at her, but I eventually manage to say, "You look unreal." And she does. From her defined collar bones to the black lace that dances across her full breasts protesting against their enclosure. To her trim waist that leads to tiny black panties that frame impossibly gorgeous hips. Her thighs are full — complimenting her hips — and her calves are toned as if she used to be an athlete. And let's not forget her beautiful, lickable skin.

Nayelli is an absolute vision.

She has the kind of body you dream about, the kind that you can get lost in. The kind you look forward to haunting you after the sex is done and over with. One that might make me cum too quick. One that might destroy my soul during orgasm and leave my body a crumpled heap on the mattress.

I lick my lips at the thought, wrapping my arms around her waist and bringing her closer to me.

If this is how I go, then so be it. I pull her closer to me and pray that our first time won't be over too soon.

*

"Where are you going?" I peer from the far side of the bed and see Nayelli bending over, grabbing her things in the dark. We went at it for so long, it has to be at least five in the morning, if not later.

"Back to my hotel," she replies plainly.

Did I do something wrong? Did she not enjoy herself? Am I not the size she's used to? I should've asked her if she's been with a white guy before.

"Are you mental? It's almost six in the morning! Just stay," I tell her. In a matter of moments, she manages to shove the anxiety from our first encounter back inside of me.

The moon casts a silhouette across her figure and I can tell that she has paused in her movements, so I take advantage of her hesitation. "Don't you want to cuddle? Cuddling is like the best part. You don't want to miss out on the best part, do you?" I really don't want to sleep alone tonight.

She finally breaks from her stance and turns back the covers to climb into bed. *Thank god.*

I watch all of Nayelli's movements as she joins me again. I'm probably staring at her like a complete moron, but I honestly can't help it. A stunning girl that I actually get on with — and not to mention she's leaving for America next week. I might as well cram as much ogling in as she'll allow me to.

I pull her supple body into me and give her a small kiss on the forehead. "That was hands down the best sex I've ever had in my life," I say simply.

"Oh my *god*," she says while lightly shoving at my chest, "please don't feel the need to exaggerate just to make me feel good. My ego is doing just fine." She tries to roll away from me to her side of the bed, but I wrap my arms a little tighter around her.

"I'm not making this up. It's true Nayelli." And it is. "Next, I guess we get married and I introduce you to my parents."

"Shut up James," She's all smiles and the moonlight glints off of her perfect teeth. This girl is so damn beautiful.

"What? You don't want that? We'd have some beautiful

mixed-race babies and you know it."

"I'm not even going to bother responding to your crazy talk right now."

"Okay, okay. Well, what do you have going on tomorrow?" I ask.

"Well, I *was* going to meet up with you tomorrow," she replies.

"What? Because we slept together tonight, I can't see you tomorrow? Is that what you're trying to tell me?" I can sense she doesn't mean it, but I play along anyway.

"Yup, pretty much." Now she's in full giggle mode — and her laugh is the cutest thing. A melodic mixture of vivacity and femininity all rolled into one, and I find myself wanting to hear more of it. I pull her into me until there is no distinction between where her body ends or mine begins, and I am overcome with a comforting wave of her body heat.

"Anyways," I say with unnecessary emphasis, "what kind of food would you like?"

"Umm... Thai food? I'm kind of obsessing over it right now. It's so much better here than back home."

"Sure, we can get Thai. I'm allergic though." But I can risk it for one night with her.

"Then why would you agree?" Her voice colors with extreme concern and it makes me chuckle a bit.

"Don't worry, if I get sick later you can hold back my hair." She shoves lightly at my arm.

"Whatever, James." Nayelli turns her back to me and I can hear the eyeroll in her tone. I lean over and give her a small kiss on the side of her cheek as amends before spooning my body against her soft frame and find no trouble drifting off to sleep.

I am at a party, it seems. But at whose house? I'm not quite sure I know. I look around to try and catch something familiar, but all I see is a front room without its furniture and packed to the brim with random teenagers. I move from the corner of the wall and find the stairs on the other side of the room.

 Where the fuck am I? I reach the top of the stairs, but still see nothing that I know. It's darker up here and I have to feel my way down the hall until I see a closed door with light peeking underneath the crack. I open the door and I'm surprised to find my school's football star, Zack.

 "Hey James," he greets with a kind welcome. I didn't know he knew my name. "Hurry up and come in so we can close the door, yeah?"

 I numbly walk further into the all-white bathroom, a bit confused about what is going on.

 The door clicks closed and Bryan, Zach's right hand school mate, steps out of the corner. He ignores me and walks up to the tile counter expectantly. My eyes follow his and notice the thin white lines of powder that were previously blending in with the counter.

 "James, would you like to do the honors of the first line?" Zach asks, holding a rolled bill out to me.

 "Really?" Bryan interjects before I can answer. "You think gay little actor boy would really do a line?" He sizes me up with his eyes. "I bet you twenty quid that he's too much of a pussy."

 His eyes never leave mine, and I feel a deep hidden rage boil to the surface of my skin. He, and everyone at school, have said just as much if not worse before. All because I'm skinny and a part of the school's theater group.

 I snatch the money from Zach and push Bryan out of the way. Too fueled by rage I don't even hesitate to think about why I'm doing it. I plug one of my nostrils and breath in deeply.

 The white dust flies up then down my cavities, mixing with

the spit at the back of my throat and creating the most foul and bitter drip that I have ever tasted.

My eyes fly open to the dark room. My chest is heaving and my lungs are blazing — desperately searching for the breath I do not have. *Just a dream.* I look from my guitar leaning against my desk to the wall of movies, confirming my existence in the present. I can feel the thin layer of sticky perspiration that has developed across my skin , and I'm grateful that Nayelli is sound asleep on the other side of the bed. *Just a dream.* I repeat this to myself in hopes that it will take my mind off the stupid encounters of my past, but to no use. Cocaine is one hell of a nasty drug. A chill runs through me thinking of the taste.

Actively choosing not to use drugs while you are conscious is a quest on its own, but it never quite stops there. There are triggers everywhere. Even in my fucking dreams. Reminding me of the young stupid James in high school that tried to be cool and do his first line. My organs twitch at the ghost of my former self — pumping me with that all too familiar itch to resume old habits. But I remind myself that I can't, or at least not right now. I get too distracted and lose motivation for my music, and if I'm being honest – my life as well

Looking around for a distraction to take my mind off of things, I carefully reach across Nayelli's body to grab my phone from the nightstand then settle back onto my side of the bed — making sure to turn down the brightness. I fire up my app and look for my previous conversation with a girl named Melissa. She has a bit of a round face, with short blonde hair and blue eyes, and one picture in particular that shows off an extremely nice shape. With a few taps to my keyboard, I confirm our date for two days from now.

Nayelli

The next morning, I turn over to see that James has left me alone. I get up and start grabbing my clothes. Damn, this is so cliché. Is he coming back? Am I supposed to let myself out? Is it weird if I shower first? I scan the ground to my right and see my body suit still underneath the computer chair. *Damnit!* I'll have to take the train in my club clothes. So not only am I facing the awkward "Hey, sex was great, you were great, but please leave," conversation, but I have also added the walk of shame to the list. Just great.

Without warning, the door flies open with James bursting back into the room. "Hey, hey! Good morning! I have an idea," he says in one big rush of breath.

My hands fly up to cover my boobs. *Oh, so now you're modest?* I let my hands drop back down. I note that his wavy hair is brushed neatly, and he's fully dressed in jeans and a layered sweater/jacket situation. How did I not hear him this morning?

"What's your idea?"

"I figured since your hotel is right next to my music shop that we should just commute together. What do you think?"

"Um... I don't see why not?" So not how I expected this conversation to go.

"Great! You'll get to meet my dad. He's going to drop us off at the station. Here's a towel if you wanna shower. You have about fifteen minutes until we gotta go." He gives me a brief kiss and throws a towel at me, then leaves the room in the same rush of movement from which he entered.

Wow. I'm for real about to meet this guy's dad. I start to pace by the edge of the bed. What am I going to say? What is he going to think of me being here? Who am I kidding, I already know what he's going to think. Last night he went to bed with no one but his family in the house and this morning he's giving me and his son a ride at eight a.m.. Not hard to fill in the blanks. *Ugh. Kill me. Please.* It's one thing to hook up with a total stranger — against all of my better judgment — but it's something else entirely when the other person's father also knows about it.

Wait. Does this mean that his dad meets all of his Tinder matches? God, that's so creepy. For his sake, I honestly hope not.

Outside, his dad is patiently sitting on the right-hand side of a tiny silver car. If you can even call it a car. Everything is so compact and narrow here. The neighborhoods I've seen — the streets — are all at least half of the width of those back in Cali.

James opens the door for me and I slide into the back seat, alone. James runs around the front and pops his head outside his dad's side of the car.

"I'm gonna scrape the ice off the windshield Dad!"

"All right then," his dad responds calmly.

Great. It's just me and his dad. He doesn't turn around to greet me or to say anything, just keeps his eyes trained ahead of him like a taxi driver. Grey hair sticks out beneath his black beanie and frames his pale neck. The rest of him is indiscernible and bundled to brave the icy morning.

Is he not bothered that there is a complete stranger in the backseat of his car right now? I could be a murderer! Or is it murderess? Then again… he could be a murderer. He and his son could be a murdering duo and they use Tinder to find their victims!

Snapping out of my infatuation, I scan my surroundings. I

try to think of survival strategies in case this situation takes a wrong turn but come up blank. He is still saying nothing; but then again, neither am I. The sheet of opaque ice covering the windows separates James's dad and I from the outside world leaving me completely vulnerable and helpless.

Damnit, I have to get out of here.

My breath leaves my mouth in accelerated white puffs that circle the small space in front of me. My hand creeps silently, steadily for the door, but before I can even get my hand to the knob, I hear a loud SMACK on top of the windshield.

My vision fills with the sight of James seductively wiping both his jacket and windshield wiper in the shape of an S across the window.

"Yup... look at him. There he goes," his father responds to the burlesque dance, "That's my son for you."

James then makes a circle with his wiper on his father's window and yells a cheery "'ello!" through the glass.

His father gives a chuckle and shakes his head at his son's antics.

I let out a deflating exhale and urge my heartbeat to return back to normal. I really should get some rest.

*

Spending an entire night drinking and sexing is not for the weak-spirited. My body sags in relief between my bed's layers of sheets and blankets. I don't think I've ever been this tired in my entire life; but I've never strayed so far from who my mother raised me to be either. I can hear her voice already. *You did WHAT? So you just sleep with any Tom, Dick, and Harry that comes along? Nayelli, you're better than that.* Everything with her is black and white: hooking up is for girls who want to cheapen themselves, sex is for the marriage bed, in sex you give a piece of yourself that you can't get back — blah, blah, blah, celibacy, celibacy, celibacy. It's a good thing I'm taking my extracurricular activities with me to the grave. Not even my sister will get to know about this, she would just end up letting it slip to Mom. I still haven't recovered from being guilted to death because I had sex with Will, and we were actually dating at the time. Thankfully, though — with the time difference and my sister's work/school schedule — we haven't been able to chat much these days.

Then again, even if my sister *could* keep a secret, I still don't think I'd tell her. There's just something so thrilling about having this experience to myself. I never knew sex could be so liberating. Or, more accurately, I never allowed myself to know. Don't get me wrong, sex with Will was good. But it was good in the sense that I didn't know there was more — and better — out there. With James, it's like a switch has turned on. Like being introduced to hunger for the first time.

Oh, James. I cuddle deeper under the covers and become lost in my own mind, thinking about the moment that changed everything.

"Why aren't we having sex again?" he asked. Fully naked at this point, we had been touching, teasing, and tasting each other for the better part of an hour. Straddling some invisible line together, but never quite crossing it.

I straddled his hips, balancing my hands on his chest and pressing my ass into him. His face scrunched up as if he was trying to concentrate.

"Because I said I didn't want to." But what was more accurate was because my mother would not approve. The small

voice at the back of my head refused to shut the hell up. It kept asking "What would your mother say about you right now?" You would think I'd outgrown my compulsion to please my mother by now, but alas, there it was at the most inopportune time.

"Right, right, right. Who would even suggest such a thing? Why would anyone even want to do that?" he joked.

I laughed and lightly pushed against his chest. Dark round eyes and long eyelashes stared silently at me; his mouth parted slightly from accommodating his faster breaths. I sat back, attempting to drink in every detail that I could.

Moonlight from the shutters bathed him in the softest of blues. In this light I noticed his lips, perfectly even and shaped with promise. I noticed the shadow of stubble across the lower half of his sharply angled face.

My fingers zinged with anticipation as I stroked his chin before continuing the journey further down. With a mind of their own, they followed a path across his chest, his muscles were broad and toned beneath the hair. Then they moved to position his large hands into the cradle of my hips. Next, they traced the divots of a defined V that formed at the base of his waist. My fingers stopped there but my eyes resumed the exploration down to what sat between the both of us.

He was so fucking beautiful. Easily the most beautiful man I had ever seen, let alone been with.

Upon this awareness, I found myself asking the same question: Why weren't we having sex again?

Slowly, I leaned over him, my breasts hovering above his chest.

He moved to kiss me, but I pulled back. My hand firm between us, I teased him at the entrance of me.

"Wait, are you sure?" His deep voice broke the silence that

had stretched on for several lifetimes.
It was now or never.
"Yes," I breathed against his lips. "Yes, I am."
The ping of my phone jolts me back to reality. *Ugggghhhh.* I forgot to turn on the do not disturb.

I crack open only a slit between my eyelids — it's James.

Jay333, 12:41 p.m.

You better not be asleep! We are suffering through this day TOGETHER.

If I don't get to sleep, you don't get to sleep. Boom.

12:45 p.m.

I'm awake.

Jay333, 12:47 p.m.

Ok, good.

We can plan out our date for this evening.

12:49 p.m.

Sure. Do you know of any Thai places around here?

Jay333, 12:52 p.m.

Yes, there's one right by your hotel but I was also thinking that we should meet at the grocery store after I'm done working.

12:55 p.m.

The grocery store? For what?

Jay333, 12:55 p.m.

Snacks.

1:00 p.m.

You want to go buy food before we go to a restaurant to eat food…

Jay333, 1:01 p.m.

I am a hungry man.

Trust me, we need snacks.

1:02 p.m.
Okay, fine. Which grocery store and what time?
Jay333, 1:05 p.m.
Tesco's on Goodge Street
I'm off at 5
He tries to keep the conversation flowing for another hour but between each reply, my body slips closer and closer towards the sweet promise of sleep until finally, I give up on texting back and welcome unconsciousness with open arms.

James

I rest my elbows on the music shop's glass counter for the tenth time in just as many minutes. My eyelids feel as if they weigh a stone each and with each passing second, I lose the battle to keep them open. But I shouldn't complain because every time I think about how tired I am, I think of the cause of my lack of sleep and it teleports me back to last night. And *fuck*, I'd trade all the sleep in the world to experience that again.

When my eyes close for long enough, I see her. Permanently tattooed in my brain is the image of her naked body, with the exception of her lace thong caressing around the curves of her beautiful ass, and her chin resting on her shoulder as her soft brown eyes glowed with a need that aroused me faster than anything ever has.

That is illegal. She is illegal. No one should look like that. I bet she can easily have any man she wants. And just that thought alone is eating away at a small piece of me. She didn't even notice the way men watched her as she moved through the city this morning. That's how normal it is for her. Men must be throwing themselves at her feet in California. It's not hard to imagine. I already feel like putty in her hands — ready to mold and shape into her every wish and desire.

Dear god James, get a grip.

But thinking I can get a grip over this girl is a vain errand. The drive of my mind and body are centered on one thing and one thing only — to experience this woman again and again. And *again.* All day I've been craving to watch how she opens underneath my touch, see the smile that lights up her face and touches her eyes — eyes that hold so much seductive promise within them.

I cut my thoughts short. Helping customers with a full hard on is probably not the best idea. But since no one is here at the moment, I take advantage of the lull in work and shoot her another message.

The last few minutes until five feel as if they might strangle me. 4:59 p.m. rolls around and I make haste locking up the shop and walking the few blocks that it takes to get to Tesco's.

I stroll in and scan the aisles for her. By the time I reach the wine aisle, my eyes are welcomed by the body that has haunted my fantasies all day. Nayelli is turned away from me, so I take two seconds to just admire the look of her ass in a pair of jeans. *Damn woman, what you do to me.* I silently walk up behind her and give her a kiss on the cheek as I wrap my arms around her waist.

"James? Oh my god, you scared me! I thought a random man was trying to feel me up." She turns around in my embrace and hugs me as if she's known me for years, not a day. After a few seconds, she lifts her head from my chest and says, "You're lucky I caught a glimpse of your face before I used one of these wine bottles as a weapon."

"Easy now ninja assassin," She looks about as scary as a blow-dried kitten, but I dare not tell her that. I squint my eyes down the aisle and ask, "Have you ever tried port?"

"No, what's that?" She asks, trying to focus her eyes on what I might be talking about.

"It's like wine but a lot better, let's grab some." We add the port to the little cart and continue down the next aisle in search of snacks.

"This is hard," she says laughing, "I'm not sure what to get because I know we're about to eat. I don't understand your need for post meal snacks."

"Hey, I won't force you. Just don't ask for any of my snacks when you're hungry later." She turns from the shelf of food and sticks her tongue out at me, to which I respond by pulling her in for a kiss on the forehead. "I don't normally do the whole PDA thing, but there's just something with you... I don't know."

I shake my head and make a note to find out what it is later.

The Thai restaurant near her house is slightly hipster looking and perfect for a date night. We sit next to each other at a bench-style table eating chicken wings and curry. We talk about the last time I played at a music venue, how her trip has been going (her mate is definitely a bit sketchy), and our New Year's Eve plans for tomorrow. The whole time I find myself saying things to make her laugh, although it doesn't require much comedic skills since she seems to laugh at everything. At one point she laughed so hard she snorted and Thai tea shot out of her nose. The restaurant dropped dead silent to look at our loud commotion, to which she responded, "My bad," and laughed some more. But in a string of bad luck on dates, it was hilariously refreshing.

After dinner, we walk the short distance back to her hotel. The streets are quiet and the lights lining them are dim, casting shadows from the buildings across Nayelli's face.

"Thank you so much for dinner. It was so good!" she yells into the cold night air.

"Very welcome. Do you like chicken?"

"Umm, yes?" Her face contorts in puzzlement.

"Then grab a wing!" I exclaim, offering my bent arm for her to walk next to me.

"James, you are so corny. Cute, but corny," she says, grabbing onto my arm and shaking her head in amusement.

When we make it back to her room, the first thing I note is how impossibly tiny it is. She obviously wasn't expecting to keep company here. The single bed is going to be barely long enough for my body alone, but I guess we'll have to make it work.

She walks down the narrow hallway that leads straight to the bed and plops down on the edge of it. Her jeans are doing wonders for her shape, especially with the way she sits slightly leaning back, putting her lovely figure on display. Nayelli doesn't say anything, only sits there, her eyes gleaming with an unspoken invitation.

I arch my brow and start unbuttoning my shirt, amazed at how easily this woman calls me to be at full attention in a matter of seconds. The sexual hold she's creating over me fucking is ridiculous. It's like I'm a teen all over again, needing to fuck endlessly and unveiling a stamina that I thought I had long since outgrown.

"Your turn," I announce once naked.

Nayelli takes her time, unwrapping her curves like a damn present. Patiently I watch, anticipation building by the second. The moment she divests of the last bit of her clothing, my body wastes no time in clinging to hers like honey.

I pick her up by her ass, wrapping those gorgeous thighs around my waste. Her lips devour mine, soft pillowy kisses on my neck and mouth are followed by light nips of her teeth.

"Sweet Jesus, Nayelli," I mutter under my breath.

Laying her down on the mattress, I go straight to work on tasting every inch of her. My tongue traces a path down her left thigh, across her pert nipples, and up her right thigh – purposefully skipping her beautiful core that's already glistening for me.

Frustrated with my movements, she tugs on my hair to lead my face where she wants it but I refuse to give in that easily. Instead I trail kisses along the sides of her lips, inching closer but not quite where she needs my mouth the most. "Keep teasing me and I will throw you out into the hall naked," she whines. "And then call the front desk and complain about a disturbance."

"All right, but if the little kid next door happens to see me… their psychological damage is on you." I tease, still trapped between her thighs. But good god I'm losing my resolve. I don't think there's anything that turns me on more than a beautiful woman with a cheeky mouth.

Nayelli's body vibrates against me with her laughter and she releases her grip from around my head. I flip her over, leaning down in her ear to whisper, "Hands on the headboard. Now."

"Since when do you tell me what to do?" she asks, a large dose of playful attitude in her response.

I lay down onto my back and slide in between her legs, holding her in place by the back of her thighs.

"What are you doing?" I can tell she's unnecessarily nervous.

"Shhhh," I respond and then in the next breath ravage her clit with my tongue.

"Oh!" she cries in response, and her hands automatically drop down to tangle in my hair.

"Hands. On. The. Wall." I state in between kisses. "My god, you taste so sweet," I murmur against her. Jesus, does this girl bathe in fucking flower petals and oranges? Every inch of her tastes so damn good.

"Are you trying to kill me? I think you are," Nayelli complains, but places her hands back where I asked.

"Just trying to help you understand how you make me feel," I answer, and proceed to feast upon her like the ravenous man that I am.

We spend the next hour not knowing where she begins and I end. It's easily become my new favorite pastime and the hours seem to tick by without our notice or care.

Utterly spent from the rigorous fucking but not tired enough to sleep, we lay naked and entwined with the sheets. Her fingers dance a waltz through the waves on my chest and I feel the open-close tickle of her eyelash against my side.

We drift through the time trading stories, wanting to know things about one another. And to my surprise, I open up and tell her nothing but the truth. Talking to her in the dark allows me to strip bare and not be ashamed — peel off my insecurities like I did earlier with my clothes and just exist as a man who knows nothing but has seen enough.

"I wasn't always this hairy," I say to the dark.

"What are you talking about? You're not even that hairy." She gives a soft kiss to my chest and I know it's to soothe my feelings.

"When I was in high school, I only had a bit of soft hair here instead of the full-on mammoth wool that you see now," I say and gesture to my chest with my free hand.

"Again, you're *not* even that hairy. But what changed? Isn't chest hair supposed to do that as you age?" she asks and gives another soft consoling kiss to my chest.

"Not really. I threw a party at my house and shaved off all of my hair in the bathroom right in the middle of it."

"Ha! Why would you do that?"

"I was high. It seemed like a good idea at the time," I respond with a slight shrug.

"Hmm," is all she says.

"Have you ever done any drugs?"

"Nope," she responds simply.

"*Never?*" I ask incredulously. "Not even weed or cigarettes. Even just one puff?"

"Never. I've been fine without trying them this far, and I don't see a need to start them now," she says very pointedly.

I'm almost six years older than her, but somehow her admission makes our age gap feel like decades. She's a baby. She has no idea what's really out there — what the world can be like, how fucking hard and devastating it can be. She's never had the need to find out.

I instantly love and hate that about her. She must be a good girl then, since her innocence to the darker side of the world is still intact. Good for her.

But then the dead-obvious smacks me right in the chest: she'll never understand what I go through; what my life was like before; what it can still be like at times.

Then again, it's not like our paths have to cross ever again. Yet, something about this newfound information bothers me a bit.

Whatever. I let it go and return to the moment.

I check the time and it's well past two in the morning, but the lateness means nothing to me. I haven't been this content and at ease in a long time. Not since my last girlfriend. Or at least in the beginning... But my ex-girlfriend doesn't matter right now. The beautiful woman cuddled in my arms and listening to music with me does.

I'm not quite sure why — and maybe I don't care enough to find out — but her presence is so soothing to me. Holding her like this makes it almost easy to forget; to envision what it might be like to get to know her; to take her out on more dates; to be the kind of guy a girl like her would want.

I bet she's the type of girlfriend to be more adorable than scary when she's angry.

I cut my thoughts off right there. Why am I even thinking about that? It is too late for me to try to be the kind of man that she deserves. I am an old, depressed record stuck on play. No one should have to take that on in a relationship; especially not someone with so much life ahead of them. When all of this is said and done, we will be two people who had a great time on her holiday. Nothing more.

All right then, James. That's enough of the fucking dark pity party. Right now she's still here in front of me.

I give her forehead a satisfied kiss and my fingers resume their rhythmic caressing of her naked back.

She's still here, I repeat and force myself to hold on only to the good.

Nayelli

"You know, I could die right now and I honestly think I'd be okay with it."

"Woah, there is no dying on my watch. I'm not going to jail over you," he responds and gives my body a small squeeze before rolling over to grab the almonds out of the bag of snacks.

"Are you seriously eating right now?" I ask incredulously.

"Of course. You were there, you witnessed what I just did. I gotta replenish my strength."

I roll my eyes at his corniness... again. I should be trying to sleep since I have to meet back up with Olivia and her family later this evening, but there's just something so necessary about being cuddled up on his chest and talking. Somehow we keep ending up this way after sex, and I find that I don't want it to end.

"I think it's your turn," he reminds me.

"Oh yeah, okay. Ummmm..." I try to think of what I want to ask him next. We've been asking questions back and forth for the better part of an hour, but there is still so much more that I want to know. "Why are you single?"

"What do you mean?"

"Well, from what I can tell you're an extremely charismatic and attractive guy and probably don't have a shortage of women who want you. Do you not do relationships or something?" I almost feel bad for whoever his ex is.

"Oh wow, going serious on me," he lets out a long sigh before he continues. "My one and only serious relationship ended almost a year ago and I just don't feel the need to get back into something again. It got really toxic, really fast — but neither one of us had the courage to break it off. I was unhappy for a very, very long time. Three years to be exact. So now, I'm just enjoying the whole not being responsible for someone else's happiness thing."

I play back his words. He's twenty-six years old and has only had one relationship and doesn't plan on another anytime soon… a small red flag raises in my mind, but he's being so open and honest about it that I choose to ignore it.

"What about you?" His question breaks the silence.

"What about me?" I regret turning the conversation in this direction.

"Why are you single?"

I can answer this question a million ways, but honestly, I don't want him to get the impression that my past still affects me. Especially after connecting with someone like him — it gives me a little hope about the guys still out there.

"In short, my first boyfriend of almost four years cheated on me and all my friends knew about it, but no one bothered to tell me. We were sixteen when we started dating. So, I guess I just want to spend time with myself and find out who the single Nayelli is."

"He's an idiot," he responds. And he is, but I don't want to talk any more about it so I opt for not saying anything. His lips kiss the top of my head and he rubs my back with soft, consoling strokes.

The space between our last words eventually lengthens out into complete silence, but he never stops stroking my back and I begin falling asleep on his chest. He finally breaks the trance and says, "Nayelli?"

"Hmm?" I force myself to say.

"I know we don't really know each other but... I really like you."

"Thank you." My face scrunches up in confusion at my own words. Thank you? *Really*? That's the best answer you could come up with? What is *wrong* with you? I think about correcting my words and telling him how much I like him too, but I take too long and saying something now will just make it more awkward.

"I have something for you," he says. In the dark, I can barely see the expression on his face but can tell that he keeps looking from me to his backpack and back again. Is he nervous?

"What is it?" I eventually ask.

"Well, I know that you mentioned it was your birthday yesterday so I got you a gift." He gets up and starts rummaging for the elusive present.

Did this man seriously buy me a birthday gift after only knowing me for twenty-four hours? My mouth drops open in astonishment and I can't quite seem to recover my cool. The only light in the room comes from the small, muted streams of moonlight slipping through the cracks of the closed curtains, so my expression is hidden — thankfully. I prop myself up on the pillows, and he turns on the nightstand light before joining me again in bed. "Now don't get too excited, it's nothing super fancy."

"Just give it here, please," I hold my hand out for the tiny rectangular box that has an even tinier red bow in the center.

He's watching me intently for my reaction, but I don't understand why he cares so much. I cup my hand underneath the box, and into my palm slides out a small metal rectangle attached to a thin gold chain.

"It's a mini harmonica attached to a necklace. I got it from my shop." His eyes are still watching me closely.

I hold up the necklace and watch as the thumb sized harmonica twirls back and forth on its chain, catching the light every time it spins towards the lamp. "It's so tiny and cute!" I tell him and crawl into his lap to give him a hug. No words can express the emotions that this tiny piece of jewelry has made me feel, but what's most pressing is my confusion. Why did he feel the need to get me a birthday gift? In the grand scheme of things, it doesn't really matter.

My life — especially dating wise — has been so shitty that James feels like a breath of fresh air. Things have been going so well, a small blossom of hope springs up inside of me that we might actually stay in touch. The possibility of being friends with him after I leave just might distract me from the state of affairs of my life back home. And even if we don't — I will still have this small, kind gift between almost-strangers.

I'm still in his lap, so he has to reach around me to grab his phone from the night table. He fiddles through it for a bit before he says, "If you ever wonder how I feel about you, just listen to this song."

"Use Me" by Bill Withers floats out of his device and into the space around us, and I adjust my body to cuddle into his side and take in the words.

*

Daylight cascades through the thick tan drapes and teases its rays across a very naked James. Lying still, I listen to the thrum of his heart's strong and steady rhythm. The taste of skin and James' soap still lingers on my lips and tongue as a form of testament to where my mouth had been last night. I roll away from him, my cheek imprinted by his hairs and my own body slightly too warm from sleeping by his side all night. My head also aches from consuming too much port.

Geez, waking up has been so rough these days. I pull the too small duvet closer to my face and try to fall back asleep, but don't make it far before an alarm begins blaring.

"Good morning," he says bright-eyed and bushy-tailed, turning off his phone alarm.

"Umm... good morning," I mumble groggily. My skin hums in a low excitement at the sound of his voice, but I don't open my eyes.

"Can you show me how to use your shower? I have to get ready for work."

"I mean... can't you figure it out? I had an extremely rude man keeping me up all night with his music and sexual antics."

"Wow, that guy sounds like a jerk. Why would you ever hang out with someone like that?"

"Beats me." I like him — really, I do — but I honestly don't think I've slept since the night we met. I can't keep going on like this.

"Just really quick?" I can hear the slight edge of begging in his tone and give up all notions of falling back asleep.

"Fine. I'll turn on your shower. Is there anything else you would like while I'm up, your highness?" I mutter, hopping off the bed and stomping — all three steps — to the bathroom.

The moment my feet touch the cool tile of the bathroom floor, my skin flares up in goosebumps. *Damnit.* I should've thrown something on. I lean into the shower and adjust the silver knobs to jet out steaming-hot water. James is standing silently behind me in the doorway, so, for added emphasis, I turn around and gesture at the now running water.

"See? Easy."

"Have you had sex in a shower before?"

An electric jolt shoots straight down my body and makes its home right in my core. How in the fucking hell does he do that?

"I mean, yeah, but…" I try my best to not look affected but end up staring at him like a three-headed goat.

"Would you like to join me?" he asks. His eyes drink me in as he crosses the threshold into the bathroom. Seconds — or maybe minutes — pass before he stops within touching distance.

Again? Is he okay? Is his penis okay? Should we consult a doctor or someone about this? At what point would you consider being at risk of having "too much" sex? Is that even a thing?

His left-hand cups the side of my face, and our eyes meet and lock — just like they did the first night, and again last night. My inner thoughts break and falter as my mind redirects towards consuming the man in front of me.

I look into the depths of his chocolate-green eyes that come alive with promise when his body is craving mine. I move my eyes down to his soft parted lips that have become my new obsession. Next, they lazily drag down his toned swimmer's body to the erection that keeps tapping me on my stomach.

There is no such thing as too much sex.

His head dips down to follow where my gaze has landed and he tilts my neck up to look at him, a wicked smile knowingly plays on his lips. Bastard. Cockiness is usually a turn off for me, but I can't help but be magnetically sucked in by him.

Slowly, painfully he's driving me mad. He keeps me on my toes — watching, anticipating, but never quite guessing what he has in store for me — and I freaking love it. Is this why they say you should date older men?

He brings his mouth down to mine and I stand on the tips of my toes to meet him halfway. Our lips and chests meet and a tickle of hair brushes against my nipples spreading a shiver across my skin so intense and alive that my legs go weak. I wrap my arms around his neck for support, and he wastes no time in grazing his fingertips across my breasts, then my stomach — until they reach their destination in between my thighs. I moan against his open lips as they kiss mine, not recognizing the needy voice as my own.

His hands never break their rhythm and his reverential kisses move to my neck — so soft and gentle — yet persistent and fervent as if he is performing some kind of litany that is meant to save us both. But I am already damned. No man will ever drive me crazy in the same way that he does. I don't know how I know that, but it's true. The few before him didn't even come close.

Breaking the kiss, he spins me around and gives my ass a firm slap. "I'll take that as a yes to you joining me?"

I don't answer him. Instead, I glance over my shoulder with an arched brow before stepping into the soothing jets of the shower.

He and I both know it was never really a question.

James

What. A. Fucking. Three. Days.

Counting moments in between when I get to see Nayelli has made me lose track of everything that doesn't involve her. Unfortunately, I can no longer afford that luxury. It's Friday — and New Year's Eve — and I agreed to go partying with my brother tonight.

I cross the street from her hotel towards the station to catch a train home. Normally on a Friday I would head straight into the music shop but will have to head in later since Stanley, my agent, messaged me this morning with a reminder about my audition tape that needs to be sent off by this weekend. It's fortunate that Alex works from home as a freelance writer because he's also my go-to for helping film my auditions.

I would make the statement that the creative gene runs in our family, but my older brother Daniel is an accountant based near the Wharf. Need I say more?

I wish I could have spent a bit more time with Nayelli if I'm being honest, but I wanted her to have a chance to rest since I woke her up so early for a shower.

Mmm. That fucking shower. The memory is like wet paint taking its time to dry in my mind. Specifically the image of her body arching to make a perfect bridge between me and the shower wall with water running down her smooth back and onto her round ass. Fuck. I won't be forgetting that for a long time.

I don't think I've had this much sexual chemistry with

someone in my entire life, and it is becoming more obvious that it's eating away at my sanity.

But dear god, those damn sounds she makes. She is the type of partner that is very vocal in her approval. And oh so giving — both eager to please and be pleased. Just thinking about it makes me want to turn around and head back to her tiny hotel room.

Every time I think I've had enough of her, I also think of how she's leaving soon — and I become desperate to chase my insatiable fill of her.

Like an addict.

The thought momentarily sobers me. I shake my head like it will somehow rid her from my thoughts. I seriously need to stop obsessing over this girl.

By the time I make it home, Alex has already set up the camera, light, and white background sheet in the corner of my room.

"Ready?" he asks.

"Sure, just let me change," I say, setting my overnight bag down near the door. "You triple-checked the filming instructions I sent you?"

"This isn't my first time, James. How else would I have known how to set up the lighting?" He rolls his eyes and sets the chair in the proper position between the backdrop and tripod. "What's this roll for again?"

I hold up a blue button-down shirt and black T-shirt, not answering right away. "You remember the movie *Guess Who's Coming to Dinner*?"

"Yeah, what about it?" he asks, still adjusting the stool position until it's just right.

"Well it's kind of a remake of that. Just more modern. And with a British actor to play the boyfriend this time." I end up choosing the blue button-down, it's more flattering.

"Oh fuck. That's kind of big, isn't it? And they're filming it here?"

"No. It's being filmed in Los Angeles." I've been keeping the audition a bit of a secret because of that fact.

"Way to fucking keep that hidden, mate. You were going to move halfway around the world and not say anything?" Alex straightens to his full height and gives me a lethal stare.

"It's not like that. It's just that this could be really big for me and I don't want to jinx anything before I know if I've gotten the part." At this, he nods his head and relaxes his posture. I give him a slap on the shoulder for good measure. "Let's get this thing over with, yeah?"

*

I still have ten minutes before I need to close the shop for the day so I head downstairs to the faithful old couch to take a quick break, leaving Eddie upstairs to do the main locking up.

After settling into the sofa comfortably, I launch Tinder to catch up on what I've missed for the day. Three new messages are waiting for me in my inbox — one of them from Melissa.

Shit. We are supposed to meet up today. I fully open her message and read that she has invited me to a party at her flat.

This should be a good distraction from well... things.

Maybe, just maybe, with the right amount of alcohol and party festivities I can keep my mind off seeing Nayelli again tonight.

My foot is uncontrollably tapping up and down and I pop my knuckles until they no longer can. I fight desperately to keep my mind from trailing back to the events of this morning again. Why do I feel almost... *guilty*? Christ. This is going to be harder than I thought. There's only a few more minutes before I have to start the closing itinerary of the shop, so I send my brother a quick text to see if he's up for a house party tonight.

*

Tonight's outfit consists of black jeans with a button-down shirt and a navy-blue jumper on top. "Not bad James, not bad" I say to my reflection in the full-length mirror by the door. My fingers try to comb the waves of my hair into some sort of uniform look but it's useless. My god, I look like a bum. Definitely need to cut my hair soon.

"Hey, are you ready?" my brother yells as he bursts into the room, almost hitting me in the face with the door.

"Christ, Alex! You almost hit me in the nose!" I back up to let him walk fully into my room, and he takes a seat on my bed.

"Oh no," he says, bringing his hands up to his face in fake shock. "Fucking chill mate, you're fine."

"My nose is already crooked from the first two times it broke. I can't suffer a third."

"Yeah, yeah. Everyone knows. You can't go a whole week without telling someone you broke your damn nose. Enough already, I was there. No need to keep bringing it up."

"You were there? You were *there*? You're the one who broke it!" Ten years, and I still don't get a proper apology.

"In my defense, there is no proof that I am fully responsible for the second incident. It was probably still messed up from the first time. And I'm sticking to that story until you can prove otherwise," he explains with a simple shoulder shrug.

"You know what…" I run my hands through my hair in

frustration but don't bother to finish my sentence.

"Okay, okay. Too far," he says with his palms up. "Now about this party you're taking me to. Are you sure she said I could come? It's not some secret sex party is it? Am I going to walk in on some kind of New Year's orgy?"

"In the best-case scenario of tonight, that's exactly what we're going to walk in on. But to answer your question, yes I'm sure you can come. Her flat mate is throwing the party as well, so it's nothing to worry about."

"All right, I'll trust you James. But it's getting a little late. We should at least head downstairs and have a drink or two before we leave." He stands up to leave and I finally notice what he's wearing.

"You have to change," I say pointedly.

"What? Why?" he looks down at his clothes, confused.

Between Alex, our older brother Daniel, and myself, Alex and I definitely look the most alike. With our main difference being — outside of the fact that he wears Clark Kent glasses — my hair is a much darker brown than his.

The point is, we are two biologically related six-foot-three white males with brown hair wearing black jeans and blue jumpers... to the same party. I'm twenty-six and he's twenty-three for Christ's sake. The time for sibling matching has long come and gone.

"Because we're grown men matching, that's why. At least change the color of your jumper mate," I explain.

"Well why do I have to be the one to change?" he complains.

"Because I'm older. Now hurry up before you make us late," I say on my way downstairs.

"Fucking hell," Alex grumbles before I hear the tell-tale sound of his door closing.

After the almost matching outfit fiasco has been sorted — thank god — we decide it's best to get some New Year's Eve drinks in our system before going out into the night. Only a crazy person would head into a meet up/party completely sober.

"All right, James. What do you think? Should we head over?" Alex asks as he rinses his whisky and coke glass in the kitchen sink.

I peer into the amber contents of my own glass and take a slow sip before responding, "Are you mental?"

"Mental? What? Why?"

"Do you really want to be those creepy bums that don't know anyone, yet are the first to show up? They'll think we're desperate."

Alex gives a drawn-out roll of his eyes before squaring his shoulders at me, still leaning against the kitchen counter. "That's exactly what we are at the moment. Desperate guy number one, who hasn't been with a girl in almost six months, and then well… there's you. And James is always going to be James."

"Hey! Don't you dare use my name as an insult."

"Jamesy baby, this is *me* you're talking to. But okay, you 'don't' have a 'problem' when it comes to women," he says using air quotes. "That doesn't change the fact that you met this girl through an app and she's invited you to her house as a first meeting. Two plus two equals a naked woman at some point this evening. Hopefully for the both of us. You even said it yourself," he explains.

A silent moment passes between us. Neither of us say a word, neither of us break eye contact. Until, finally, I kill the stare down. "Sometimes I really wonder if your brain is aware of the shit that comes out of your mouth."

He gives one of his signature shoulder shrugs before asking,

"So what's your plan if we're not going straight to the party?"

"Well, I was thinking we could meet some of my friends at a bar for a bit and then head over."

"It's New Year's Eve. I'm down for anything that's not staying home," replies Alex.

"Then it's a plan."

*

After what seems like ten years and too many whiskey-cokes with my friends down in Soho, Alex and I arrive at the east London flat of the Tinder girl.

"Stand behind me," I whisper to Alex.

"What? Why?"

"Because she doesn't know you. I don't want your face to be the first thing she sees. Just stand on that porch step," I point right behind me.

"She doesn't know you either, James," he quips defiantly.

"You always have to be difficult, don't you?"

"Oh my days mate, will you please just knock on the door? I'm freezing my left nut off out here and you want to worry about standing in a bloody formation." He bounces his weight up and down and blows his breath into his hands.

"So dramatic," I murmur to myself, then proceed to knock three times.

Not even a minute later, Melissa opens the door... wearing baggy pajamas that completely hides the fit figure I've seen in her photos. Her hair is also pulled up into a messy bun that appears as if she just woke up from a nap. Alex and I exchange a look between each other but say nothing.

"Hey. Melissa, right?" I double check the house number. Do

I have the correct address?

"Yup! And you must be James. And James' brother." She nods and politely smiles at the both of us. "Come in."

We cross the threshold with more than a little hesitation. "So, is everyone in the... kitchen?" I look around the hallway but can't see much. All of the lights are turned off except the one highlighting the kitchen.

"Umm, I think my flat mate is. We just opened a bottle of whiskey; would you like some?"

We nod and follow behind Melissa the few steps to the kitchen.

"Hello," her flat mate greets, also in her pajamas. "I'm Paige." She's a too thin brunette with freckles and huge owl eyes — definitely not my type. We shake hands with her and stand silently around the stainless-steel island in the center of the room. The silence grows thick and encompassing. I can feel it surrounding me.

"Right, the whiskey," Melissa says and grabs two glasses from a nearby cupboard. She pours each of us hefty glasses and places them into our hands.

The girls continue to exchange looks back and forth, and I concentrate on taking slow sips out of my glass. I peep out of the corner of my eye Alex doing the same. He may be a loud-mouthed little shit to me at home, but he's never been much of a talker in these kinds of situations.

"So where's the party?" I eventually ask.

"Oh. We canceled it and decided to have more of a chill night instead," answers Melissa.

I can see Alex raising his eyebrows at her statement but trying to hide it behind his glass. I know what he's thinking.

"Okay, good to know." Information like that would have

been nice to have before we got here. "Umm," I try to think of something to lighten the catastrophic awkwardness. "Did you two want to hang out, then? Maybe watch a movie?" They exchange another glance.

"Actually," begins Paige, giving Alex and I the nastiest up and down look I've ever seen. It's so clear she does not like what she sees. Could've been less of a wanker about it though, if you ask me. "We're going to bed."

"Great," replies Alex, downing his glass and making his way to follow behind her.

She turns around and stops him with her hand to his chest. "I'll go grab the blankets for the couch. It's the least we can do since you traveled all this way," she says with a smile but it's heavily sarcastic. She turns and exits out the kitchen, Melissa hot on her heels.

Alex's mouth drops to the floor. "What in the —"

"They think you're ugly man." I shake my head, not quite sure what to make of the last five minutes of my life.

"*Me?*" he yells. "How do you know it's not *you?*"

"I'm the one with the app, remember? She's seen my photos."

"You're such a prick," Alex huffs, helping himself to more wine.

Melissa is at least nice enough to come back and hang out long enough for us to finish a bottle of whiskey between the three of us but it's dreadfully painful and awkward. Thankfully, she's eventually called upstairs by dodgy Paige and abandons us for the evening.

How Alex is snoring comfortably on the leather loveseat across the living room is beyond me. I've been staring into the darkness from the larger couch for the last three hours, chastising myself for such a fail of a night.

I pull up snapchat to help pass the time and see that my last recipient was Nayelli.

My night would have ended *so* differently if I had spent it with her. It almost hurts my soul to think of the night I could have had over this one. This... this is the most absolute shit night I have *ever* — oh.

The night with the fairy lady plays unbiddenly before me.

Maybe Alex is right. I need to do better.

I snap a quick photo of my face in the dark and send it with a message, hoping Nayelli's still awake.

Forty minutes pass and no response. She's probably asleep, it is pretty late after all. Giving up, I set my alarm to coincide with the first tube out of here and try to get some rest.

Nayelli

Dark patches dotted by platform lights flash by. I stare at nothing and everything outside the window, waiting for the St. Paul's stop. I'm headed to a Mexican restaurant by the name of Wahaca's to meet Olivia and her newly arrived family. If the margaritas from the cantina are any indicator of the Mexican cuisine here, then I know that I shouldn't get my hopes up too high.

The computerized British accent announces my station so I hop off the train and wait my turn in the *queue* to ride up the escalators and stand politely on the right, following the example of the other strangers sardined around me. After forty-five seconds of uninterrupted escalator riding, I feel as if I'm emerging from the depths of the underworld. How far down does this station actually go? A few brave souls race up the steps on the left-hand side. They must be running to an emergency because there is no way in hell I'd run up these steep ass stairs. Not even for work. It's never that serious.

After an eternity, I eventually surface to a dark winding street called Cheapside. The wind instantly slaps through my three layers of clothing and down to my bones causing me to instinctively wrap my arms around myself for extra protection. I don't think I'll ever get used to this kind of cold. It's not natural.

I walk in a random direction just to get my body moving against the cold. Checking my map, it shows the restaurant literally on the other side of the street of the station, situated in a mega mall of some sort. I scan the colossal steel and glass building bathed in orange street lamps until my eyes land on a neon blue sign that spells Wahaca's.

Making my way through the mall, I get lost in all that's happened since I last saw Olivia at the club. She's never going to believe me when I tell her. I actually met someone that I like and they aren't a complete bag of shit. I could kick my own ass for liking someone who lives so far away, but maybe — just maybe — he might be okay with seeing where this goes. I can't be the only one who feels like there might be something here... right?

I can't wait to talk all of this out. A second opinion is exactly what I need right now.

After pausing for a moment to steady my nerves and giddiness, I open the door to find an expansive, yet hipster, Mexican-themed restaurant with new-age art in desert yellows and oranges and wall paintings of roosters. Almost immediately, I spy Olivia and her family seated at the back right corner of the room and make a beeline for their table.

I hate it when I'm right. Have these people never heard of cumin? Or seasonings in general? I look across the table at everyone's plates: a full spread of enchiladas, tacos, refried beans, you name it. All imposters putting on a display. None of it tastes remotely close to the Mexican food back home in Cali. I let out a small sigh and put down my fork — effectively giving up on being polite and trying not to waste food that Olivia's mom is paying for.

At the table, I scan from Olivia, to her mother, to her grandmother, and finally land on her two sisters. In each face, a trace of one or the other. All with darker brown hair, except for the grandmother who boasts her natural hair in all of its silver glory.

I don't really hear the words being passed between them; I

just take in their presence. Three generations of women having dinner together in a foreign country. My heart constricts wistfully at the sight and a flutter of sadness swims inside of me and settles nowhere. I will never have a moment like this. Not with my own mother and grandmother at least, they have an irrational fear of flying.

I nod and fake a smile with all of the appropriate cues but absorb nothing. Again, I flow from one face to the next at the table until my eyes land on Olivia's which happen to be lasered in on me. Well, not so much me, but my neck.

"What is *that*?" she asks, venom dripping off her last word.

"Umm, it was a gift. For my birthday. James got it for me." I grasp the tiny harmonica hanging from my neck. For protection? For strength? I'm not sure. Granted, Olivia has not said anything to me all night, but I didn't expect her first words to sound so agitated.

"Wow, so what's next? Are you guys going to get married or something?" she asks in the same tone.

I squint my eyes at her before answering in the most sarcastic voice that I can muster, "Yeah, something like that." What is her deal?

Her answering eye roll is a severe one, and I notice her mother's eyes questioning the exchange. My heart cracks at Olivia's attitude. Shouldn't she be happy for me? She, more than anyone, knows the terrible luck I have had with men.

The waiter comes by to deliver the bill, and I find myself running through the possibilities over and over again as to why Olivia could possibly be upset. Is it because her Tinder experience hasn't been positive and my one date was?

Still deep in my own thoughts, my mind drifts back to our shared apartment. Olivia and I are sitting at the long narrow table in the kitchen of our old apartment. I was gushing over one of the guys who works with me as a campus tour guide. I think he was the first guy I had a crush on since the breakup with Will.

"Do you have a picture of him? Let me see," Olivia asked as I scrolled through Facebook trying to find him.

"Found it!" I exclaimed, coming across a tagged photo of him. "Isn't he the freaking cutest guy you've ever seen? He's really sweet to me too."

Olivia took the proffered phone in hand, and studied it for a long, silent moment. She handed back the phone and said, "Yeah, you definitely have to take me to your next tour guide party. Hook it up and introduce us."

Did she just...? But certainly she heard the part about me having a giant crush on him. What made her the better match for him — because she's skinnier than me? Because she's white, like him?

At the time, part of me probably agreed with her. Which is why I pretended like she didn't say anything offensive and dropped the subject.

We gather our belongings from the table and descend down the hidden escalator at the back of the restaurant. Olivia is two steps ahead and hasn't looked in my direction since asking about the necklace. How are we supposed to go out for New Year's Eve if she won't even look at me?

We are halfway down before she snaps her head around and asks, "Did you sleep with him?"

I look at her mother and grandmother, just behind us. Apparently they didn't hear her, so I respond with a quick "Yes," in as serious and hushed a manner as I can.

Olivia snaps back forward and resumes ignoring me. I've never seen her act like such a brat. At least never towards me.

My nerves are singing inside of me — their synapses laced in betrayal and heartbreak. I want to forget how she looked at me over dinner. How she spoke to me at the table, and again just now. But my insecurities have climbed into my chest and made their home. Why did she encourage me to meet him if she was going to act like this?

I try to hide my pain by asking these questions, but I know what just happened. I know that I wouldn't have gotten the same response if things had gone differently — if instead he had fucked me and dumped me, just like her guy did.

But the reality that Olivia doesn't know how to be happy for me unless she's happy as well hurts too much for me to accept.

So I bury Olivia's transgressions with the rest of the growing pile from this trip and pretend I'm having a great night.

My toe catches on the carpet of the hallway causing me to stumble into my hotel room. I jam the key into the light switch and scan the room for the new puffy coat I just bought. There's no way I'm going to last through midnight walking around the streets of London without more warmth.

I spot it tucked underneath my suitcase, both black and blending into each other.

I switch out coats and check the time. It's only 10:30. Perfect. I'll make it back in time to meet Olivia.

Before we parted ways, she complained about not being in the mood to party. Even though I only have two days left here and bought tickets to a masquerade, in advance, for the both of us. Instead, Olivia suggested we ditch the $100 tickets and pop a bottle of champagne in front of St. Paul's Cathedral. I roll my eyes and stuff my phone into my jacket pocket, but feel it vibrate and take it back out.

"Hello?"

"Hey Pumpkin, happy almost New Year." The tension in my posture instantly eases.

"Hey Mom, happy almost New Year."

"How's your night? What are you about to get up to? I know you must have big plans for spending New Year's Eve in London."

Her questions, although perfectly innocent, make my face crumble. I immediately sit down on the edge of the bed, my spine curving into a C over my lap, my chin tucking into my left hand.

"Nayelli? You there?"

"Yeah. I uh," I dig deep to find the courage to not be a cry baby over this. Once I feel the knot at the back of my throat dissolve, I allow myself to talk. "I've had a rough night."

"Really? What happened?" There is so much love and concern in her voice that the feeling as if I'm going to cry consumes me all over again.

I dive into the melodrama that has been Olivia and I for the past week. Glancing over James, of course. I don't think she could handle that. She'd lecture me about my behavior straight through the New Year. I end the long recount with Olivia's attitude and hostility over dinner.

"You said this is your friend, right?"

"Yes." My voice sounds small, even to me.

"Well, to me, it sounds like she has an attention problem. Is she an only child?" My mother, the oldest of four, believes that your birth position can tell you everything you need to know about someone's personality.

"She's the middle of three girls," I respond.

"Oooohhh. That might be even worse. Did she mention anything about your weight loss?"

"Hmm," I correct my posture and sit up straight. "No. No,

she didn't. But people don't just go blurting things about other people's bodies, mom."

"But she was your workout buddy, was she not? She saw you struggle at the gym, you told me how you two used to exercise together last year. A supportive friend would have said something. Even if it was something small like 'You look really nice.' It's not rocket science, Nayelli. From what you've told me, your friend has a problem with you — and her other friend — receiving attention. She thinks it all belongs to her."

When she puts it like that, it does make a lot of sense. Even so, a part of me still wants to believe that she's just having a bad... week? Holiday? Half year? Now that I think about it, she did say that she's been miserable since September when she moved here.

"You don't have to agree with me," she continues after I don't say anything. "But I'm telling you, that's her problem."

"Yeah, I hear you Mom." My phone buzzes. It's Olivia asking me how far away I am. "Hey, I gotta go. I'm supposed to meet back up with Olivia to pop a bottle of champagne for New Year's."

"Okay, but first, you know what I'm going to say, right?"

"No?"

"On the count of three I'm gonna need you to turn that frown upside down. You ready? One... two... three..." An honest smile breaks across my lips. She's been doing this to cheer me up for as long as I can remember. "It worked, didn't it? Bet you feel better already."

"Thanks Mom, I love you."

"I love you too. Enjoy your night."

In the back of the uber, I check the time on my phone for the twentieth time in the last five minutes. It's only 10:45. We should have plenty of time to make it over to the Cathedral, but Olivia never texted me back after I told her I was on my way and it's giving me massive anxiety.

"This is your stop, yeah?" the driver asks, pulling up to the curb.

"Yes, thank you!" I slam the car door behind me and race up the hotel's marble steps, noting that it reminds me of Chuck's penthouse in Gossip Girl. I power walk across the matching beige marble reception area and find the golden elevators around the corner. I hit the button for the ninth floor, tapping my foot incessantly.

The seconds feel like minutes and I bounce from foot to foot in anticipation. The doors open at last, and I bolt out of the elevator, find room 963 and knock briskly. My breath sounds harsh blowing through my nose, but at least I made it.

"Oh, hey." The door opens and it's Olivia's older sister. Her chocolate brown hair hangs loose at her shoulders and she's wearing her glasses and pajamas.

"Hey." I scan the room from the hallway. "Where's Olivia? Is she ready?"

"Oh, umm," the sister trails off. "She already left for the Cathedral. With our youngest sister."

I close my mouth, realizing it dropped open. How could she?

"I'm sorry, would you like to come in and wait for them to get back?" The tone of the older sister's voice is sympathetic, but not surprised.

"Umm sure," I answer defeatedly. What other option do I really have? I'm in a foreign city alone on New Year's Eve.

Kary steps aside for me to enter the room. There are two messy all white double beds and the NY ball drop playing on the TV. She takes one bed, I take the other, and before the countdown even has a chance to begin, I fall asleep.

I jolt awake at the sound of the door hitting the wall. Looking around, I see Kary in her same spot under the covers watching the news. People are kissing, dancing, celebrating, and overall enjoying the New Year.

"Happy New Year!" Olivia yells to the room, her little sister trailing behind her. I never realized how much Savannah looks like Olivia's blonde mini me until seeing them stand side by side. Olivia walks to the chair in the corner of the room, dumping her jacket. She turns around, finally noticing me. "Oh. Hey."

"Hi," I reply, short and barely civil. My supply of understanding has run out and all that's left is a boiling rage inside my chest. She's pushed me well beyond my breaking point and if I say something, it will be mean and hurtful. So, I say nothing and stare.

"Soooo did you want to go back out or something? It's not too late, I don't think," she says nonchalantly.

"No, I don't. It's already after 2:30 a.m." I grit my teeth hard enough to make them ache.

"Fine. I guess you're headed home then." Olivia crosses her arms over her beige sweater, her obsidian lined eyes staring a hole into my head.

"I guess so." I jump out of bed and grab my things, not bothering to look in anyone's direction. Needles prick the back of my eyes, but I don't cry. Not yet. Not in here. I can't let her know how much she got to me. I have to keep the upper hand and more importantly, my cool.

I leave the room and her wretched bratty face behind me, slamming the door as I go. Well, so much for keeping cool.

Out in the hall, my heart sinks into my gut and my legs move like they are made of lead. A solid five minutes pass before I reach the elevator.

The whole ride down to the lobby, I ask myself the same questions over and over again. Why did she leave me? Why didn't she wait a little longer? Wouldn't it have been better to at least have the champagne in her family's hotel room? Together?

I retrace my steps across the gold freckled marble, only this time, I veer left to the plush burgundy couches by the entrance. My whole body curls into one of its corners and I connect to the hotel's WiFi to call an Uber.

Once connected, my phone buzzes with a delayed message from Olivia.

We left. New Year's wasn't going to wait for you.

After placing an order for an Uber, I pull my knees closer to my chest and wrap my arms even tighter. When that's not enough, I rest my mouth against my knee, grazing it with the tips of my teeth. I need something, anything, that will ease the sting of hurt and frustration that have rooted deep inside the cavity of my chest. What did I do to her? Why is she treating me like this?

I want to scream; I want to yell; I want to curse at her like a sailor for being such a shit friend — but I do none of these things.

Instead, my tucked away body stares through glass sliding doors into the black night, silently waiting for a man named Daniel in a blue Prius.

*

Early the next morning, I dread the day before the day has a chance to begin. What the hell was that with Olivia last night? Should I even try to see her again before I leave? I stare at the blank screen on my phone, mulling it over.

A message from James pops up asking if I would like to

come over to walk his family's dog with him since his parents are going to be gone all day.

Duh.

But before I can respond with a *hell yeah, I'll be there* he sends me another message.

Jay333, 12:41 p.m.
False alarm. Parents actually aren't going to be gone. Mom is walking the dog and will be back soon. Still feel free to come though. No pressure, but invite is still open.

I contemplate meeting this man's mother. On one hand, his dad didn't seem to mind me and I would assume his mom is probably of the same disposition. On the other hand, from what I know of mothers, they definitely tend to be more protective. But what's my alternative? Wait around in my hotel for Olivia to text me? And even if we do meet up for my last day, then what? More unnecessary attitude and party pooper mentality?

I let James know I'll be there soon. It's my last day in London, I might as well spend it having a good time.

*

"Mum, this is Nayelli. Nayelli, my mum," James announces as I walk into the living room. His mother is adorable and sweet looking with an oversized hipster tan cardigan and trendy black glasses.

"Hello Nayelli, nice to meet you," she greets with a cordial, eye-crinkling smile to accompany her British accent.

"Hi, nice to meet you as well," I reply, not quite knowing what to do with my hands or feet. Her hair is cropped short into a pixie cut and she has a small smattering of gray that disrupts her chestnut strands. In her face, I see so much of James. But where he is hard and angled, she is soft with age: attractive hazel eyes, inviting face, and a slightly understated nose and mouth.

My brain is incapable of knowing how to proceed with James' mother. When I met his dad, all I had to do was get into the back seat of their car. Do I sit? Do I have to curtsy or something first? Do they kiss on the cheek here? My smile soon turns into a nervous grimace.

"Please, do sit down," she says, ending my embarrassing stance.

I sit on the empty couch to the left of the one she is on and fold my hands in my lap. James, who is silently watching this humiliating endeavor from the entryway, plops his large self, to the right of his mother. Abandoning me *again*? Wow this guy really has a thing for leaving someone he barely knows to face his parents.

"Would you like some tea?" she asks.

Oh, that's really a thing here? How freaking *cute*. "Yes, please. Thank you," I answer, giving her my most polite smile. She leaves the couch to grab it and James follows right behind her. Really?

I turn my attention to an old western playing on their small TV. Not long into it, a familiar thought hits me: who does she think I am? Did James tell her about me? Did his father say something? Did his father and mother have a conversation about the American chick who keeps showing up to their house to have sex with their son? Dear god, I hope not. My fragile ego would never recover.

Is she in the kitchen chastising James and judging me? My coat is hanging on the hook by the door, but the front door is in direct eyesight of the kitchen where James' mother is grabbing tea.

Their house isn't even walking distance to the nearest train station. I'd have to call an Uber. But do I have time to call one before they come back? I hear footsteps coming towards the living room, effectively ending my escape plot.

A few more footsteps and his mother returns with a fully decked out tea tray that I've only seen in my favorite old British movies with my mom. She sets the assortment between us on the low wooden coffee table. A bowl of tightly packed sugar cubes; an array of loose-leaf tea with a metal contraption that holds it in the cup; a large white porcelain teapot of hot water; a matching smaller porcelain pot that holds cold milk. His mother pours a steaming cup, then hands it to me with a saucer underneath.

With each warm sip of tea, my apprehension eases. Notes of lavender and other earthy leaves linger on my tongue, sweet and smooth. I know that this is probably normal for them, but I can't help but feel a little special that she brought out the works for me.

"So are you on holiday Nayelli?" his mother asks.

"Yes, Ms…" Wow. I don't even know what to call her. Maybe just keep it simple and say James' mum? Or Mrs. James' mum? Am I even allowed to use "mum" or is that cultural appropriation?

"Nayelli?" James' voice breaks into my inner spiral.

"Oh, um. Yes. I'm on vacation from school visiting my… uh… friend."

I could kill James for springing his mother on me at the last second, but I know why I'm here. Hell, I would've still come even if his entire extended family was here.

Ugh, I'm so pathetic.

I peer into my tea cup and briefly close my eyes in chastisement for being so desperate for this man.

The things we do for men who give us good sex.

James

Nayelli and my mum are busy chatting away over tea, covering a wide expanse of topics like elected officials and American TV shows. Some of her responses are punctuated by her infectiously goofy laugh. Her curls are pulled back into a bun, so I get to admire her face in depth. Like how the light breaks in through the curtains behind her, dancing and warming her smooth skin with golden tones.

Just look at her: all calm, cool, and collected. There hasn't been one awkward pause in their conversation since she got here. I'm impressed. But in hindsight, not the greatest idea. She could have done or said something weird in front of my mum — but she didn't. Instead, they are discussing the different coastal towns of California.

"You're from Santa Barbara, then?" she asks Nayelli.

"Well, not from there, but I do go to school there."

"Wow, lucky girl that you get to go to Uni on the coast. I've been to Los Angeles but never made it over to Santa Barbara. It's quite beautiful, I've heard?"

"Oh man, it's one of the most stunning places to watch a sunset. And the Mexican food is to die for, unlike…" her voice drifts off and I raise a brow at what she could have possibly meant. "You definitely have put it on your list of places to visit," Nayelli advises.

We've socialized enough to be polite, right? I stand up and look at Nayelli. "Hey, let's go upstairs?"

"Okay. Yeah, sure," she replies a little confused, "Thank you for the tea," she says to my mum.

Nayelli rises from the couch and her fitted grey dress comes into full view, stretching and sliding across her hips. I'm surprised I let the conversation with my mum go on for this long. *Christ, woman.* She walks in front of me and my legs strain in a heroic effort to keep myself from running up the stairs with her.

Once upstairs, Nayelli steps away from me and into the only light in the room. My hands reach for her face but fall at my sides. The center of them itch, mourning her absence and craving to touch her again.

She gives me a slight smile before removing her dress, her tiny under things following shortly behind. The sun bathes her skin in golden orange and I admire her figure in all of its rawness. *Sweet Jesus.* I twitch to life like a motor engine, instantly hard in my jeans. Fuck. What was that? Three seconds?

She sits at the edge of the bed, facing away from me and sitting on her heels. The curve between her waist and hips is caught in between light and darkness, half of her silhouetted and left for my imagination to fill in. She turns her face and rests her chin on her shoulder, her eyes sliding over to me as she waits for me to join her.

Nayelli's sumptuous curves and subtle movements mirror *The Birth of Venus* in motion; her sensual energy is like a magnet sucking me in and paralyzing me at the same time.

Shit. I realize I'm still standing in the same spot with my mouth hanging open, fully clothed.

After stripping down to nothing, I walk up behind her to the edge of the mattress. My lips make love to the soft skin between her neck and jawline first. The taste of her skin is infused with notes of orange and ginger. *Always so fucking sweet.*

"Mmm," she hums and leans her neck over further.

Her small sound is all the encouragement I need. Nothing else matters in this moment but pleasing her, pushing her to the edge, helping her understand how powerful of an effect she has on my body by mirroring the sensations within hers.

My teeth lightly graze against her shoulder while my arms wrap around her. I bite my lip at the heaviness of her breasts in my palms and give her nipples a twirling stroke with my fingers.

"Mmm," she approves again.

"Face down," I instruct. She hesitates but follows my directions, her ass taking on the shape of a peach before me. I lick my lips and a lightening rich excitement snaps through me. All of my muscles contract together as a need to be inside her drives so deep within me, I have to close my eyes to compose myself.

Whew. *Calm down, James.* A minute man isn't a fun time for anyone. My breath slides between my lips and I count to ten. Feeling less like a loaded gun, I continue my pursuit.

The bed sighs beneath me as my knees fold behind her body. I wrap one arm around her waist and plant a kiss to the small of her back before allowing my other hand to part and stroke in between her legs.

"James. Yes," she breathes into the sheets, her fists clenching beside her face.

"Christ, you're so fucking sexy. Should I?" I ask, positioning myself at the entrance of her.

"Yes," she echoes again.

Slowly I advance, filling myself with her warmth and softness. She gasps. A small breath of pleasure caressing the dark air around us.

Fuck. It will be a very long time before I forget that sound.

We assume our familiar position: naked post-sex in the bed, talking in the dark, Nayelli in my arms.

"How was your New Year's Eve?" I ask.

"One of the worst I've ever had." Her response is dry and serious.

"Really? Why?" She's on holiday in a new country. What could have been bad?

"Well," she takes a deep breath before continuing, "you know how I came here to visit my old college roommate?"

I nod but then remember that she can't see me with the lights off. "Yes, yes I do."

She proceeds to recount her evening of being stood up on New Year's Eve. Apparently her person from Uni didn't care enough to wait for her and left her to bring in the new year alone. She hasn't heard from her since, even though it's her last day here.

I can hear the hurt in the way her voice drops low, her syllables laced in pain and confusion. My arms curl tighter to give her body a reassuring squeeze, hoping to provide at least a temporary comfort and hating whoever was so intentionally unkind to her. "I hate to tell you this," I begin carefully, "but that's not your friend."

"I... I don't know. She's been weird this entire trip. I just don't understand why."

"Well, it's your last night here. Don't worry about getting that sorted right now. So, friend aside, did you at least enjoy your time in London?" Her body turns in my embrace and she beams a huge smile at me.

"Of course. I met you. And I know I messed this up the first time but," her eyes look down, her warm fingers drawing circles where her gaze connects with my skin, "I like you too James."

I can't bring myself to say it this time. It was easier the first day, new. But now that we've clicked, all I can think about is how I'd like more. And that makes me feel... weird as fuck. If I'm being completely honest.

Nayelli's lips find mine, and I forget that she is leaving me. That I like her. That I... Her mouth is plump, soft, and giving. Always so, so giving. She licks my bottom lip before lightly teasing it with her teeth. A low sound resonates within me and vibrates across both of our lips.

"Let's get a little sleep," she ends the kiss and settles back into her previous position.

Her soft breath blows across my chest in a steadying rhythm until it smooths out completely. I tuck my arm beneath my head, knowing my body is not quite ready to fall asleep. My thoughts drift to my ex.

My mind unwillingly plays the beginning and end of that relationship. How emotionally codependent we became. How getting over her took almost everything in me. The fucking depression that came with it all.

I fill up my lungs until they almost want to burst with fire then release the built-up air in one giant sigh.

I can't do that again. I just *can't*. And it is with that thought that I at long last drift off to sleep.

Her chest continues to rise and fall in the tell-tale cadence of sleep. I've been awake for a few minutes but don't have the heart to wake her just yet. She's still curled against me, her mouth blowing small puffs of air against my skin. I lazily draw patterns with my fingertips across her naked back and look into the dark space of my room.

I think back to the first night she was here, making beats with me on my synths board at one a.m. like it was just another regular night for us. I think of how our conversation flows so smoothly between one another — over dinner, on the tube, after sex. How she was so calm and natural talking with my mother, as if that was a normal situation for her.

Is it the normalcy that I'm drawn to? It's not like I've had a taste of what normal is before. But it's more than that. It's like she fits — as if there is a small carved space in my life that she has plugged herself into. Not to mention that spending time with her is just so... easy.

Then again, aren't all new things easy?

Still, I find myself wanting more of her. To know her a little better.

I run my hand down the length of her spine and give her hair a soft kiss. She really is quite attractive. But it's more than me being attracted to her, it's the chemistry. I've had sex with enough women to know that. The pull that I've been feeling to her all week — to see her face, to feel her against me, to lose myself within her. I honestly can't remember a time when I've wanted anyone as much as I want her.

I continue my soft strokes against a sleep-laden Nayelli and feel the moment's contentedness drifting through me, making me light. With her asleep in my arms, I just feel good. It isn't much, but it's all that I know right now.

But is allowing myself to feel this good a mistake? The last thing I need is to start becoming attached to someone who is so unavailable to me.

Disappointment mixed with regret ebbs its way into my chest and taints my reflections of the woman cuddled up to me. It might have been nice to know her but as always, my life never seems to give me what I want when I want it most.

Nayelli

"Nayelli. Nayelli? Nayelli. Nayelli, it's time to wake up love."

"Hmm? Why?" I answer, still in between states of consciousness, while James kisses my shoulder. Wait. Did he just call me? Oh, right. I'm in England. That term is casual.

I've talked with enough men from here — virtual and otherwise — to figure that out. My hope that he feels enough for me to give me a term of endearment deflates, but at least I am fully awake. Discouraged, but awake.

"Aren't you hungry?" I feel the timbre of his voice rumble through his chest.

"No," I respond pointedly, "I'm tired."

He chuckles and the hairs underneath my face tickle my nose. "Dinner is well past cold. We can sleep again later."

"There's dinner?" Who made it? How long have I been out?

"My mum made it. Come on then," he rolls me over lightly "I'm starving."

Holy mother of — His parents! How could I have forgotten about his parents? I get up to throw my clothes on and send up a small prayer that they didn't hear us. And — even if they did — that they aren't the kind of people to say anything about it.

I pause before entering the dining room, the light of the TV in the next room catching my eye. I peer into the living room and see the entangled lump of James' mother and father curled up on the couch watching a movie. His father's arm is draped across the shoulders of his mother. His mother's head is leaning into the chest of his father.

Damn.

I realize I've never witnessed this image before, the simple affection and ease shared between married partners. My parents split up before I can even remember. My dad re-enlisted into the military and has since spent every two years being stationed from state to state. He calls every now and then to keep up with my life but I hardly see him.

I continue staring at the couple, wondering if I will ever have this for myself. I want to stay and memorize the feeling of this sight before me, but force myself to join James in the dining room.

"Sit down, I'll make a plate for you," he yells from the kitchen.

"James?" I hear his mother call.

Oh god. Did she see me creeping on them?

"Please pour Nayelli a glass of wine to go with her dinner."

I love this woman.

James returns with two plates of roasted chicken, red potatoes, and asparagus followed by a white China gravy boat and a glass of red wine as per his mother's instructions.

"Prepare to have some of the most delicious food of your entire existence," he tells me while taking his seat on my right.

His obsession with food makes the side of my mouth quirk up and I shake my head at him, remembering my first night here and how he kept trying to feed me because it was the "Jewish mom in him". Even though I'm pretty sure he said only his dad is Jewish. Also, I'm pretty sure they celebrated Christmas. This family is interesting to say the least but I let it go, my hunger more important.

I go for the chicken first, but before I can bring it to my lips he interrupts with, "Wait, wait. Try it with the gravy." I pause and let him pour it onto my plate before dipping my forked piece into the tan sauce. "Mmm, some damn good chicken and gravy isn't it?" he asks as the food enters my mouth.

I almost choke on chicken and gravy and laughter. But he's not wrong. It's savory and delicious. Here I was, believing the hype that Brits can't cook but James' mom can definitely throw down. Well, on this at least.

"It's really good," I'm finally able to get out.

Not long into our meal, I see the cutest ball of auburn fluff that I have ever laid eyes on.

"Hello!" I greet instinctively.

James looks around for the intruder and sees that his retriever has joined us for dinner. "Oh. That's Benson, our dog."

"Hi Benson," I greet him again. "Aww, aren't you such a handsome guy." I ruffle Benson's ears and he smiles up at me like he loves me. Is my dog voice on? You better believe it. Do I care? Absolutely not. He immediately rests his head in my lap and I become ambidextrous for the sake of scratching his head with my right hand and eating with my left.

"Don't start thinking you're special," James cuts in, "he's just whoring himself out for food."

"HA!" I laugh and snort loudly. "You want to hate on me so bad," I tease.

"Really?" His eyes are challenging mine. "Benson," he calls, holding out a piece of chicken. The dog abandons me immediately. "See?" he smirks triumphantly.

"You just can't let me be great, can you?" I rumble under my breath.

"What was that?"

"Nothing," I mutter around another bite of chicken.

We finish our food and head back to his room. I fumble around in his closet to grab my boots while James watches the endeavor from his bed.

"What are you doing?" his voice breaks my concentration.

"Grabbing my shoes." I'd love nothing more than to spend my last night with him, but I know that it might be too much. I'm not anyone to him. Not after tonight.

"Stay," he says simply.

"You don't have to say that just to be nice." I remember James calling himself a gentleman when we met, but I don't want any of his pity or whatever it is that causes gentlemen to feel compelled to do something.

"I'm not just being nice. Please, stay." His voice is honest and open and weakens my resolve to leave.

"I didn't bring any of my things. And I have to leave first thing in the morning." My heart deflates in defeat. I can't stay. Even if I didn't feel like a freaking pity case.

"Look, obviously I'm not going to force you. You can do whatever you want, but I'd really like you to stay."

My eyes search his and in them I find whatever reassurance I'm looking for. He really does want me to.

Something about this admission allows me to drop the guard that I've been putting up, if only a little. It's going to be a hell of a push to get to the airport tomorrow, but something tells me it will be worth it.

"Okay, I'll stay." He opens his arms to me and my hands stop their aimless pursuit. I race over to the bed to jump into his lap. Wrapping my arms, legs, and entire body around him.

"Thank you for being so cool with my mom earlier." His tone is completely earnest.

"Uh, you're welcome?" My forehead wrinkles a bit, trying

to figure out how else he thought I might act in front of her.

"I'm serious." James glides his hands down my back. Still holding me, he stands up and our eyes meet in a way that is somehow so natural between us. The light from the shuttered window streams across his face at different angles. His eyes pendulum from hazel, to slightly emerald, to brown, and back again. He turns slightly towards the last rays of seeping daylight and I am in awe of the beautiful mix of green with flecks of butterscotch that stare back at me.

Sliding down his body to stand, I force my physical attraction to this man to simper. Besides, I'm sure my lady parts are on strike at this point.

But James' features reflect a look that is both dark and ablaze.

Welp. That was a valiant effort while it lasted.

My lips part open to compensate for the dip in my oxygen supply. From my fingertips to the pads of my toes, I feel my body heat up its synapses in preparation for what is to come, newly primed and dispositioned to be ready for anything at the sight of that look he gives to me so freely.

How long are we standing in front of one another? A minute? Ten? The heavy burnt-orange rays that illuminated his room mute down to nothing but shadows.

"You," his baritone fills the weighted silence between us.

"Yes?" I respond, my voice drowning in a thickness that makes my words curl across my lips and leave my mouth slowly.

One step. Another. My pulse crests to a new height with each fall of his foot. He takes his time until there is only the slightest separation between my body and his. Time, breath, movement — everything is still. His hands reach out to cup the sides of my face, as if he's capturing something precious. My heart is suspended and motionless between the cage of my ribs; wanting to float at the way he looks at me, touches me, fucking covets me — wanting to sink at the realization that tomorrow I leave and all of this ends.

The moon completely takes over the duties of its predecessor and my eyes adjust to make out the edges of his stubbled jaw and the seriousness of his stare. His eyes implore into the depths of my own. This man will be the death of me, I know it. The intensity of his gaze makes me shift my weight slightly, but I can't look away. Trapped and tethered by the line of desire that pulls me to him and keeps me there.

His full lips claim my cheek, forehead, neck, then mouth. It tickles in the most sensual of ways. His hands never stop cradling my face, as if only the touch of his palms are tying us both to reality and keeping me from disappearing.

He tilts his head back, "You," he resumes from before, "You, Nayelli, are so, so beautiful," he says, his voice's cadence as slow and heavy as my own.

*

Leaning my head back against the wall, I tuck my toes underneath the white down comforter for warmth. Of course I ran out of socks on my last day here. Since James insisted I spend the night, the least he can do is part with a pair of socks. But he's currently grabbing me breakfast from downstairs and I dare not move my feet from under the covers.

I'm dozing off to the show *Adventure Time* playing in the background when he finally comes back into the room.

"Ready for some super fancy bacon and eggs in bed?" he asks enthusiastically.

"Yes please," I answer. His enthusiasm is infectious, if only slightly.

Each passing moment brings me closer to my departure and simultaneously adds to the forlornness buzzing at the back of my mind.

You should've left him alone after the first night. Now you like him. Idiot.

My phone rings in my hand and relief washes over me for the distraction it brings from my thoughts.

I check the caller ID, then answer it. "Hey." James turns from watching *Adventure Time* and raises his eyebrow at me.

"It's my mom," I mouth at him.

My mother is barely able to ask if I'm ready to come home before James blurts out, "Hi Nayelli's mom!"

My eyes almost explode from their sockets. This is it. This is how I die.

My mother's frantic voice catches my attention, and I tune back into our conversation. "Hello? Hello? Nayelli! Who is *that*?"

A deep, spiritual, bone-deep sigh escapes my body and I close my eyes before answering, "That's James."

"James! And *who* is James?" My mother yells. James can hear her freak out from his spot on the bed and starts cracking up laughing.

My heart works overtime in my chest as I try hard to think of a way to explain to my overprotective Baptist mother the week-long sexcapades her child has had with a man she just met.

"It's hard to explain."

"Hey, did you tell her about—"

"Shut up. Shut up! Shut *up*!" I yell.

"Why?" he asks, confused. Then, realization quickly dawns

in his eyes and he adds, "Ohhhh you thought I was going to say something about all of the *sex* we've been having!"

I hang up on my mother.

How in the hell am I going to explain my way out of this one? And knowing my big-mouth mother, she is probably already on the phone with half of my family members telling them I've met my future husband while abroad. I get up from the bed, give him a threatening double-fingered *I'm watching you* signal, and loudly stomp to the bathroom.

So much for keeping this a secret.

The drive to the station is filled with a suffocating silence. Gone is the vibrant, goofy man I've spent the last week with and in his place is a contemplative, dour stranger. I rack my brain for something to say, for words that will lighten the oppressive tension hanging over us but come up short.

We sit outside of Wimbledon station in his tiny two-seater for what feels like hours. It is too early for the sun and my breath can be seen in small intermittent clouds of mist. Neither one of us moves; neither of us is willing to say a word because we know once we speak, the magic will die and we will return back to our previous lives, carrying on as if we never met.

"I have to go." I break the silence, yet it feels like it's not the only thing I've broken. Regardless, I have to leave soon or I'll miss my flight. I reach across to kiss him on the cheek and try my best at an awkward side hug. "Thank you so much for an amazing time this past week. I'm really happy that I've met you," I smile at him. But he says nothing, only stares. I turn to open the door and he catches one of my hands between both of his — making them feel so small, yet so warm. We lock eyes, his filled with some unnamed emotion.

Slowly, he brings my hands to his lips and gives it a brief

kiss. "Have a nice life Nayelli," he whispers softly.

My heart shatters into a million pieces, with each piece sinking into my flesh, stabbing me from the inside out. The shock on my face unthaws and I muster up the strength to throw a weak smile in his direction. I grab my bags and scramble to get out of the car. My brain turns on autopilot, I can't risk dwelling on what just happened. There'll be plenty of time for that on the flight.

I rush into the train station, forcing myself not to look back. A steady beat pulses in my ears, drowning out the shuffles and grunts of the morning commute as I briskly make my way down to the train's platform. I focus my gaze on the ground, towards the unending paint that tells you where to stand. The scene from the last few minutes is stuck in my head on repeat, and with each replay a rhythmic chant in my head persists: *idiot, idiot, idiot.*

James

I had to tell her to have a nice life. What else was I supposed to say?

My hands grip the wheel a little too harshly and I can feel the leather of the steering wheel chafe against my hand. The dull ache in my palms is a welcome distraction, but not enough.

What more could we have been? Nothing. What more could I have offered her? Nothing. I hardly have anything to offer myself on most days, let alone others. And it is in that answer of nothingness that I try to find some sort of solace. So what we had a really good time? It's not that big of a deal. She's a girl I met off *Tinder* for Christ's sake. You go there for one thing and one thing only. I know that and so does she.

But then why did it feel so weird to say goodbye?

Maybe she's just pretending to be amazing and the girl I met is nothing but a lie. Maybe she's actually stuck-up with an extremely ugly attitude. And has a harem of men back in California that she uses for sex and money.

Yeah, right. Nayelli is perfect, she would never.

I can lie to myself all day, but it won't change anything. Whatever it is that happened between us this last week, there is still something that I do not possess the power to change: she doesn't live here and never will.

I look out the window at her bundled retreating form one last time; she still hasn't made it to the inside of the station. Fuck. I shouldn't have looked. With no little effort, I force myself to stop watching her. I shake my head sharply from side to side, hoping that the memories of her will fall out onto the seat where she sat only a minute ago.

The car pulls from the curb and I allow the distance between us to become a barrier around my feelings.

Out of sight, out of mind.

*

I sit down on the leather couch that has probably seen one ass too many. The beer-stenched living room is packed with a lively bunch of people enjoying their Saturday night.

My eyes scan around the room and return back to the whiskey-coke in front of me. There's no one interesting enough to talk to or that isn't otherwise occupied with the hope of the night ending with a shag — how disgusting.

Holy fucking hell. Not even a whiskey is drowning out my negativity — a very serious and depressing sign if I've ever seen one. I lean my head against the back of the couch and let out an impressive groan.

"Aye mate, you all right?" My mate Chris asks me. He invited me and some other friends out to drink and swim at his house tonight. I swam a few laps, drank a good amount, but feel just as shitty as I did this morning. Which, if I was smarter, would be *another* huge flashing sign from the universe since swimming is normally a cure all for me and has been since I competed in secondary school.

"Yea, yea. Cheers, mate. Just kind of tired is all. I might call it an early night," I respond. I check the time on my phone and do the quick time zone calculation for California.

"You sure everything's cool? Not like you to be so quiet.

And that's the tenth time you've checked your phone in the last hour." Chris's round eyes squint down to tiny points that are set into his even rounder face.

The blue of his irises is bright and jumping out against his flush face, meaning he's probably one drink away from his limit. It also means that sober Chris won't remember to pressure me about this later.

"I met this girl from America and she left this morning. And now..." And now, what? You told her to have a nice life for fuck's sake. "And now I just don't know." I'm not stupid. I know I like her. I know I'm still thinking about her and wish that I wasn't. I know I don't need any distractions. Yet, that still doesn't quite capture things correctly. My mind has exhausted itself in working overtime to put a label on how I feel. A little sad? Horny? Stupid? Definitely stupid after the way I treated her this morning when she left. *Fucking idiot.*

"Bloody hell, James! A girl? This is about a *girl?*" He shrieks over the noise of the room. "Hey Kenny, get over here and hear this. James has a crush on a girl and he's all bent about it!"

"All right, you can kindly fuck off now Chris," I smirk. Should've known he would be an asshole about this. I don't even know Kenny that well.

I take advantage of Chris's sidebar conversation with Kenny, who has now made his way over to us, to make my exit. I throw on my jacket, drain the last of the whiskey-coke mixture in my cup, and stand from the couch.

"Hey, I have an early day at the shop tomorrow so I'll catch you guys later," I say over my shoulder, heading straight for the door. Out of the corner of my eye, I see Chris making a pucker with his lips and blowing air kisses. Without stopping, I throw up my middle finger in his direction and exit out of the house.

Once outside, the bite of the winter air greets me all at once and it is a welcome distraction from my blackened thoughts. I wrap my arms across my chest and tuck my head against the wind, keeping my eyes glued to the dimly illuminated pavement. The shadows of buildings and overarching trees dance in the night's gentle breeze, and I'm reminded of walking down a similar street after our Thai date night. Craving the opening I have now provided, my brain takes off once again on the Nayelli infatuation train. I reminisce about running my fingers through the wild, untamed curls that is Nayelli's hair, then how she'd look under the light of the moon, her skin bathed in an ethereal glow with her signature mischievous smile resting upon her beautiful face.

I become so entranced with piecing images of her together this way that I almost run into a pole. Stopping for a moment, I size the pole up like it has offended me with the utmost disrespect. Thank god for my cat-like reflexes or it really could've taken me out.

I resume my walk to the station. "Christ," I whisper, my breath curling into the air. "I know I've talked loads of shit about you not being a real thing. But if you are some kind of magical fairy man, *please* help me be less bat shit over this woman."

I peer into the depths of the streets looking for a sign, anything that might indicate I've been heard. But of course, nothing happens. It never does.

*

Once I make it home, I pathetically – and unsurprisingly – turn on my Mac and try to FaceTime Nayelli.

Is she ignoring me? It's my fifth time calling her with no answer and I begin to panic. Nayelli really might be done with me for good.

Focus, mate. I pull in large breaths, filling my chest to capacity and then push them forcefully out of my mouth, hoping that my nervousness will filter out with each exhale. Deep down I know what I told her is the right thing to do. "Have a nice life," I mutter into the still air in my room and rub my stubble, attempting to wipe off some of my angst. The crestfallen look on her face after I told her to have a nice life has haunted me all night.

Speaking of haunting, the image of her naked silhouette in the shadows of my bedroom during our first night together is still imprinted behind my eyelids. And not to mention that sensation — that addicting feeling of happiness that she carries with and around her — is noticeably *gone*.

My computer screen is displaying our FaceTime history. I've called her five times since I returned home from Chris's party.

"Fuuuccckkk." I shift my weight back in my chair. I shouldn't be calling her. If she is smart, and she is, she won't have anything to do with me. But maybe I shouldn't have ended things on such a final note? All of the whiskey I've had tonight isn't helping me forget like I hoped it would.

What if we try to be friends? Like long-distance pen pals or something. Men and women still do that, right? That wouldn't be too distracting, I'm sure.

I spin in the computer chair and survey my room. Ghosts of our fucking play across the walls, her essence stamped on every surface of this place. The double bed in the corner of the room is the same exact bed that it was yesterday, and yet the bed — hell, the whole room — feels so different.

I swivel back around to the computer and click on her FaceTime contact to call her one more time.

"Hello?"

Air leaves my mouth is one big rush — I didn't realize I'd been holding my breath. I maximize the chat window so that her face appears larger than life on my Mac. *Why is she so damn pretty?* "Hey, guess what?"

"What?" She responds with a wrinkle in her brow.

"You're pretty," I say matter of fact.

She rolls her eyes and lets the tiniest smile dance at the corners of her mouth. *Damn that mouth.* Flashes of her plump lips come to the forefront of my mind and my thoughts fill with the dark ways I could enjoy them if she were here instead of a million fucking miles away.

"So I have something to run by you," she says without making eye contact, her face is void of emotion. "Well… never mind," is all that comes out.

"No, you brought it up. Go on with it. What's up?" Now I'm worried. She said she was on birth control, right? But for the life of me I can't remember if she said, "mhmm" or just "hmm". Either way, it is several unprotected fucks too late now. There is no way in hell I'm ready for a little person. Fuck. I've really fucked up this time. *Fucking idiot.*

Before I get too deep into my mental crisis, she cuts the silence. "You know how I was supposed to come back for my friend's birthday? Well obviously she hates me now, but maybe I could come back and see *you* instead…"

Come back and see *me*? Like my bloody long-distance girlfriend or something? Anxiety creeps down my throat like a fucking spider. My heart thumps against my ribs and a sweat breaks out above my brow. She wants to date me? *Me*? No. Fuck no. No. This is not the direction I wanted to take things. When I made up my mind to call her, I had convinced myself that I'd be okay with talking from time to time, maybe even persuade her to FaceTime sex me or send a naked photo or two. Never had I thought about taking it any further than that. She lives halfway around the world, surely she understands how infeasible starting a relationship would be. "Well," I let out a long breath in hopes that I can think of what to say. "I don't know what I have going on. I'll have to check my calendar to see if I'm even free. When would you be coming?"

"Around the end of March. For spring break," she answers in a tiny voice. "I'm only bringing this up because if I do come back, it would be *specifically* to see you. No one else. Would you be okay with that?"

Her eyes are meeting mine now. Their crescent shape cut into me through my computer screen. I can see the light of hope and infatuation brimming in them and all of my lust and excitement from earlier calms down to a soft whisper.

I can't do this. No, it's not that I can't; it's that I don't want to. Who in their right mind would let their feelings grow for someone under these circumstances? She's already invaded my subconscious in more ways than I should have allowed as it is.

"I'll get back to you on it," I gotta let this thing die — and quickly. Her face looks a tad bit defeated, but it's better this way. It's better that she knows not to get her hopes up about me and that there can be no us.

Soon after, I end the call and climb under my big white blanket — chastising myself for even calling her in the first place. She likes me. That much is obvious and only adds to the fact that I need to leave her the fuck alone. She doesn't deserve some half assed fling with a bloke who can't even be there in real life.

Besides, there's always the expectations that come along with it. Feelings, commitment, affection — the whole lot of it — makes me sick to my stomach. And knowing how women work, those are all of the things she would probably want. Friendship is out of the window too. Or at least the type that I would be interested in. She seems too nice of a girl to be into the NSFW things I had in mind.

    I clear my throat of some unknown irritant and grab my phone from its place on my nightstand. I click on the soft glowing red flame and start swiping through pictures that are within a thirty-kilometer radius of myself. Maybe this time I'll have better luck.

Nayelli

I drag my body across the threshold of my house and look around the small living room: the black futon to my left, the green leather couch across from me, the TV mounted up above the fireplace. Everything is the same. And yet the blood in my veins is alive with a pulse that shouts at me to leave and whispers to my heart that a part of me no longer belongs here. Somewhere. Anywhere. But not here.

 I let out a long, deep sigh. It's too early for this. I haven't even been back for a full twenty-four hours and already the depression is kicking in. Returning to my room, I turn on my phone light and see that my roommate is still gone. *Good.* I can feel bad about myself without being interrupted. I lay down in my twin-sized bed by the window and cuddle one of my pillows, ignoring the morning's looming responsibilities for the moment. But the second I close my eyes for a touch too long, the past week begins playing in my mind. Waiting for me behind my eyelids are all of the confusing and intense moments with James, and of course all the drama with Olivia too.

 I text her to let her know my flight landed safely — she replied with a thumbs up. I figured she didn't care about me anymore when she made no effort to see me on my last day, but it's crystal clear now: our friendship is over. *Ugh.* I should be used to losing friends by now, but it still cuts a fresh wound each time.

 Maybe I just need a hot shower to wash the memories of

London off me.

I stand up again and force myself to take a long, slow, deep breath. *Iiiiinnnnn. Ouuuuuttttt.* Once I feel a tad bit of normalcy return, I strip out of my clothes. Call me darkly sentimental but these are the same clothes I was wearing on the plane from London — and the same ones from when James FaceTimed me on the cab home just to tell me he didn't want me... again. The only reason I even answered was because my phone alerted me to five missed calls from him once I landed. I thought that maybe during the flight he'd changed his mind. That maybe he felt what I did and made a mistake in telling me to have a nice life. That maybe we'd... never mind. It doesn't matter any more, does it? Because he got all sketchy at the prospect of seeing me again.

There is no denying it, his sudden flightiness is beginning to seriously hurt my ego. Like... a lot. How much of myself am I willing to sacrifice in hopes that something with James might just work out? It scares me that I don't know the answer.

Sigh. The clothes from my flight are still in my hand, curled against my chest. I walk over to my laundry hamper and bury the offensive items at the bottom. Grabbing a towel from the closet to wrap myself in, I walk to the shower, crank on my new FKA Twigs playlist and turn the knob as hot as it will go.

I send up a little prayer that maybe, just maybe, a hot shower will cure me and wash away all traces of my infatuated stupidity.

*

A few days pass and I find myself opening WhatsApp to look at the message I sent James. *Again.* I sent it on Wednesday and here it is, Sunday, with no response.

Ugh, rejection is a son of a bitch. Even in the form of an unreplied text. I should've known he would freak out about me suggesting I come back to see him. But I didn't think he'd flat out ignore me. All I said was *hey* – who's too stuck up their own butt to respond to that?

I don't regret asking to see him though. I *had* to. I can't explain why but it feels like we have some unfinished business and the feeling won't stop nagging at me until I find out exactly what *this* is. What do I really have to lose at this point anyway? What does he? But alas, in lieu of a double text, I set my phone down and attempt to sleep a little longer. I spent last night out in Isla Vista with my housemates, partying the night away and could really use the extra snooze.

All too soon, a lawn mower's engine revs on and off outside my room's window. I try my best to ignore it, the dreadful state of wakefulness looming just above my body. The engine grows louder, approaching closer to my window, and I abandon the hope of any more sleep. "Uggghhhhh."

Frustrated with life, I begrudgingly roll over, grabbing my phone from the window sill.

Waiting for me is a text from James. My heart lurches into the back of my throat. He wants me to call him on FaceTime. *About damn time.* I race to the bathroom to give myself a thorough once over. Dark eyeshadow has smudged and traveled past the lines of my eyelids and mascara clumps to the apples of my cheeks. My hair: curly at the roots and straight pieces at the bottom from all of the sweaty dancing last night. *Dear god.* I look like an absolute train wreck. Why do I do dumb shit like fall asleep in my makeup?

No number of wipes can save me, so I opt for a full-on shower. Fifteen minutes later and I'm sitting on my bed with my legs folded beneath me, hovering above James' green call button on FaceTime. My pulse thuds soft but fast at the back of my throat. I take a deep breath in hopes of strengthening my nerves and press the call button. *Here we go.*

"'Ello there! How's you?" James asks, his eyes giving me a once over.

"Umm...good. I'm good. How are you?" I can't bring myself to look at him directly. My eyes focus past my Mac and on the clothes that pile on and around my roommate's bed across the room.

"Hey, everything all right?" his large eyes scrunch in concern.

I steady myself with another deep breath. It's now or never. I shift my gaze directly to him. "You ignored me... I asked if you wanted to see me again and you *ignored* me. It's fine if you don't want to but just say so," I finish the last of the words with one big huff. The thrum of my heart has moved from my throat to behind my ears. It's loud enough for me to hear the tiny arteries whooshing and whirling. I hold my ground, refusing to say anything else and for a painfully long and silent time. James, all the while, stares at me and says nothing.

"I uh," the fingers from his left hand rake through his dark brown waves and he looks at something on the floor of his room. "Look, Nayelli. Are you trying to court me?" he asks seriously.

"Am I trying to *what*?" I snort. What in the hell is that supposed to mean?

"You know, court me. Like boyfriend and girlfriend."

"What? No!"

"Oh, thank god. Okay, good."

His chest heaves in relief and he finally looks at me again. We've barely met. I'm not crazy. But the truth behind his words sink deep into my skin. He doesn't even consider me dateable. *The fucking jerk.* I would make an awesome girlfriend and screw him for thinking otherwise.

"You know what," I squint my eyes and square my shoulders, "I don't think we should talk any more."

"What? Why?" James' eyes bulge in panic or shock.

"You live over six thousand miles away. I'm not saying that I'm trying to *court* you, but if you aren't even open to seeing where things go then I don't see a point in keeping in contact with one another."

"Not even as friends? I think it'd be nice to be friends." His voice sounds so small and choked, but I dare not let my resolve break.

"I have enough friends. Friends that live near me. Thank you for a wonderful time, and again, I'm glad that I got the chance to meet you. Goodbye, James."

I slam shut my screen before he has the chance to respond, the image of his mouth hanging open haunting me. I delete my FaceTime app from my computer then snatch up my phone to do the same, followed by muting his contact so that I can't receive notifications from him. I'm not mad enough to block him completely, but I still need some space while I figure my shit out. I also know myself and therefore know to keep temptation at bay in case he decides to text me anytime soon. I'd undoubtedly answer the phone and try to find the good in him like the deluded masochist that obviously I am.

I pace in front of my bed, restless energy circulating through me. I snatch my laptop and aggressively cancel my spring break flight to London in hopes that it'll release whatever is building up inside of me but it does nothing but make me think of how horribly I've missed judged things. First with Olivia, and now James. Damn, how could I be so freaking gullible? What was I thinking?

I need to get rid of this... this pinned up frustration. Ugh!

Yes, that is it. I'm freaking *frustrated*. And a run will do just the trick — never mind that I just showered. My usual trail along the beach is the only therapy that will help shake off this revolving door of rejection.

In no time, my feet find their own rhythm against the asphalt of my street. Renovated houses along *Del Playa* speed by morphing into two-story blurs with palm trees guiding my route to Sands Beach.

Panting and nearly out of breath, I pause in my stride, bending to place my hands on my knees. The two miles that it takes for me to reach the steps leading down to the shore still aren't enough to calm me down. *Damnit.*

How many times will I allow myself to go through him telling me he doesn't want me? I continue down the wooden steps to the beach.

My feet plunge and pull against the wet sand, some of it scratching and sticking to my bare ankles. The waves crash hard against the beach, reaching out with the tide and threatening to lick at my shoes. Harder and harder I push around the bends of the cliffs until I run out of shoreline. My pace slows to a complete stop and I find a rock to sit on nearby. Salty air sticks to my face and tongue from breathing through my mouth. My lungs sting with oxygen loss, my breaths coming heavy and uneven.

The tangerine sun hangs boastful and high above the sea while a golden retriever plays hide and seek with a tennis ball in between the cerulean waves. Tucking my knees into my chest, I rest my chin on top of them and take in the view.

The only time I am happy to live in Santa Barbara is when I am here.

James

The screen's been black for a while now but I can't seem to make myself move from my computer desk. How did I manage to fuck up *again*? It was a goddamn offer of friendship for fuck's sake. Who would get so angry at that?

My fingers run through my thick mop of hair and an exhausted sigh forces its way out of me. My curls are starting to be more pronounced and touch my neck and ears. I really did need a cut soon. Long hair always makes me look like a haggard bum. And that lazy sod is staring back at me from the blackness of my Mac screen. Why can't I do anything right? Or, better yet, why can't I just leave this girl alone?

No, no. That's not it, it's not all on me. Nayelli doesn't want to leave me alone either, she fancies me just as much. Although, I'm not quite sure why.

I lean back in my chair, my fingers steepled atop my head. Why *does* she fancy me? She lives in California, by the ocean at that. There's no shortage of shirtless attractive men running around, I'm sure. And she's... well, any man's fantasy. By a long shot.

Just look at me, a struggling nobody living at home with his parents at twenty-six. And twenty-six might as well be eighty in the up-and-coming musician realm. I have absolutely no clue when the fuck I'm gonna "catch my big break", but I couldn't imagine myself doing anything else with my life. I love music that much.

But with each year that passes the window of opportunity closes even more. *Christ*. And with each year my looks go too. It's only a matter of time before I begin to noticeably bald. Then what? Will she still want me then?

Time slips by as I reminisce at my desk on all my shortcomings. And to no one's surprise, anxiety sets in about our call.

What did she do after she hung up? Was the "Goodbye" she said goodbye forever? Or goodbye for now because I'm too pissed to speak to you at the moment?

My mind goes fucking mental coming up with all sorts of possibilities — what if she's on tinder back home? Who am I joking, of course she is. Does she have someone significant in California? I haven't shown her anything that would make her consider me as an option if she did. Do I even want to be an option? It's not like I can afford to fly out and visit her. *Fuck.*

I cannot offer her much, this I know. At the same time, I can't just let her go. So what do I do? Stay away because I know I can't add to her life in any meaningful way? Once she realizes that she'll forget about me and move on in less than a week — and that thought alone makes me want to break out hives.

Fuck. Thinking in circles like this is starting to make my mind melt. I have to figure out what I'm going to do and fast, before this situation literally drives me mental. I shake my mouse, turning on my screen. Her FaceTime contact is still up from our last call. I just have to explain that she took what I said the wrong way, that's all. My finger clicks dial without hesitation.

The call rings until it notifies me that she isn't available, so I dial again. I don't care if I have to call her a hundred times. We are going to work out some form of agreement. I won't tolerate any other option.

We got on too well to just be nothing to each other, and there's absolutely nothing wrong with a little bit of fun between two adult friends.

Right?

Of course I'm right. There's no harm being done here. And I'm sure she'll come around to seeing it that way too.

"James?"

"Ahh!" I jump in my chair at Alex's intrusion. "Christ mate, do you knock?" I ask, clutching at my invisible pearls.

"I was just coming to see if you were ready," he says, leaning against the doorframe with his arms crossed.

He's going the traditional dress route, with a crisp light grey shirt tucked into dark blue slacks and a belt. His hair is styled in the manner of James Dean, and of course, he would not be caught dead without his Clark Kent glasses.

"Really, I have to know. What were you thinking when you bought those glasses?" I ask.

"Give it a rest, mate. Are you ready?"

I grab the blazer off the back of my chair and head to the full-length mirror. Donning on the midnight blue blazer — that was not cheap by any means, thank you — I give myself one last look over. I adjust my white shirt in the waist of my dark blue jeans, then the cuff of my blazer. There is never much I can do about my hair but cut it, so I give it a few rake-throughs with my fingers and call it a day.

"All right, let's get on with it," I say to Alex and we head out into the breezy evening air.

The journey from Wimbledon to Lancaster Gate Station is mostly spent in silence. Alex stays on his phone and I plug in my earphones to keep my mind from thinking about a certain lady in a different time zone.

Upon exiting the station, the purple sky greets us once more. The London nightlife creates a vibrating hum along the streets as people move to and fro without sparing a glance, too focused on their plans for a Friday night out.

We arrive at the door to Scullery at Old Mary's where an intimidatingly large gent dressed in all black asks for our names before letting us through. Soft jazz music and candles set the mood while different people mill about with polite smiles and cocktails in their hands. I've been here once, but the contemporary farm benches and tables have been rearranged to accommodate the larger gathering.

The subtle grandeur is awe-inspiring. The type of place that makes you feel fancy and proper from the moment you step inside.

"So this is how they're treating struggling actors these days?" Alex's head cranes back to take in the copper art pieces, light fixtures, and candles that adorn the entire room. Food overflows on a back table next to a makeshift bar serving cocktails by a silver-haired man in a bar keep's outfit.

"Trust me, the last gig I did had nothing like this," I whisper. My role is in no way a big one on the show, I played the female lead's ex-boyfriend. Still, it's an upgrade from the last Netflix gig I did where I was on screen for a total of ten seconds. In a way, being here brought a validation I didn't know I was seeking. I am finally on the right track, finally doing things right, and my work is *finally* picking up momentum.

And thank fuck because it was about goddamn time.

We meander our way to the back of the room towards the bar, stopping every now and then to say hello to a producer or the likes. The main cast and their significant others are taking up most of the attention so the greetings are brief and uneventful.

"Hey man, how's the night treating you?" Alex asks as we approach the bartender, leaning a forearm on his table.

The man stares at Alex's arm on his table until he removes it. Alex stands and dusts fake lint off his clothes as if nothing happened.

After looking between Alex and myself with scrutiny, he eventually answers. "Eh, not bad. Gig's like these normally aren't. What can I do for you?"

"Happen to have a Satan's Whiskers?" Alex asks.

"Coming right up," the man answers, or Steve as his name tag says, and begins assembling the drink.

I give Alex the most incredulous look I can muster. He shrugs his shoulders. "A bloody Satan's Whiskers, mate? And just *who* are *you*?" I ask.

"What?" he shrugs again. "You're the one that invited me to this proper event. It's only right that I get a drink that fits the occasion."

Steve slides Alex his drink, then shifts his attention to me. "What about you, mate?" he asks, his overgrown handlebar mustache moving in time with his words.

Alex takes a sip with his pinky up and smiles in satisfaction. "For Christ's sake Alex," I mutter discreetly under my breath. "A whiskey coke for me."

"I really can't take you anywhere," I say to Alex.

"You knew that before you brought me here," he responds, dragging out yet another long sip with his pinky up.

Steve hands me my drink but doesn't take his eyes off Alex. He raises a brow, as if asking me if he's all right. I shake my hand no.

"Cheers, mate." I leave a note and nod my glass to him,

hurrying to get Alex and I away from the bar before he tries anything else.

We move around the different areas of the room and mingle a bit more, but the conversations are almost mechanical. It's mostly with some of the spouses of the extended crew so the questions end up being the same. *Who are you here with? Oh, what part did you play? What is your favorite episode?* Etc.

"Alex, are you good here for a bit? Need to take a trip up to the loo."

He gives me a brief nod, not paying much attention as he's deeply engrossed in conversation about the mechanics of successful writing and production.

I slip away and head towards the stairs that lead to the toilet.

It's dark at the top of the stairs, the only light source illuminating the sign of which door is for which toilet user.

I'm in and out in a blink, but upon exiting the door feel a hand caress my shoulder.

I freeze in place. Sharp needles of adrenaline imprint into my shoulder where the hand lies. I force myself to control my breathing and stifle my initial reaction to jerk or yell. My eyes glance to the manicured fingernails and tell-tale diamond band on her left hand. *Oh.*

"Are you enjoying the party?" she croons in my ear.

I thought the day we wrapped up on set would be my last time having to deal with this.

I stiffly remove her hand from my shoulder, making sure to only touch her where absolutely necessary. "I was," I say, turning around. "How's your evening, Elaine?"

Her grey shaggy bangs cover most of her eyes, but even in this dark abandoned space I can still see the depraved debauchery within them. "I would have to say that it's a lot better now,

James," she purrs.

She moves a little closer, resting that godforsaken hand upon my chest this time. Peering down, I catch a glimpse of the cleavage spilling out of her form-fitting black dress. Christ, I think I'm going to be sick.

Swallowing the bile that hovers at the back of my throat, I ask, "Is your husband here?"

"Pfft," she exclaims, her breath caressing my face. "Now why would you ask a silly question like that?" she smiles, the position of her teeth somehow wicked. I don't indulge her with a response. "He's downstairs," she finally answers. Chuckling at some inside joke while playing with the lapel of my blazer.

It's always a dangerous game turning down a co-star that you have to work extensively with, especially when they are far more well-known than you and their husband is a director that could make or break you. I've been tiptoeing around this woman's advances for months, but it only seems to excite her more. I wouldn't be surprised if I wasn't the only one she's done this to.

I catch her hands to still her movements. "I'm sure he's looking for you. Besides, I have to get back to my brother," I say tersely.

Elaine leans in even more, closing the distance between us and resting her chest on top of mine. "A kiss goodbye then?" she whispers close to my lips.

I want to throw this old bitty off me, but I know that isn't very gentlemanly so I opt for the only other thing I can think of. Leaning my head back, I let out the largest, fake sneeze I can muster — knocking her forehead with mine in the process.

She jumps back, "Ow! Fucking hell, James!" she says, grabbing her forehead and leaning against the wall in pain.

"Ohhhh noooo Elaine, I am so sorry," I say, putting on the

best performance of my life and faking concern for this vile woman. "What a freak accident, am I right? I'll go get your husband for you."

I dash down the stairs without giving her a chance to object. I hear a loud "James!" on my way down but don't hesitate in getting the fuck out of there. By the time I reach Alex, he's back at the bar. I join him, leaning against the bar counter, huffing and trying to catch my breath. Steve shoots daggers at me with his stare and I immediately straighten up, removing my arm off his bar.

"Where have you been? Was there a queue or something?" Alex asks.

"Later," I force out under my breath.

"And why are you out of breath?" He gives me an up and down.

"A double of Jameson, neat." I say to Steve.

"Ooohh, it's a rough story then," Alex says, followed by a long pinky sip of his drink.

Taking a closer look at his glassy eyes, I arch my brow. "How many of those have you had, Alex?"

"Mind your business, mate. The show is about to start," he says, grabbing my drink and ushering us towards our seats.

Since we're a bit larger than most of the people in attendance, we sit towards the back of the screening. Set up at the front is a large white canvas with an accompanying projector in between the seats and speakers strategically placed about the room. The lights dim, the show's creator and executives stand at the front, and the room calms down to only murmurs.

"'Ello everyone, it's nice to see all your lovely faces once more," one starts. They take turns indulging in a funny memory or two and end with a call for applause at the hard work of everyone to make the show possible. Upon taking their seats, the room cuts to black followed by a glow from the projector and the show begins.

Watching myself on screen is always an out of body experience, almost as if it's not me on the screen but a past life. Even though you're there during the filming, there's so many cuts and breaks and splicing together that you never know exactly what the final product looks like. But I have to admit, I didn't do too bad.

The show continues but instead of watching, I train my ears to assess the room's reaction to my lines. The show is obviously a comedy but I wonder if anyone else finds me absurdly goofy on screen? It's almost hard for me to watch. But from the resounding chuckles, I can say that yes they do. And given the nature of portraying an insanely meat-headed idiot boyfriend, I can also say that it's a good thing.

What if this opens doors for me and I'm able to keep this going? What if my next gig is even bigger than this one? The questions stir within me an excitement I was too scared to have because they also make me ask the opposite: what if I never land another gig again? Especially after that whole debacle with Elaine.

I am zero out of a hundred in the answered prayers department but feel compelled to tempt the kindness of the universe anyway. *Please, if anyone is there listening. Let this show be the break I need... and while I have you here, please keep the crazy lady away from me.*

The show finishes and people begin to clear out, no doubt getting home to relieve the sitter and the likes of such. Alex and I follow suit, making our way back to the tube to get home.

We walk in silence again, too deep in our own thoughts of

the night.

"Not bad my friend," Alex eventually says, clapping my back with two hard pats. "A little cheesy, I'll admit. But not bad. And — dare I say it – I'm *proud* of you." He smiles and means it.

"I'm sure I should've recorded that, but thank you nonetheless," I say, giving him a pat on the back as well.

"Well?" he asks, glancing at me out of the corner of his eye.

"Well what?"

"What's next?" he says, his walk never breaking stride.

"The hell if I know," I answer. And I truly didn't.

"I was hoping you'd say that," he says, a grin on his face.

"What do you mean?"

"Well, after schmoozing up to that producer, I pitched our show that we've been wanting to write. And he may or may not know a certain BBC producer that would take a meeting with us if we can finish our script in the next couple months."

I stop and he's forced to stop with me. "You better not be joking or I will fucking kill you, mate." There's no way our luck could be going this well. Could it?

"Woah, there." He holds up his hands to show he means no harm. "I'm being serious. So by tomorrow you better get to work because I'm not letting you blow this for us," he says, nudging me and continuing our walk. "Things are looking up, James. Just you watch."

I hope like hell he's right. "Sure," I say, and continue the rest of the journey in silence.

Sitting against the window of the train, I pass time by gazing out into the dark void of nothing. So much is on my mind, it will take me several days to sort through it all. Alex wanted to spend the commute pre-planning our script structure but I asked for a moment. I'm just too overwhelmed.

Speaking of overwhelmed, my thoughts drift to my conversation earlier this evening.

It's almost midnight which means that it's well past 3pm in California, yet still not a peep from Nayelli. If she would just answer the phone, she'd know that I meant no harm in what happened earlier. I was just being honest in my feelings — women usually loved when you did that.

Fuck she seemed so pissed with me though. I might have really fucked up.

Once again I don't care to think too deeply of why, but the thought of her never talking to me again makes me nervous. At the very least we should end things on better terms and not with me feeling like an idiot.

The urge to ring her again makes my fingers itch. If I keep calling, she'll have to answer eventually. Right? Right.

It's brilliant, really.

So when I get back to my room, that's exactly what I will do — call until she picks up. No matter how many times that may take.

Nayelli

That Friday, I arrive at the dull brown eight-story tower that houses the Literature and Languages departments. My classroom is on the first floor, so I find it and enter with ease.

Maybe it's my enthusiasm on the topic, but without thinking I sit in a seat in the front row of the class. Digging through my all white Jansport, I retrieve my notebook, colored pens, and a thick translated version of *Inferno* by Dante Alighieri. My eyes look to the other twenty faces in the room but land on no one familiar.

The class doesn't begin for another five minutes, so I grab my phone to pass the time. Waiting for me is yet another text from my mom.

Just tried calling and you didn't answer.
Call me back.
Hello?
Made it back safely.
Call me back.
So you don't return calls or texts now?

We haven't formally talked since I hung up on her at James' house. I don't want to ignore her, truly I don't. At the same time, I can't bring myself to explain anything about James to her — especially when I'm not even sure what's going on myself. I also don't want to face the inevitable shaming she's bound to unleash on me for having sex with a man I barely know. I can't keep putting her off forever, though, so I type out a message saying

I'll call her tomorrow morning.

"Sanza speme vivemo in disio," the strange words caress my ears and although I haven't a clue what they mean, I am entranced by the voice. Who knew Italian sounded so hot? But then, a thought hits me.

Is this class *in* Italian? Motherfu-

"This," rumbles the deep voice from the back of the room, "comes from Canto 4 of *Inferno*. But before we get into that, let's talk about the man himself, Dante."

Soft clicks of chocolate Italian leather loafers increase in volume as Professor Matthews travels through the rows to the front of the room. He places his chestnut leather briefcase on the desk in the corner then unties the cashmere sweater about his neck and places it on top of the desk as well.

"Dante was born as Durante di Alighiero degli Alighieri in the city of Florence, Italy in 1265," Professor Matthews pivots and walks towards the center of the white board. "This places us in medieval Florence that had seen decades of unrest between the opposing factions of the Ghelbs and the Ghibellines."

After writing the two names on the board, he faces the class again to break down their feud further, but what I study is his appearance. He's tall and physically fit with a sharp nose, slender jaw, and greying hair — or in other words — the poster child for a silver fox. He flows into Italian again and if there weren't twenty other students around me, I'd probably swoon. I shake my head to clear my thoughts. Who do I think I am?

For the rest of the class I focus on color-coding my notes and only looking up at Professor Matthews when absolutely necessary.

The class is two and a half hours long, and halfway through Professor Matthews pulls out a film for us to watch about 15th century Italy. Darkness soon enshrouds the space and without his voice as an anchor to my surroundings, my mind drifts to the events that led me to taking this class in the first place.

Reading has been my escape for as long as I can remember, so when I had finals work and roommate drama up to my elbows, I read to forget it all. It was then chance — and Amazon Kindle — that brought me to a novel by the name of *Gabriel's Inferno*.

At first, I wanted to roll my eyes at the shy virgin caricature who had a "thing" with her emotionally unavailable professor. Surprisingly, however, the book pulled back layers like a striptease and transformed into a story I didn't expect. What brought these two stereotypical characters together wasn't lust, nor proximity, nor the thrill of breaking the rules. No. It was Dante.

Lovesick, idolizing, borderline stalker Dante. I was intrigued; I was curious; I was hooked.

Who was this damned, love-tortured man writing poetry about a Beatrice he could never have? And why did he resonate with me so deeply? I guess I could have googled him but I needed an elective and this one happened to fill my requirement.

Professor Matthews flips on the light switch and my gaze swivels to him. I lose my train of thought as he lapses back into his beautifully spoken Italian, but just as quickly snap out of it.

Oh my god.

My life is so horribly boring that I'm trying to recreate a book in real life. This is low... even for me. I have officially hit rock bottom.

Professor Matthews dismisses us from class with an Italian farewell. I hardly notice it this time, too submerged in packing my things and an immense grief over my own pathetic life.

I really should get out more.

*

"You're still not dressed!" Bri yells as she balances two shot glasses overflowing with either vodka or tequila. She is a sweetheart in comparison to the rest of my household, and pretty much the only one I interact with.

Her question forces me to look down at myself — blanket over legs — still in my pajamas. She walks from the doorway over to my side of the room and hands me a shot.

"It's your fucking birthday party, you better get up and start drinking bitch!" She clinks glasses with me and takes hers straight to the face. Two of the other three girls that live with me also had birthdays over winter break, so they decided to throw a combo birthday party the Friday after school started back.

"All right, all right." Damn. It's going to be *that* kind of night. I flip the covers off me but make no further movements to get ready.

My roommate Bri is probably two inches shorter than me, but definitely can out drink me on any day. I normally like to space out my alcohol but can tell that my usual method isn't going to be of much use tonight.

I pinch my nose and take a deep breath before tilting both my head and drink backwards. The burn immediately tingles down my throat and makes its rapid journey to my belly where it settles and warmly toasts me from the inside out. *Ugh, definitely vodka.* I hate vodka. It reminds me of my sophomore college days, filled with fruit-infused flavors of Skye that Olivia and I nearly choked on and ultimately threw back up. Before that thought can go any further, I force myself to think about the destination, not the vehicle that gets me there. Besides, the alcohol is free.

Bri is on her side of the room and I give her petite stature a once-over to get an idea of how I should dress for the evening. She's wearing a cream sleeveless blouse that stands out against her cinnamon-tanned skin, and a pair of dark wash jeans with heeled-booties. Her dark hair is flowing free down her back, with her handmade waves out on display.

"You look really cute," I say to the back of her. She's rummaging around in her makeup bag, but stops to throw me a quick smile before continuing her search.

Muted yells of people drinking and waiting for us to join the festivities seep underneath the crack of the door. I have to make a decision once and for all: to mope or to party. After a few seconds of deliberation, I decide to give James up. I am twenty-one years old damnit, and this is *my* party. Well, sort of. And you only turn twenty-one once! James was right about there not being an us. What was I thinking? James and I never had a chance and he could see that. It took me an extra week, but now I can see it too. I need to get back out there and enjoy my life because no one else will do it for me.

I jump off the bed with a new spring in my step and race to the closet to get dressed. I should be out there having fun. He's not the only guy in the world.

"Bri, will you go grab us some more drinks while I grab my clothes?"

"That's what I'm talking about!" she cheers, abandoning the room for more shots.

"Damn, Nayelli! You look like a fucking goddess, girl!" Our neighbor Luke wastes no time complimenting me when I join the group in the kitchen. He's dressed up in his black button-down and jeans and is bobbing his short sandy hair to some song by Tiesto that's playing.

"Aww, thank you," I respond, and walk over to give him a

big hug. He's closer friends with my other housemates, but whenever I see him, he always has something nice to say to me. Unfortunately, however, his comment catches the attention of my other housemates drinking around the table, and they all turn around to look at me.

My black bandage halter top makes an "X" across my body: the top of the X cradling around my breasts, the bottom of it crisscrossing around my navel. My black leather pants hug my hips and thighs in all the right ways, and my black wedge heels give my shapely legs some height. Then, to spice up my all-black ensemble, I added a gold chain that travels down the middle of my cleavage and circles around to rest on my waist. And to complete the look, a trendy gold head chain frames my freshly straightened hair in a tiara-like crown. I even decided to put in a little extra effort and wear makeup tonight.

I look damn good and I *feel* good too. Or at least I *did* before my housemates decided to gawk at me like some kind of Loch Ness beast.

"Are you seriously going to wear your tits out like *that*?" Hunter screeches over the music. She's also dressed in all black, but decided to wear her long auburn hair in a high ponytail.

"Obviously," I mutter with a huge eye roll, and walk over to the tile kitchen island covered with plastic handles of alcohol, soda, ice, and cups.

"Leave it to Nayelli to always want to be the center of attention," I hear my other housemate, Sofia, tell Hunter. The bitter taste of irritation bubbles up on my tongue, but I ignore them and focus on pouring my drink.

If it isn't my tits she has a problem with, it's my ass; and if it isn't my ass, then it's some other bullshit like, "breathing too seductively" or whatever the hell else she wants to make up about me.

I've always been open about the fact that I've been on a fitness journey since my freshman year. I tried to give up my bad eating habits when I lived with Olivia and two other girls last year but the buffalo chicken cheese fries at 2 a.m. kept calling my name. Flash forward to this school year and I finally decided to put my health first. Right after moving in with them I started working out and eating healthier and was so damn proud of myself. It was my first time taking my health seriously since starting college, and I soon found a balanced groove that was sustainable for me.

It took only two months for Sofia to start noticing my results and everything about me has been a problem since. I even saw her copying my exact meals for a while – something I would've found endearing if she wasn't such a bitch. She even hated a turtleneck that I wore once because it "wasn't ugly enough for an ugly sweater party." Like are you *kidding* me?

As for Hunter... let's just say it was complicated. She was more of a sour patch kid, giving me whiplash. We didn't interact much but when we did it could range from her being the sweetest person ever to her deciding to hop on the Sofia hate train – like tonight – and it made me not care for her. I'm sure if we were met under non-roommate circumstances, I'd probably like her. But you know how the saying goes, living with friends can ruin friendships.

I gulp down my red solo cup full of Tequila and Sprite in two seconds flat — an amazing accomplishment given that it tastes like ass — and escape to the backyard where the real party is underway. I know about five people out of the crowd of fifty that have shown up, four of them being people I live with, but it's safe to say that the company of strangers is better than that of my salty-ass housemates.

The alcohol sets into my blood and the tiki torches and Christmas lights that line the perimeter of our backyard begin to merge into a singular faint glow of soft yellow orbs. I half-see the world through my lowered eyelids, and somehow it feels better this way. The DJ-sized speakers on opposite ends of the patio surge with a fierce beat that hums across my skin and jolts through my body, spurring it into movement. My hips are fluid and languid in their sway to the rhythm of the music that's blaring. I don't even know what song it is or if I like this music.

But nothing — not James, not Olivia, not my crazy housemates, not my cheating ex-boyfriend, not even the hell-like bubble that is my college town — matter any more.

Tequila has that effect, you know. Making you forget about everything except your own body in the current moment. And right now, my body is a thermostat turned up way too high. When did it get so freaking hot? Dancing in the middle of a crowd of people may be a fun idea in theory, but I desperately need some fresh air.

I wiggle out of the traffic jam of people dancing by the speakers and take up residence by the outskirts of the lawn. Leaning against the scratchy wooden fence, I close my eyes and attempt to summon a breeze from the nearby ocean.

"Heeeyyyy birthday girl! Wanna take a shot?"

Fuck. They found me. I open my eyes and it's Luke who is making his way over to me with Bri, Sofia, and Hunter.

"Noooo thank you," I reply with my eyes closed. There is something about fresh air that forces you to feel the extent of your drunkenness all at once — and I am barely hanging onto the edge, ready to fall into the abyss of blackness at any moment.

"Don't be a party pooper!" yells Sofia.

"Yeah girl, we already poured you one so that means you have to take it. House rules!" Bri says while shoving a previously hidden shot glass in my face.

"Since when?" I ask, snapping my head in her direction.

"Since now," Bri shrugs.

"Fine. But after I take this shot, you have to leave me alone." Do they not understand that my tolerance is that of a child compared to theirs? But of course they do, they make fun of me for it all the time. They just don't care.

I shouldn't have left the safety of the human mosh pit. They wouldn't be able to find me so easily in there.

"Cheers, bitches!" Sofia calls out, while raising her red cup into the air.

I roll my eyes, clink my cup with Bri's and Austin's, and drink the contents in one swallow. *Damnit.* It's vodka again.

My taste buds and esophagus are completely numb at this point, but I feel it. The explosion; the boom; the "a-ha" moment that your body feels when your brain finally connects to your stomach and realizes all the damage that you have bestowed upon it.

"I gotta go," I muffle through my hand over my mouth.

"Are you okay?" Bri asks while touching my shoulder in concern.

"Yes... no! I gotta go!" I break away from our small group and run, with very little grace and sobriety, to the glass sliding doors of our patio. I haul ass down our narrow hallway and stop in front of the closed bathroom door, only to jiggle the handle and see that it's locked. *Fuck!*

"Are you almost done?" I yell through the door.

"NO!" a chorus of girls responds. I am thoroughly fucked.

I walk the short distance down the hall to my bedroom and close the door. I open the window to let in a breeze and sit on my bed in the dark and just... breathe. *Stay calm. You won't throw up if you just breathe and be calm.*

I'm not sure how long I sit there, but it's long enough for me to feel tired. I slip out of my leather pants and heels and throw my head chain onto the floor, not bothering with the rest. Climbing underneath my duvet, my bed is a cool embrace, and I let the soft thump of music and partying lull me into a deep sleep.

*

"Nayelli? Are you in there? Nayelli, open up!"

The sound of hard taps against my door breaks my sleep.

"I know you can hear me! Open up please!"

"Who is it?" I sit up straight in my bed and rub my face, feeling slightly less drunk than I did when I first closed my eyes.

"It's Blake!"

What the hell?

I get up and open the door, but cannot for the life of me think of why he's here.

"Babe, I've missed you!" he says while folding his six-foot-five body down to envelop mine.

He holds me in the middle of the room for a long minute and I think back to the last time that we saw each other — a few weeks before my London trip — when we ended things. Or at least I thought we did.

Our last conversation took place on my living room couch and went a little something like:

"Blake, who is Mya?

"Mya? Oh, *Mya*. Yeah, we're friends."

"Well, I just so happen to have found out that she wants to murder me."

"Really? Why?"

"Ohhhh, I don't know. Maybe because YOU ARE SLEEPING WITH THE BOTH OF US? Along with all the other girls in this school, apparently. Just a guess. And it's made me reconsider things."

"Aww, babe. Don't let other people get in the way of us!"

"It's over, Blake. I don't think we should see each other any more."

He's the tall, blonde, surfer-type with sage-green eyes that every girl at my school wants, and according to my newly learned knowledge, most of them had. We were never anything serious, but sharing someone with half of the university is just a little too much for me.

"What are you doing here?" I ask, ending the too-long hug.

"I needed to see you, and you haven't been returning my calls," he cups my face and stares intently into my eyes.

Breaking the intense effect of his gaze, I look out the window to the moon that is pouring light through the window pane. "You don't *need* anything from me. Besides, I thought we agreed not to see each other."

"I know, I know. But don't you miss me? Even a little bit?"

I don't.

But I don't tell him that. I just stare into those eyes of his, knowing why he's here.

Blake drops to his knees in front of me, and I watch as he softly kisses his way across the expanse of my hips. My nerves are vibrating with sensitivity at his touch, and I can't help but to think of *him*. I think of how he seduced first my body, then my emotions, and then just... dropped me. Like opening up the vulnerable parts of someone and then cutting them off without warning is the norm.

And while standing in this dark room with someone else, I

want that too. I want to be as free and as unaffected by him as he obviously is of me.

"Can I?" Jackson asks, his mouth hovering inches above the lace of my panties. His breath — slow, and purposeful, and swirling — ignites a spark to the memory of what it is like to be with him.

I thread my fingers through the wrong soft hair, of the wrong head, and gaze into the wrong eyes. His warm breaths are close enough to affect my conflictingly aroused skin, not making my decision any easier.

I *tsk* under my breath and shake my head at the option before me.

Do I really want to do this?

*

An all-consuming dread erupts over my body the moment I wake up.

My eyes dart to Bri's side of the room and determine that it is just a lump of laundry that fills her bed. Where in the hell has that girl been? I haven't seen her since last night at the party.

Propping myself against the cool wall, I rub my face and think of all that I have to do for the weekend. Not much, I decide. Still, I want to do *something* to keep my mind busy and not thinking about my clusterfuck of a dating life. Maybe I can go for another run? A budding soreness from dancing in heels all night tingles down my thighs as I shift my body. Running is out, along with anything else productive for the morning, so naturally I land on scrolling through my cell's notifications.

Two missed calls from my mom and a message asking, "Hello? Earth to Nayelli? I've *still* been trying to reach you." My finger hovers above the call button but every time I try to press it, I hear James yelling about "All of the sex we just had".

"Get over it. You're a grownup who has sex. She'll live," I grumble to myself. My lungs fill with the deepest breath I have ever taken in my life, and on the exhale I press call and squeeze my eyes shut against the inevitable verbal lashing.

"Nayelli Madison Hayes! It's about *damn* time!"

"Hey mom, I—"

"How am I supposed to know you're okay if you don't answer me? And why have you been ignoring my calls in the first place? That's not like you," she says. I can hear her feet tap against the kitchen tile, a testament to her notorious pacing. She can never stay in one place while she's on the phone.

"I wasn't *ignoring* them. I've just been really busy. Getting back into my school routine and stuff, you know?"

"Mm."

It's clear she doesn't buy it so I switch subjects. "How's Grandma? What have you guys been up to? Are she and Papa getting along?"

"She's good, and you know they're not. Yesterday she said she's going to file for divorce and that she's 'serious this time' but she's been saying that for the last five years. Now stop avoiding the subject, you already know what I'm going to ask you," she says pointedly. By the tone of her voice, she probably has her arm wrapped around her waist while she leans against the kitchen counter. It's a move I've seen so many times during her conversations. It's her *I mean business* stance.

"Fine," I sigh in resignation. "Give me a sec, okay?"

"Okay, but you better not hang up this phone," she warns.

"I'm not!" I yell at the phone and set it down on the bed. Throwing on a pair of shorts, UCSB tee, and sneakers I grab my phone and head out the front door. I don't want to risk Sofia's nosy ass overhearing me.

"Hey, I'm back. Just had to throw on some clothes for a walk," I say.

"Good thinking, you don't want that terrible roommate of yours in your business."

I laugh at the uncanniness. She and I can be so alike sometimes. "So now that you're alone, tell me all about this James person. Who is he? How did you meet? Where were you when I called?"

"Well he—"

"Did you have *sex* with him Nayelli?" she asks incredulously.

My footsteps falter on the pavement and I fumble for a response. "Huh?" I ask, pretending I didn't hear the question.

"You did. You took too long to answer," she replies indignantly.

If you already knew then why did you ask? My eyes roll at her tone and a forced breath filters through my lips. I resume my pace down the tree-lined Camino Del Sur, desperate to get to the beach. If I have to have this painful conversation with my mother, I might as well do it with a beautifully distracting view in front of me.

She breaks the silence with a sigh of her own, tired of me not owning up to her accusations. "You know I'm right, so there's no need to lie."

I roll my eyes again. "I'm not lying, I haven't said anything."

"Same difference. So tell me about him," she says.

Once again, meeting up with a stranger from an app just doesn't sound like the best thing to tell your overprotective mom, so I opt for what James came up with in case someone asked.

"We met at the grocery store."

"The... grocery store?" she asks.

"Mhmm."

"Ok, well walk me through it. You were standing in the aisle and he just... walked up to talk to you? How did it go?"

"Umm, well..." Jesus, she's really about to turn me into a liar. "I was standing in the wine aisle and he came up to me and started talking with me about Port. He was cute and funny, so when he asked if I wanted to try some Port with him I said yes." Why does it feel better to lie when it's something that kind of, sort of happened?

"So a man you don't know comes up to you at the grocery store, asks you to try some Port with him, and you say *yes* and go *home* with him and have *sex* with him?"

"Mom!" I yell, causing some girls biking past to turn around.

"What? I'm just trying to understand," she says innocently.

"Well, it wasn't like that." My annoyance eases at the parting between the Del Playa houses, revealing the large wooden staircase that leads down to the beach. Salt hangs heavily in the air and a muted whooshing fills the silence of the afternoon. Arriving at the top step, I snatch off my sneakers and take the stairs down two at a time.

"Then what was it like?"

"You really won't let this go," I realize.

"Let what go?"

"This whole James thing!" I say, exasperated. "We met, we hung out, I had a good time. There's not much else to say."

"Are you going to see him again?" she asks, her voice softening at my frustration.

"I... I don't know." I stop my aimless walk through the sand and sit down in a small tucked away cove of rocks near the stairs.

Waves lap one against the other in the distance with seagulls flying overhead in broken patterns.

"Why don't you know? Did he say anything about seeing you again?" The chair to the dining room table scratches against the tile. A soft thud comes through the phone as she settles into her chair.

"Yes... no. It's complicated." I draw up my knees and tuck my chin into my folded arms.

"Nothing in life is truly complicated. If it seems that way to you, it just means you're too close to the source to have a clear perspective. Just tell me what's going on. Maybe I can shed some light, you never know."

Damnit, the lady always makes sense. Besides, with Olivia out of the picture, who else could I really talk to about this? "Fine, you're right. But brace yourself because it's a bit of a long one," I warn, then dive into the full story of me and James sparing only the details of the rampant rendezvouses.

To her credit, she gave what I had to say her full attention without judgment, only stopping me to ask clarifying questions. I finish explaining our most recent encounter — about a week ago — that ended in me muting him so I can't see when he texts or calls.

"Mm," she responds, but doesn't say anything else for a while. I hold my breath for an eternity, waiting for her to impart information that will fix this mess. Eventually she says, "You may not like what I have to say."

"Oh... okay?" I chew the bottom of my lip. What in the hell is that supposed to mean?

"I think you are one of the most beautiful girls in the world, but of course I do, I'm your mother. And even though you are beautiful, there are other beautiful girls who don't live six thousand miles away."

"Mm," is all that comes out. She's right, but I'm not sure if I trust where she's going with this. I dig my toes deep into the grainy sand, steeling myself for what might come next.

She lets out a short sigh before continuing. "What I'm saying is no man sends themselves through so many changes if they don't even like you. If he thought you were just some piece of ass, he would've left you alone the moment you got on your flight. Since he didn't, it is very clear that he likes you... a lot. I just think it's tripping him out that after such a brief time together, you've made an impression on him that he can't shake. And trust me if he could shake you, he would. No one in their right mind wants a person they're interested in to live half the world away. *Especially* when you both don't even know each other that well. Which is probably why he's so hot and cold. Because he's trying, but failing miserably, to let the experience of you go," she explains.

"But what am *I* supposed to do about that? I didn't ask for this either." Switching positions, I lean against the cool rocks, suddenly tired.

"Nothing. You don't have to chase any man, baby girl. Keep standing up for how you want to be treated. Don't compromise *any* of your standards. And if he doesn't want to treat you how you ask him to, you know how to walk away."

"Yeah," I agree with the second part, but not the first. People don't play games when they like someone. He's only bothering me because of the sex. Hell, even *I'm* still thinking about that sex. Ugh, it was just so damn h—"

"Nayelli," my mom's voice breaks through my reverie, and thankfully so. I focus on the crashing waves. "You are the prize. No matter who it is that you're with. I don't care if he's the richest, most talented man in the world, you will always be the prize. Okay?"

"I know." Her motherly pep talk does its job well and soothes me. I stand and dust cold sand off my butt with my free hand. "Thank you, mom."

"I mean it," she says sternly and it makes me laugh.

"I know you do. I love you," I say.

"I love you more. I'll talk to you later, okay?" And with a click, she's gone.

I jog back up the stairs until I am once again greeted by asphalt and palm trees. The talk with my mom left me with a lot to think about, but one thing is certain: I don't have a single thing to worry about. I just need to focus on me.

*

"Hey girl," Bri greets with a smile.

"You're alive!" I answer, joining her in our room. Her thick hair is piled high on top of her head in a bun and she's wearing a tie-dye tee and shorts. She calls it her *I have things to do around the house* uniform.

"Ha! Yeah, got a little caught up with Dan." Dan is her fling of the month. She never keeps guys long, they bore her. And to be honest, I don't blame her. The guys around here aren't that great. "Where are you coming from?" she asks, surveying my tee and shorts with sand still stuck to my legs.

"Oh, nowhere. Just went for a walk at Sands. I'm actually gonna go rinse off and make lunch. Would you like some food?" I ask, grabbing my towel and a change of clothes out our closet.

"Ooohhh," she responds, clapping her hands excitedly. "You know I love when you cook. What are you making?"

"I'm thinking grilled chicken sandwiches?"

"Count me in!"

"Sounds good," I smile, and head to our bathroom.

The shower and cooking don't take long, but I'm also too distracted to pay attention to the time passing. I bring our sandwiches back and we enjoy them together with some Odesza softly playing from her laptop.

Bri fills me in on her disappearance with Dan. Apparently he came to see her at the party and they've been holed up at his place ever since. I nod and laugh at all the appropriate times during her story, but honestly it just makes me think about James.

There's a knock on the room door followed by Hunter and Sofia poking their heads in.

"Hey, need some groceries?" Hunter asks.

"We're heading to the store right now," Sofia adds. Neither of them look at me.

"Oh, that's perfect. I actually do need a few things," Bri says, grabbing her purse and heading to the door with the other two girls. She turns back as if barely remembering I was there. "Wanna come?" she asks.

"No thanks, I have some studying to do." For good measure, I grab my laptop and open up my tabs.

"Okay, see you when we get back," she smiles.

"See you," I say without looking up. The door closes and the engine of Hunter's Toyota Rav starts up shortly after.

I only make it through five minutes of studying. Too distracted by thoughts of James, I find I'm just not in the mood and give up.

Was I too harsh with him? Being friends wasn't such a terrible idea, was it? It's not like we can be much more living so far apart. Maybe I overreacted. My phone stares back at me from the window sill. Filled with anxiousness, I lightly chew the inside of my cheek, the uncertainty of my decision gnawing at my gut until I can't stand it.

Unsurprisingly, I give in and convince myself to unmute James' contact.

I scroll down to refresh my notifications and see that I have *forty-seven* missed calls from James. I snatch my laptop into my lap, redownload FaceTime, and call him.

"James?" The moment our call connects, my eyes scan to see if there's any kind of physical crisis that I can spot. But no, he's sitting at his desk wearing a navy-blue Captain America T-shirt.

"Nayelli," he responds casually.

"Are you okay?"

"Yeah, fine. Why?" His response is deadpan and I honestly can't tell if he's kidding or not.

"Soooo," I give him a scrutinizing look to see if he'll offer up any information. He doesn't, so I plunge right into the obvious problem. "You have no idea why I have forty-seven missed calls then?"

"Oh, geez! Forty-seven calls? Wow, that is quite a number," he pauses and covers his mouth with four of his fingers, as if in deep deliberation. "Nope, no idea who did that," he shakes his head for extra emphasis.

Oh my *god!* This man is infuriating. "James, quit messing with me! My phone says that you called me forty-seven times. Why?"

"Listen, I don't know who this other James is that's calling you, but he sounds crazy. I'd be careful honestly."

"Goodbye James."

"Nayelli, wait!"

"What?" My finger leaves the pad, the mouse hovering above the end call button. I fold my arms across my chest, already tired and my day is barely starting. I don't need this right now.

"I'm sorry, okay? I just," both hands rake through his hair this time, "I'm really sorry. And I'd like for us to still talk — if that's okay with you, that is."

The story of Icarus pops into my mind before my answer does — am I also doomed to cyclically tempt my fate towards the point of my own destruction?

A sigh escapes my lips and another image pops into my mind. This time it's Blake and the look of disappointment etched onto his face when I sent him home shortly after he stood from his knees. I wanted to be able to do it but I just... couldn't. And ended up falling asleep alone.

"Fine," I answer. His posture relaxes into the curves of his chair.

"Good," he breathes and then doesn't speak again for a while. "Have... have you... um," he struggles to get the words out.

I arch my brow, but say nothing. What now?

"Have you been with anyone else since you left?" he asks, his amber eyes penetrating me through the screen.

"No," I answer too quickly, not even bothering to wonder why he would ask that.

The corner of his mouth lifts in a bit of a smile. "Me neither," he admits.

Both brows raise in small shock. Is that some kind of feat for him? It hasn't even been two weeks since I was there. Does he want a pat on the back for keeping his penis to himself for ten days?

I cross my arms and start to give him a piece of my mind but catch myself, my mother's words from earlier rushing back to me. He could be with other people, but he's not. I obviously could be as well, but look at me. He doesn't know what the hell he's doing and neither do I. The frustration fizzles out of me. My hands leave my sides to rest atop my thighs. I look at him again and find an amused smirk on his face, no doubt in response to the emotional rollercoaster he just witnessed on my face.

This man is the most frustrating yet thrilling person I've ever met. I smile back and shake my head.

Moments pass but we just sit there, taking one another in.

The silence between us impregnates three times over until I can barely stand it, but he still says nothing. His eyes never leave my face, but the emotion in them visibly shifts — reflecting warm pools of maple colored whiskey that caress me through the screen and intoxicate me.

I remember this look. I remember it well.

I now understand what his eyes are asking me, what his mouth won't. It's the same look he gave me before stripping off my clothes after the club. Moving my fingertips to the edge of my spaghetti strap, I slowly slide it down my shoulder. The answering glow in his irises and the soft pop of his lips opening tell me that I have guessed his desires correctly. His lips part open further as he fixes his gaze on my impending one-man show.

If I stop to think about what I'm doing, I'd probably call myself an idiot and spank my own behind for being so foolish over this man. Fortunately for me, I can't seem to think beyond the look on James' face. All I can see is the pure, unfiltered thirst that matches my own lust for this man. His eyes train on my every movement, cycling between my face, body, and back again. He licks his lips and in this drawn-out moment, I know that he'd give me anything I wanted. And just that thought alone feels so…

powerful. Powerful, and dangerously addicting. Have I ever had this much of an effect on a man?

The fact that I have to ask lets me know that I haven't.

My camisole finds its way to the floor. Topless and hung in suspension between excitement and fear, I wait. My stomach sinks with nervousness and excitement, like I'm jumping out of a plane for the first time. I do not recognize the confident vixen in the miniature square that reflects back at me, breasts exposed and thighs folded so that the drastic dimensions of waist to hip are on full display. But looking at her, and noticing the way James looks at her, makes me feel damn near invincible.

"Turn around," his voice is thick and sharp, cutting through the heavy quietness. His finger twirls in the air, mimicking his verbal instructions.

I shift my body's weight onto my hands and knees and turn to do as I'm told. But before I can make a full one-eighty, I swear I hear the click of the front door unlock and panic. Turning to hide, my foot connects with the edge of my laptop and it flies onto the wooden floor with a loud crash.

"Are you okay?" I whisper, peering over the edge of my bed at the fallen computer.

"Me? You! Are *you* okay? And why am I looking at a laundry hamper? Where are you?"

"I think I heard someone."

"Okaaayyyy, well can you at least—"

"Hey girl! I'm—" Bri stops mid entryway after swinging open the door.

"Ohhh my god," I mumble into my hands, covering my face. I pull my legs up to my chest in an attempt to cover up.

"Umm, I had to come back for my wallet," she says, grabbing it off her nightstand. "Am I interrupting something?"

she asks, confused.

"No!" I answer. "I was just, umm—"

"'Ello Nayelli's friend!" James yells from the floor.

"Hi. I'll umm… see you later." Bri slowly turns to leave.

"No, it's okay!" I jump up to stop her, forgetting my half-naked situation with my tits jiggling everywhere. Instinctively, I grab them to stop my boobs from moving. *Kill. Me. Please.* I give up the innocent act and grab my laptop from the floor. There's no use in pretending I wasn't about to have a naughty FaceTime call, I've been caught. Embarrassment courses through every single one of my veins, not allowing me to say anything else. I stand there and look from the computer screen to Bri, praying she'll be cool and end the awkward silence.

She throws me one last shocked glance before disappearing completely, closing the door softly behind her.

"Well, I'd say that went fantastically well."

"Shut *up* James."

James

"Hey, do you like surprises?" Even through my computer, Nayelli's eyes have a sparkle of mischief in them.

"No, not really." I swivel to the left in my computer chair.

"What? Why not?" Her mouth frowns deep in disappointment.

"Well, there's this level of expectation that you have to meet. You have to be the right level of surprise for the occasion and sometimes the surprises are just shitty. But then you have to fake excitement for the shit thing anyway. It's just too much work." Her forehead furrows a little further. "Why do you ask? What's up?"

"Umm, nothing. Never mind."

"You have a really bad habit of that, you know."

"Of what?" Her brown eyes pop wide open like saucers. I cover my mouth with my hand, the doe-eyed expression amusing me for some reason.

"Starting to say something and then backtracking with a 'never mind'." It's actually starting to get a little frustrating. Why won't she just speak her mind?

"Oh. Well, don't worry about it. It wasn't important anyway."

I squint my eyes at her. "Okaayyyy, if you say so."

"Yup. Anyways, I gotta go. Have a good night James." She blows me a kiss and is gone off my screen.

I awake the next morning feeling more relaxed than usual.

Groggily, I reach around towards the nightstand on my right until finally making contact with my phone. The first message awaiting me forms the edges of my mouth into a simple and genuine smile. *That sly devil. She fucking remembered.*

Happy birthday James! Hope
you have a fantastic day x
12:00 a.m.

She's punctual too, making sure to message exactly at midnight. A few of my other friends have sent their wishes too, but it's hers that holds my attention.

Holy shit. I hope that was just a coincidence and she wasn't waiting around to send that.

Whatever. She's an adult. She can make her own decisions.

Throwing my robe over my pajamas, I race downstairs to the kitchen.

"There he is!" my dad greets.

"Happy birthday to *you*!" my parents sing-say together. My mother sets her signature teal coffee mug atop the beige tile counter and grabs both sides of my face, giving it a big kiss. My father follows her kiss with two solid slaps on the shoulder before returning back to his own mug.

Sundays are always late mornings for our household, so breakfast is barely starting. "Have a seat sweetheart. There's also some mail for you on the table," my mother instructs with one slender finger.

I grab a glass of pre-poured orange juice and sit at the table in front of a package that boasts the letters "USPS". My eyes dart to the sender and confirm what I already know. I tuck the white parcel underneath my arms and head back up towards my room.

"Happy Birthday! Wait, where are you going?" Alex stops me on the stairs.

"Just to my room right quick. And don't you dare touch the food before I'm back." I maneuver around him and close my door behind me.

Not wasting another moment, I tear open the package to find a small tan paper sack. I empty the contents and out falls ten Marvel-themed guitar pics. "She didn't..." The Hulk, Iron Man, Thor, freaking Wolverine — the whole immediate gang all here.

This girl has a better memory than I thought. I remember one of our post-sex conversations veering in the direction of comic book superheroes, but that was months ago at this point.

I arrange the pics into the shape of a heart, snap a pic, and send it straight to her. I hate to admit it but it is a pretty good gift. Especially from a foreign woman I met through an app two months ago. But Nayelli is just like that it seems — full of surprises and everything that is good. *Too good.* My eyes automatically narrow in suspicion because I haven't been able to find her crazy yet; no one is authentically this nice of a person. No matter, I'm sure the ugly will come out one way or another. It always does.

The rest of my birthday passes by like any other day with the exception of being punctuated with gifts. My family's never been one to make a big fuss about throwing proper birthday party's but they are fantastic at giving presents to celebrate the occasion. My parents have bought me a flight to Amsterdam for the summer, as well as given me quid for my stay and food. Alex, on the other hand, was a typical prick and gave me an envelope with a handwritten receipt detailing the money I owe him. Surprisingly, I didn't let his antics trigger me. Call it growth at my new age of twenty-seven.

Later that evening, my family and a few of my mates round out the day with me in Chelsea for a birthday dinner at Benihana.

It's a bit basic in terms of birthday choices, but there's just something about a man shaping fried rice into a beating heart that really does it for me.

It's still a bit early for the evening by the time my family and I make it home, but Alex has talked Chris, Eddie, and a few others into getting a nightcap at a bar in SoHo.

"Would you like a little top up before heading back out?" Alex calls to me from downstairs.

"Yeah, just give me a minute." I yell back, and close the door behind me to my room.

I rush to hop onto my Mac and call Nayelli. I still need to give her a proper thank you for my present before I get too deep into my cups.

"See? Surprises aren't *that* bad." Nayelli says as we join on FaceTime. She's sitting on the ground in a room I don't think I've seen before, the beige door and ugly green carpet momentarily catches my attention but not for long. I can't stop staring at her.

"Dear god," I whisper. "Really? *Really* Nayelli?"

"What? What's wrong?" Her eyes scrutinize the room, looking for what I'm talking about.

"This is how you look when you're at *home*? Unbelievable." Her fingers inspect the thin sheer fabric that caresses around her cleavage and wraps around her waist. I can see straight through to her belly button for Christ's sake! It also doesn't miss my notice that she's wearing the harmonica necklace I bought her for her birthday.

"Oh," she says. "My housemates are having a Valentine's Day date night at their friend's place. We just got done watching *50 Shades of Grey* and now they're setting up for a party that's supposed to start soon. But back to the point," she rolls her eyes, "how'd you like your surprise?"

"It wasn't a surprise. You basically gave away that you were sending me something. Come on now Nemo, you can do a better surprise job than that." How many times have I sat in my room FaceTiming her since she's left? Probably too many to be healthy at this point.

"Nemo? NEE-MO? Like the *fish*?" Her chin drops down in incredulity at my new name for her.

"Well I wasn't thinking about the fish per se, but it's a fitting nickname for you I think."

"You thought *NEMO* would make a good nickname for me? Are you *serious*?"

It was supposed to only be a joke, but her expression and offense are too good for me to let it go. "Yup. That's your name now," I reply, barely able to keep from laughing.

"Unbelievable," she mutters and crosses her arms underneath her chest. I lick my lips. *Damn, she looks so damn lickable.*

"Where are you?"

"In one of the bedrooms at the friend's house. Why?" she smiles knowingly.

"You know why," I answer. She bites her lip and lowers her eyes. Christ there is nothing sexier than those eyes and how they look at me. A soft "Fuck," leaves my mouth.

"I can't," she replies, her face alive with mischief.

"You sure? Not even for a little bit?" Was that begging I just heard in my own voice? *Jesus Christ, James. Get a fucking grip.*

"I'm sure." She laughs, no doubt at the sound of my desperation.

"All right then Nemo, enjoy your party. I'll speak to you later. And don't forget to remind me that I have some news for you."

"What news?"

"I might've secured a gig in L.A. It's not Santa Barbara, but it's close, right?" It's the most exciting news I've had all year, to be honest. It also means that allowing myself to continue things with Nayelli might not have been in vain. Nayelli and I have been getting on surprisingly well long distance and just... wow, this could really change things.

Her mouth hangs open for a long moment before she responds. "Umm, YES. That's practically down the street from me! Well, in comparison."

Excitement warms my face. She seems genuinely interested in this — in me. And I might actually get to see her, smell her, kiss her — fuck, okay. Dangerous thinking. And she said she had to go. "I still have one more round before the final decision, but we'll talk about it later, once I know more. Okay?"

"Okay! Good luck, I hope you get it." She blows me a kiss and is gone.

*

To describe the past few weeks after my twenty-seventh birthday as perfect would be an understatement. A dream, or a vision, or downright magical would better suffice because there is no way this is my reality.

I ignore the gray blanket of clouds draped across the skyscrapers and stroll down the streets near my shop, looking for a lunch spot with a stupid grin on my face. Car exhaust and cigarette smoke careen across my senses but today it doesn't bother me. This morning after breakfast I didn't even remark to Alex about how cold it is for it to be March.

If you told me on Christmas morning that my life would be going this smoothly, I'd slap you and call you a liar. And yet, I've made it to the last round of casting for what will be the biggest role of my career, my second Netflix show airs this week, and Alex and I have enough saved up to begin flat shopping. Life is *good*.

A French cafe with a navy-blue overhang catches my attention. Peering up to read the name on the awning, I see that it's *Savoir Faire*. A bit pricey for their French onion soup, but it's one of my favorites so why the fuck not.

It's not busy, with only one other couple tucked away in the back corner and another sitting in the window. I seat myself at a table next to my favorite wall — the sky blue one with painted ladies in puffy dresses dancing the can-can. The waiter in their pristine white button down and slick black hair takes my order of French onion soup and a baguette then disappears, leaving me to myself.

My phone vibrates on the table. It's a FaceTime call from Nayelli, now saved in my phone as Nemo with a fish emoji.

"Hello?" she says once we connect.

"'Ello you. What's up?"

"Are you busy? I can call back later," she says.

I roll my eyes before answering. There she goes again with the backtracking. "I'm working at the shop today but stopped to grab some soup for lunch. Tell me what's up?"

"Well you said you speak French, right?" she asks.

"Indeed, I do."

"Okay, but like do you really? Or is it another one of those times where you're being sarcastic? Like, do you speak real French or some made-up James type of French?"

This makes me laugh. Definitely sounds like something I

would do. "No, no. I am fluent. Only Americans think other languages aren't important to learn."

At this, she rolls her own eyes. "*Anyways.* I need a second opinion on an assignment pretty please. It's about the French Revolution's impact on John Keats as a poet. And I know you mentioned you just finished that book about him and that he's one of your favorites."

Again, she surprises me with how much she pays attention to me. I take a second to study her. Her curly hair is pulled up high in a messy bun, allowing me to gaze unobstructedly at her sensual eyes and full mouth. She's wearing an oversized grey jumper that is hanging off her shoulder and still somehow showing her nipples through the thick fabric. *Sweet Jesus.* Looking at her has to be one of my favorite things. I clear my throat and sip water from my glass before speaking. "You wrote the paper in French? Do *you* even speak French, Nemo?"

"Stop calling me that! And yes. Duh. I'm a French studies major, remember?"

"Ahh, right. Right. It's coming back to me now." I do not remember that.

"Well—" she cuts off when she sees the waiter setting down my food.

"Thank you," I whisper to him before he leaves again.

"I'll go so you can enjoy the rest of your lunch. I'm gonna send it now and then just call me after you've read it, okay?"

"Sounds like a plan, Nemo," I give her a knowing smile.

Her eyes lower down to a squint. "Bye James," she grumbles and then hangs up.

A smirk graces my face. She's just so damn cute when she's grumpy.

It should come as no surprise that since discovering I might be moving to Los Angeles I have been abundantly reckless. Weeks have gone by with Nayelli and I talking most days, and it is a dynamic I didn't think I would like but I am happy it exists all the same. Especially since so many of the calls end with her naked and me orgasming. I thought maybe I'd get tired of only seeing her through a screen, maybe even become frustrated, but with the looming decision over us that could alter things indefinitely all it's done is make me starve after her even more. I know I'm jumping the gun and being an idiot, but can anyone blame me? I've never been known for my patience or my foresight.

Besides, what's done is done. I'm sure it'll be fine.

My full attention refocuses on the delicious cheese and onion combination of soup in front of me. The seasoned broth warms my stomach and I know I made a proper choice with my lunch decision. Time is passing quickly and I realize I need to get back soon, so I try to finish the rest as fast as I can without burning my tongue.

"James?"

My spoon freezes in the air mid bite. I know who's face belongs to that voice before I look up from my bowl. The baguette in my stomach transforms into cement and my appetite vanishes. I grab my side, feeling like I'm going to be sick.

"Aren't you going to say hello?"

My head slowly straightens with my eyes following shortly behind. "Hello, Emily."

"What are you doing here?" she asks, standing at the chair across from me, refusing to sit.

"I work near here. You know that," I reply deadpan. I've been teaching music lessons at the shop for close to seven years. Three of them were while we dated and lived together.

"Right, right. Well? How are things? Any closer with your music?"

She looks just as I remember. Too large eyes the color of wet sand and small button-like features making up her nose and mouth. Her dark curly hair is still far too big for her frail body but her skin is much more vibrant and livelier than the last time we saw each other. The same day we decided we were miserable friends to one another post-breakup.

"Oh, you know. Same old rubbish. Nothing to report really." God, this is torture.

"Ah, I see," she says, with all the judgment in the world loaded into her statement. With a slow dramatic sweep, she wipes her face with her left hand and the light reflecting off the multi-faceted ring catches my eye.

"Congratulations," I say, tipping my head in the ring's direction.

"Oh," she drops her hand down to inspect her ring, almost like she forgot she was wearing it. "Thank you. And what about you? Seeing anyone these days?"

Her voice is light and casual, but the kindness is forced. I take my time, rolling my near-empty water glass between my fingers and contemplating my answer. She stares at me, her eyes searching within mine for an answer that she didn't ask aloud. *Is it the same girl I caught you sexting during our relationship?* My throat constricts to the point of almost agony. I can't be here right now. Not with her. It's too much. Even after all this time.

"Listen, I know this doesn't mean much to you now but I am really sorry. You know, for how things went and all that. And I wish you all the happiness in the world, you deserve it." I stand, still looking into those innocent, large eyes. All at once, my past transgressions and failures play in her eyes. What has really changed about the man that was with her not that long ago? The guilt of my former stupidity threatens to swallow me whole right here in this restaurant.

"Hmm. Thank you," she says, crossing her arms across her peacoat. It wasn't the answer she wanted.

"It was nice seeing you again, Emily. Take care." I lean down to kiss her cheek, drop a note on the table, and leave the cafe without looking back.

*

Outside, the street lights flicker on and the sun fades to purple behind the music shop's building. A chime rings with a text from my agent and it's the worst timing for the bad news. I pause at the glass storefront finishing locking up, but can't seem to make my feet move once it's done.

I scroll through my contacts needing... I don't know. Just to vent to someone after the events that occurred today. Alex answers on the first ring and a breath I didn't know I was holding leaves my body in a gust.

"Hey mate, you busy?" I ask, pacing along the sidewalk like a madman.

"Not any more, I just finished up with writing for the day. What's up?" he replies.

"I..." The words get stuck on my tongue.

"Everything all right, mate?" His voice drops down to a whisper on his side of the phone. My parents must be home.

"Yeah, it's just... I uh. Shit. I fucking ran into Emily." I finally let out the air that was building in my chest.

"Whew," Alex lets out a long whistle. "You okay, man?"

"I thought so. But then my agent just texted me saying they

went with another guy for the part."

"The one in California?" he asks.

"Yeah. If they had happened separately... but they didn't. And now..."

"I know, I know. Meet me at the pub around the corner from the house. I'll buy you a drink and we can talk."

"Thanks, Alex. See you in a bit."

Alex is surprisingly right. Going for a drink is exactly what I need because after my third whiskey coke, the tension in my shoulders begins to ease and my massive anxiety roils down to a simmer.

"So," Alex pauses to sip his gin and tonic, "what next? How do we help you move on? But for real this time."

"It's not that simple, Alex." His shaggy, sandy hair is flopping in front of his glasses and he has to keep pushing it back. "And why don't you just get a haircut?"

He squares his broad shoulders at me, "Stop deflecting James. This is about you. Do you know why I'm here? Talking to you about your one-year old breakup?"

"Why?" I ask genuinely.

"Because mate, I care. I know I give you a lot of shit, that's just how I am, but it would kill me to see you fall back into the depression you were in right after you and Emily split." His face, so similar to mine but more youthful, scrunches in deep concern. He waits for me to protest, but I stay silent so he continues. "After you moved back in with mom and dad, you stopped living. You wouldn't even pick up your guitar unless you were giving a lesson. You stopped singing, going out with your friends, hanging with me if it involved leaving the house, cracking your dumb jokes. You just weren't the brother I've always known and grown up with. It was hard to watch. For me and for mom and dad."

"But you don't understand—"

"Fuck, James! Yes. I do. You fucked up. We all do. How were you supposed to know Emily's father would die three months into you guys dating? You did the best you could but how old were you, twenty-three? Not nearly old enough or experienced enough to deal with something that traumatic on your own. And you let her become dependent upon you for her happiness and well-being, setting unrealistic expectations for the both of you. You loved her, you wanted to make her happy. But that wasn't the right or healthy way to do it. You know that now. Take it as a lesson and move the fuck on. Stop always looking for a hole to fall in or a whip to beat yourself with, it's getting old mate."

He ends his rant and drains the rest of his glass before ordering another. I study the contents of my own tumbler and take in everything he's said. Deep down, I know that he's right. It's just so hard to accept and far easier to pick apart everything I've done wrong up to this point.

"She was my first real thing, you know?" I don't break eye contact with my glass while I speak. "I never knew being with someone could hurt so much. And that not being with them could hurt so much more. I swear to god, Alex. I never want to hurt like that again." Failing Emily in the way that I did — not being able to make her happy any more, hurting her when I was supposed to be doing the opposite — stripped me of everything I liked about myself. "What kind of person cheats on a girl who's just lost their father?" I ask. The most pathetic of all, that's who.

"Listen," he swivels in his bar stool to face me, clasping my shoulder roughly and looking directly at my face until I look back. "Given the chance to turn back time, would you do that immature prick shit to her again? Hmm?"

"No," I answer.

"Then you've grown. And that's all that matters. Making mistakes doesn't make you a bad person, James. It makes you human. It's when you know better but don't do better that makes you terrible."

"I guess," I answer and turn back to my drink.

"There is no guessing about it. And I'm here so that you don't forget it." He turns back as well, resting his elbows on the bar counter.

"Since when did you become the older brother, huh? I'm supposed to be the one giving you advice." I nudge him in the side with my elbow.

"Since you needed me to. Things really will get better, I hope you believe that. You are not the same person or in the same place. And as far as your gig in California, it just wasn't meant mate. But everything else you've been working on and towards still stands. You have your Netflix show airing and who knows what opportunities that could open up for you. You are doing so much better than you give yourself credit for."

"You're right," I say.

"I'm sorry, I don't think I heard you correctly."

"I'm not repeating myself."

"Aaaaannnddd he's back ladies and gents," he chuckles.

I shake my head at his nonsense. Talking with Alex is definitely what I needed. As well as a wake-up call to the messiness of getting involved with someone too deeply.

I slowly sip on the last of my drink, knowing what I have to do. I have to concentrate on me and only me. And yet, I can't help but feel a small nugget of regret settling into my stomach at the thought of letting Nayelli go... again. I push past the feeling.

It's what I have to do.
Didn't get the gig.
8:53 p.m.
The LA one?
9:17 p.m.
Yuh
9:20 p.m.
Oh no! I'm so sorry. Have time to FaceTime? My cheering up skills are pretty fantastic.
9:21 p.m.
Actually out for drinks.
Have a good night x
9:39 p.m.
You too x
9:42 p.m.

Nayelli

The fifteenth alarm of the morning goes off. I resist the urge to snooze it one more time or I'll be late. I stretch to get the morning rolling. Groans, mumbles, and joint pops fill the still air. Sitting up does nothing. Tiredness still swaddles me like a newborn blanket. My eyes are puffy and filled with sleep and blinking feels like a monumental task.

In these precious minutes before my day begins, I hate everything and everyone. If people are supposed to be productive in the morning then why is waking up so damn hard?

The weight of my boring world bears down on my hunched shoulders. I sit in bed and stare at nothing, losing more and more time to get ready. Since my trip, I can't help but notice how static my life was... is. Wake up with just enough time to make it to class, tune out in every class except Dante, hit the gym, then go home to study.

That's it. That's my life.

How did I let it become so boring? I used to cringe at the thought of routine. Or maybe I've always been this monotonous and only notice it now because of how much I loved my time in England. *That* was living.

Checking the time, I have exactly ten minutes to get my shit together and get out of the door for class.

My bare feet pad lightly down the hallway to the bathroom. I am usually the first up and the last one home, so I make sure to stay quiet — even though the courtesy is never returned.

In the mirror, an unbidden smile curls around my toothbrush as a memory pervades my thoughts.

"No, no, no. You're doing it all wrong." James gawked at me in disgust. "Why would you rinse your mouth with water after brushing? You'll wash out all the stuff that's supposed to help your teeth. You Americans just don't make any sense," he scoffed. I bit my tongue and held back my remark on the British's relationship with dentistry.

Shaking my head, I spit the white foam into the porcelain sink, skipping my normal after brush rinse. I stare into the mirror again. Somber eyes stare back.

It's been like this for almost a month. And it's been almost twice as long since James stopped talking to me completely. He didn't even tell me that he didn't want to talk to me any more, he just... stopped. Right after a short exchange of messages where he said he didn't get the part in L.A.

For the first few weeks, I just thought he was really busy. But somewhere in between the dodged FaceTime calls and the nonresponsiveness to texts, I finally put it together that I'd been ghosted. He didn't even give me the courtesy of a "this isn't working out", the freaking asshole.

And ever since that realization, I've been in my own personal hell. With each day that passes, some tiny moment comes back to me. It floats through me — at first — then fights for my undivided attention until it consumes me. Like this morning with that stupid exchange about brushing teeth. But just like that, my day becomes ruined because he is all I can think about even though I wish I wouldn't. Maybe if he officially broke things off I'd have some closure, but since he didnt I obsess over every possibility and "what if" until I have exhausted all potential outcomes — both in this lifetime and the next.

Is it healthy? Probably not. But I am a woman in college with zero dating candidates. So, I allow myself to indulge in what I cannot have because I assume that eventually, hopefully, I will get tired and move on.

For the most part, my day at school passes by like all the other ones. Except today is Thursday which means I get to end my day with Professor Matthews and Dante. My neat, color-coded notes stare back at me as other students filter into their seats. My blue, purple, and pink pens are aligned neatly next to my black journal, ready to tackle all that is Dante's *Purgatorio*.

Right at 1:30, Professor Matthews strides in with his Italian leather briefcase and matching sable leather loafers. His cashmere sweater is a deep oceanic blue today and compliments his cobalt eyes extremely well. I still have yet to figure out if my fascination with this class has to do with my love and empathy for Dante or the man teaching me about him. He just makes everything that is Italy and Dante so damn cool and fascinating.

Not to mention how he makes me wish I spoke Italian.

The lights dim, the projector cuts on, and we are plunged into awe-inspiring art meant to illustrate *Purgatorio*. Professor Matthews wastes no time in jumping into today's lesson and I find myself drawing parallels.

With the current state of my life's affairs, I thought I'd identify more with Dante's work in *Inferno*, however, learning about the stuck souls doomed to repeat their fatal life mistake over and over again until they learn from it and reach penance is hitting an unignorable nerve.

After class, I make my way to Professor Matthews's desk as he's packing up to leave.

"Professor Matthews?" I ask a bit timidly. I don't think we've had a single personal conversation this semester. Not unusual for me in my classes, but still. Doing so now is giving me a touch of anxiety.

"Oh, hello," he looks up from his things with a bright smile that reaches his eyes. A smile that communicates he really loves what he does for a living.

"Do you have any appointments left for office hours this week?" I don't need help with anything, but I thought it might be nice to talk to him a little more about Dante.

"I'm actually about to head to my office, would you like to walk over and we meet now?"

"Sure, thank you." I gather my things and follow out of the classroom behind him.

We walk in silence across the courtyard towards the five-story building constructed in the same adobe brown as the classrooms it's connected to. His office is on the fourth floor with the rest of the Italian department as well as the French department. To have taken so many French classes, it's a wonder I've never made it up here. Then again, none of my classes were exciting enough to make me want to spend more time on campus than absolutely necessary.

I trail behind Matthews down the carpeted hallway in silence, noting absently the brown and gold name placards attached to each door. Some only have one name, but most have two. I wonder how it's determined who has to share and if any fights have broken out over office space.

Finally, we make a left at the end of the hall and he opens the first office door on the right. The room is sparse and spacious with only one oak desk, a mahogany leather chair, and a floor to ceiling bookcase that takes up the whole wall. There's no way all the books belong to him.

He sits behind the desk and gestures at one of the two black chairs in front of him.

I sit in the chair closest to my left and dump my backpack in the other. In an effort to not fidget, I cross my leg over my knee and fold my hands carefully into my lap.

"So," he begins with a small, patient grin, "what brings you in?"

"Well," I stare past him out the large window and gather my thoughts. Why am I so nervous? "I was hoping you could give me some tips on how to prepare for our final. I know you mentioned being able to recite cantos from both *Inferno* and *Purgatorio* and it's making me a little nervous." I release a small exhale after. It's true, he's requiring so much memorization of the books and I don't want my perfect grade to be ruined if I choke on our final.

"Really? Nayelli, you have absolutely nothing to worry about." Matthews relaxes his posture and sinks into the groaning chair. He steeples his hands across his head and the image it creates looks so expensive. What I wouldn't give to be a well-traveled and learned woman who speaks another language, affords finer things, and my job is to talk about something I love every week. *What a fucking dream.* "You've aced every single quiz so far. It's clear you're a very bright young lady. The final is going to be in the same exact style as our midterm. So, however you prepared for those, do the same for this test as well."

"Whew," my shoulders visibly relax and I smile. The midterm was pretty easy so the final should be a cake walk too. I can't explain but the cantos really speak to me for some reason, making learning them and their significance all the easier.

"Is that all?" he asks.

"Yes. Well, no. I also wanted to ask what inspired you to teach this class. As well as how long you've been teaching it?"

"Um, okay," he chuckles and crosses his arms across his chest. "I guess the short answer is that I lived in Italy for the later part of my 20's, then went back in my 30's to complete my doctorate. During that time, I got to visit the Uffizi often and well, it's just one of those places you have to put on your list to visit in your lifetime."

I nod, but I've only heard of the Uffizi in passing.

"Anyways, one day I stopped by and there was a Dante exhibit. Botticelli, Stradano, you name it. Centuries of great art that this one man inspired. It was amazing and incredible; and is the reason that I've been teaching this class for the last fifteen years."

"Fifteen years?" my jaw drops.

"Correct. The Ufizzi will always hold a special place in my heart. Every other year, I make sure to stop by during my summer research travel."

"Wow," I lean back in my chair. "I wish I could do something like that." My mind flashes to my brief trip to England and all of its richness. There's just so much to learn and experience in this world.

"You can," he says plainly.

"I can? How?" I quirk my brow and cross my arms. It's too late for me to learn Italian well enough to go to school there. Or any other non-English place for that matter.

"What year are you?"

"A junior."

"I thought so. Study abroad this summer. There's plenty of programs to choose from. Just do your research on where you want to go."

"But don't most of the programs require you to be near fluent in the country's language?"

"Not for the summer programs. Those are a lot laxer in their requirements and are more so meant for students like you to explore and experience a new culture for a few weeks."

"Hmm," I nod, considering. "I'll have to look into it then."

"Please do," he smiles. "There's nothing quite as fulfilling to the soul as international travel. I recommend it for everyone at least once in their lives."

We wrap up our conversation shortly after that.

It's about a mile from the language building to my house and I spend the whole walk more nervous and excited than I've allowed myself to be in a very long time.

What if... what if I spent my entire summer somewhere new and exciting and different. What kind of experiences await me in a new country? What kind of friends?

I wonder and fantasize the whole way home and promise myself to keep an open mind to all things new.

*

"Nayelli, are you going to keep beating around the bush or are you going to actually tell me?" my mom asks.

"Tell you what?" I feign innocence but I know what she's getting at. I drove home to spend time with my mom for a couple days and the conversation has started the same way each day.

"What you're going to do about *James*. That's what," my mom's tone is beyond exasperated with my faked naivety.

But where do I begin? She knows everything. Well — almost everything. My mom has been so intrigued with the fantasy of her daughter caught in a star-crossed lover situation with some hunky foreign musician man that it's all she seems to want to talk about. Then again, I shouldn't be surprised, *The*

Notebook on repeat is her idea of winding down on a Saturday night.

"There's nothing to *do*." I respond.

"What do you mean there's nothing to do?" she scoffs. Her eyes peer over the mug between her hands, assessing my solemn disposition. She starts going on about the same old stuff like, "the games a man will play when his heart is invested," and blah blah blah.

I completely tune her out and divide my attention between my coffee and the pattern of flowers on the yellow table cloth. Every now and again, I add an appropriate "mhmm" out of respect.

Once my mom's mind is made up about something, there is no telling her otherwise. So even though I have given up on James — *again* — she still calls me almost every day to ask about him. *Has he reached out to you yet? Well run me through your last conversation again, word for word. Have you text him? And he still hasn't said anything?* In her mind this was "all a part of the process" and eventually he'd "wake up when he realized he doesn't need to run from what he wants". In her mind, we were the classic romance trope that had their path of trouble before their happily ever after. It's exhausting.

And if I'm being completely honest, it's probably the reason I am having such a hard time letting go of the memories — and of him in general. How can I move on when this lady wants to talk about everything James every day?

I have to leave back to school this evening, but before I go I need to pull my mom aside and give her a serious talking to. I'm putting my foot down on this whole James obsession. Enough is enough. It's mid-April for Pete's sake. The both of us need to let go and move on. Hell, it's clear that James already has. Keeping some misplaced hope alive that things will turn around for us is just getting sad and pathetic at this point.

By the time I make it back to Santa Barbara, it's almost midnight. I grab my overnight bag from my car and trudge across the porch. Opening the door, loud rumblings of drunk shenanigans drift in from the backyard.

"Nayelli!" Bri greets, bursting through the kitchen to join me in the living room. She gives me a hug, her swimsuit soaking my T-shirt.

"Is it just the house back there?" I nod my head towards the hot tub in our backyard.

"Nope!" she hiccups, clutching a full Cook's champagne bottle. "We invited some guys over and they invited their friends over, and now it's a ten on three dude sandwich out there." She hiccups again. "Ooh! You should come join us."

"No thanks, I'll pass," I say, leaving for our room.

"You always pass. Come *on*. It's Sunday and I know you don't have homework. Drink and hang out with us."

It always surprises me how oblivious Bri is to the whole Sofia and Hunter want me to get Regina George-d (aka get hit by a bus). Especially when men are involved. I turn down any invite that involves them, and yet she keeps inviting me anyway. It's kind of sweet in a weird way.

"Here," she says, handing me the champagne bottle. "I'll grab another, you start drinking."

"But—"

"I said drink, Nayelli! And put your bikini on. I don't want any excuses. We end school in a few weeks and you've never taken us up on hanging out. You owe me one." She stands with both hands on her hips, her deep brown eyes glazed over, her feet planted and unmoving.

I think about all my pinned-up emotions and the moping I've been doing for the past month. Drinking might not be the worst idea.

"Fine," I agree.

"Yay!" She jumps up and down and claps her hands. "See you outside."

*

"Fuck, you're sexy."

"Shhh, be quiet."

A couple fumbles into the room, lips connected and bodies entangled in an unidentifiable cluster. One of them bumps into the black plastic IKEA nightstand and knocks all its contents on the wood floor. Small crystals of amethyst, band stickers, and a weed pipe roll in separate directions.

The crash causes my eyes to flutter open as I try to figure out where the fuck I am.

Damnit. Untangling myself from my roommate's laundry and shoes, I curse drunk me for passing out in my freaking closet. I didn't even last long in the hot tub. It was another awkward situation of everyone knowing everyone else with the exception of me. So I nursed some tequila and ginger ale and a bottle of Cook's and listened to the conversations around me. Then Sofia got weird with sexual innuendos and I took that as my cue to chug the last of the champagne and go to bed. I do remember needing to use the bathroom at some point and must've mistaken the closet for my damn bed on the way back.

"Shhhh!" My roommate tries to shush the loud mess on the floor.

"No one is going to hear us Bri. They're all in the hot tub

still," a guy says.

I freeze. Thankfully it's pitch black, the light from our window only reaching as far as their bodies on Bri's side of the room. I weigh my options: jump up and alert them to my presence or wait for them to leave.

Shifting my weight to stand, I see the man drop his pants to the floor. "Your turn," he instructs.

Shit, shit, shit.

There is a soft sigh of swim clothes sliding off bodies and onto the floor. Shortly after, the sounds of kisses and licks and touches echo off the quiet walls.

I should crawl to the door. It's only three steps away from the closet.

Becoming hyper-aware of every limb on my body, I silently move, shifting onto all fours. Slowly, I place one hand out of the safety of the closet.

"It's okay Kevin," I hear Bri soothe. My body and breath go still. "How about we take a break?"

"No," he responds, "this is not happening tonight, Benjamin!"

Did he just call his penis…?

I retreat back into the closet, cupping my mouth to keep my laughter trapped. I want to look away, to give this moment as much privacy as one can while sitting unknowingly in the closet, but I just can't look away.

The guy is now slapping Bri's ass aggressively and yelling, "Come on! Come on Benjamin, you can do this!" He proceeds to unsuccessfully stuff his marshmallow into her parking meter — over and over. It's like Spongebob trying to help Patrick open a jar all over again.

My lungs burn with suppressed laughter. I think I even hear

Bri chuckling with her face pressed into the covers, her ass still high in the air.

But what is most impressive about this situation is this guy's resilience. He has yet to slow down. Ass slapping with his marshmallow and all. Isn't he tired? Can't he hear her laughing?

As if cueing into my thoughts, he pauses, probably realizing that Bri's noises are giggles and not encouraging sex sounds.

"Damn. You're not enjoying this, are you?" Kevin asks, sitting back on his heels.

Bri sits next to him on the bed and pats his shoulder. The silence between the three of us stretches on forever.

Eventually, she begins to get dressed.

"So, probably no second chance then?" he asks, still naked on her bed.

Bri shakes her head no, then hands him his clothes. He dresses quickly and they both exit the room.

Finally free to leave the closet, I hop into my own bed but struggle to drift off.

My body and mind are exhausted, yet an hour later sleep still refuses to find me. Bri returned about thirty minutes ago and is softly snoring — alone — in her corner of the room.

I can't seem to shake the revelation I had during my professor's office hours. The next stage in my life is not in Santa Barbara. There is *more* for me than this.

There just has to be.

Making sure to be quiet, I grab my Mac from the nightstand and tiptoe to the living room. The room is too cold for my tank top and shorts, so I wrap myself in the nearby quilt before settling into the futon.

My heartbeat rises and flutters against my ribs as I pull up the site I need.

The first part is impersonal, asking questions like name, date of birth, how did I hear about them, etc. I click and type away without a second thought. But then, arriving at the more detailed questions, my fingertips stutter.

I haven't talked to James in — well I don't even know how long.

Then again, this isn't about James. This is about me. Not wanting to appear like I am running off to make my life better with a man, I've been hesitating to do this. But after today, and if I'm being honest after my entire three years here, it's clear that my circumstances won't change for the better unless I do the actual work to change them. Something has got to fucking give. I literally cannot go on like this. And if things just so happen to work out with James as a result, then that's just a bonus.

I finish my application to study abroad in England in thirty minutes flat. My heartbeat picks up its rhythm with my increasing nervousness, but I know that this is the right thing to do. I had never felt more alive than I did last winter. England was the first time I had ever felt like I could make my own way in this world, that I could be free and adventurous and explore who I want to be instead of who people expect me to be. It was only two short weeks, but it was the happiest I had ever been in my young adult life. I'd be a fool not to see what else it may have in store for me.

Staring at my confirmation receipt, a million emotions run through me. Fear, excitement, anxiousness — all zipping through me with energy. But the deed is done, and I make a vow with myself. Change is scary, but no matter how scared I may become between now and leaving, I have to follow this through.

All that's left to do is wait.

James

"All set?" Mum calls from the bottom of the stairs.

"Yeah. Is Alex not coming?" I pause at the landing, expecting Alex to appear behind me at any moment.

"Not this time, it's just you and me sweetheart. Now let's get going before the shop fills up. You know how Tesco's can be on a Sunday."

"Ooh, you're absolutely right," I grab the keys and my wallet off the foyer table then follow mum out to the family car parked on the street.

Thankfully, the universe is kind and there aren't many out on the road or in the Tesco's parking lot. Giant blue and red lettering greet us as we enter, me pushing the buggy and mum already obsessively studying her list with a furrowed brow.

This is the first time I've been to the shops with her in quite a while, and for a moment I am reminded of how she would have to bribe Alex and I with chocolates to behave while inside. It feels just like yesterday and yet a lifetime ago all at once.

"So," Mum starts, her short auburn hair is covered in a white cap that's completely obscuring her face while she keeps her eyes trained on her list.

"Yes?" I eventually ask after she makes no further attempt to speak or look at me.

"It's been a while since we've talked alone, you and I." Each word sounds thought through and chosen carefully.

"I guess you're right," I respond, stopping the buggy against a long line of black crates neatly filled with a rainbow assortment of fruits and veg.

"So," she repeats, "I noticed your late-night visitors have stopped making an appearance." Kind brown eyes focus unflinchingly upon my face.

"You... you know about them?" I ask, dumbfounded. I could've sworn I was sneakier than the pink panther himself.

"James dear, one must be a tremendously heavy sleeper to not hear the commotion you and your guests sometimes make. By the way, it wouldn't kill you to start closing the front door more gently."

To buy time, I become suddenly interested in gathering the tomatoes and basil from the list. "Hmm," is all I can come up with, pushing the cart further down the aisle to bag the courgettes.

Her tennis shoes squeak against the linoleum floors as she trots up to my side.

"Would you like to tell me what's changed?"

"With what?"

"You and your guests," she replies patiently.

"Well," I stall a bit more. I hardly noticed it myself, so the answer doesn't come quickly.

"You didn't notice?" she asks, following along to the bread aisle.

"No, I guess not," I answer honestly.

"In that case, have you had any major life changes recently?"

"Mum, seriously?"

"What?" she asks, her eyes widening innocently.

"You know what. I'm not one of your clients. You don't need to go all 'therapist mum' on me."

"James."

"Mum." Her eyes continue to hold my own in that firm but patient manner that she's mastered so well through her years as a therapist. I heave a huge sigh, as if my breaths could solve everything wrong with me. My shoulders sag in resignation but I continue pushing the buggy to the pasta aisle. I blindly reach for the spaghetti and answer, "I've decided to take myself seriously again, that's all."

"Okay love, and the last time you said those exact words, you didn't leave your room for three months."

"Fair enough," I laugh, and she joins me, easing a bit of the tension. We continue slowly down the aisle with mum lightly patting my shoulder for support.

"It's nothing like that," I reassure her.

"Then what's it like?"

"It's… it's," I blow out my reserved air and place my hands on my hips in thought. Until now, I didn't realize that I haven't expressed to anyone what I've been feeling these past months. Not even to Alex. The little heart to heart we had that time at the bar was an anomaly. He's usually heckling me about one bad decision or another and I let him. Whether I do it on purpose to avoid fully expressing myself, I'm not sure. At the moment it just feels easiest — like a dance we both know so well that we're afraid to try anything else. It's comfortable.

My parents, on the other hand, have always believed in us being our own people and making mistakes — as well as giving us the space to do so. Especially my mother. For as long as I can remember she has always been there for us through everything; and always without judgment, always without condescension. So when she asks me what's really going on with me, I tell her. And in a bloody Tesco's of all places.

"I get distracted easily, as I'm sure may come to you as an

utter surprise."

Her eyes twinkle with humor, but she doesn't comment. She nods her head for me to continue while she gathers supplies for homemade biscuits.

"And I just, I don't know," I run my fingers through my hair, struggling to find the words. "I guess I'm just tired of always being distracted, or *allowing* myself to be, is the better way to describe it. I feel like all the drama, the chaos, the late-night visitors — I welcomed them gladly because if I wasn't giving my life my all, it would hurt less if I failed."

At the last bit mum pauses her movements, sugar in hand.

"Oh James," her hand briefly cups my face, a small smile breaking across her lips. "That was a job well done confronting your inner habits that are holding you back from what you truly want."

"Oh my days, what did I say about being therapist mum? Next thing I know, I'll have a bill taped to my door for two hundred quid."

"James, I'm serious." She gives my arm a reassuring squeeze. "Last year I could not have said that. I am so proud of the handsome and talented man you're forming into right before my eyes. But a word of advice, if I may?" she asks, placing the sugar next to the chocolate chips and motioning for me to follow her.

I nod.

"I understand that when your life's passion is to create, it can be scary and intimidating to present your full self to the world. But you have decided that there isn't anything else in this life that you want to do. So *do* it. Refusing to fully commit and dipping one toe in will only make you unhappy — it will also ensure that you are unsuccessful. If you're going to make a successful career out of *anything*, you have to actually devote your time and patience to it. There's no other way so stop lying to yourself and saying that there is."

"But…"

"And another thing," she pins me down with a harsh stare and hands upon hips. "Taking yourself seriously does not mean you need to become a hermit priest and forsake all women. Promise me you'll work on finding a balance this time?"

I stare at the aisle beyond her shoulder and weigh the weight of her words before returning her gaze and responding. "I promise."

She looks at me for a moment, making sure she's satisfied with my genuineness. "Okay, good. And just to be clear, I'm not saying I want those awfully loud chits back rampaging through the house again just — just don't lock yourself away from the world. Find some people who are worth your time and take it *slow*."

"You got it." I bend down to kiss her hair then join the queue at the front of the shop, feeling lighter than I have in days.

Later that next week, I find myself taking my mother's advice and socializing with one of my Tinder matches. Outside of the house, of course. It'll be a long while before I feel brave enough to sneak someone in after finding out that I was unsuccessfully stealthy and my parents have heard everything.

Not long into the date, however, I realize I may have made a mistake in being here.

"Where did you say you work again?"

"A music shop. Near Oxford Circus." I've told her this four times.

"Ah, right. *Right*," she says, pointing her martini olive at me with a toothpick.

For fuck's sake, why am I here? Granted, I love this bar in Brixton. It's spacious, although dark, with neon colors setting the mood. Their trademark sign lights up, *so it goes*, in pink. The tables are quite intimate with a single candle and the food is goddamn delicious. It's the perfect date spot in one of my favorite neighborhoods.

And this chick is bloody ruining it.

Chelsea twirls her empty martini glass by the stem between her fingers. "Do you think…" she trails off suggestively, her dark eyes round like saucers.

"Uhhhh," I let out an enormous sigh, not even attempting to fake my irritation. "Sure," I smirk and scoop her empty glass on the way to the bar.

"Another one?" the bartender asks as I hand him the glass, his enormous beard moving more so than his mouth. Who really needs that much facial hair? Observing him, I try not to comment on the neon purple hue of his bald head.

"Yeah, thanks."

There are no stools at the bar, so I'm forced to stand and watch him prepare the drink.

"Extra dry, right?" he asks before shaking the drink above his head.

"Yup." It's not a busy night and this is my third time up here for this same fucking drink.

"Open or closed, mate?"

"Closed." I snatch my card back, then immediately apologize. It's not his fault.

Back at our table, I hand Chelsea the drink but don't sit down. She doesn't even notice. She takes a huge swallow and resumes texting on her phone. I stand there for another minute, staring at the back of her sleek, black hair. She still doesn't bother to look up. Upon closer inspection of her phone, the tell-tale flame and chats give away that she's in the middle of a Tinder chat.

What in the — I clear my throat. "Chelsea."

"Yes?" Her head lazily rolls back to look up at me.

"Are you..."

"Done with our date? Yes. It's almost 10:30, but Todd showed up a little early for his time slot."

My mouth hangs open and I forget how to use my feet.

"Chelsea?" A tall blonde man asks.

"Yes! You must be Todd," she stands and leans past me to hug him.

"Is this your friend?" he asks, grabbing a seat at our table.

"Oh, he was just leaving. It was very nice to meet you, James."

Chelsea doesn't spare me a second glance, too engrossed with Todd and her martini.

I grab my coat from behind Todd. He doesn't even flinch so I don't bother to warn him about what she's doing.

Outside the bar, I decide on a taxi instead of the tube. To hell with the extra quid. It's Friday, but I don't want to be out another moment.

Once home, I resume writing out a scene for me and Alex's script. Hours pass with the likes of James Blake, Little Dragon, and Bobby McFerrin's *Don't Worry, Be Happy* playing quietly in the background. Still, even with all the concentrated effort, I'm only able to get a few pages done. I was supposed to be much further along in the episode, but I can't concentrate. Haven't been able to for a long time if I'm being honest. *Shit.* Alex is going to murder me. And will probably sleep like a baby after, too. Our meeting with the BBC producers is only a few weeks away. We should be doing edits for the show pilot, not still writing content. My fists slam into my desk followed by my hands sliding up to cradle my face.

This is exactly what I didn't want. A distraction.

Even Alex can tell that I haven't been myself. Hell, he was the one who suggested I go on that god-awfully horrid date tonight. *Well, James. You know how the saying goes. No better way to get over someone than by sliding underneath someone else.*

Whoever came up with that saying is a goddamn liar.

I slip off my clothes and put on my sweats. Not even remotely tired, I crawl under the blankets anyway.

It's been a couple months and I've felt every passing second of it. When is it supposed to get easier? Or do I just keep obsessing over her until one of us dies?

Sure, it probably doesn't help that I stare at her photos almost every day. Dedicating my mornings to a frozen glimpse of her on Instagram like a fucking devout worshipper drawn to a shrine, but at least I haven't contacted her. A simple task that turns harder by the day. Especially on drunken nights when I have to give my phone to Alex for safe keeping, just to be sure.

What would be the point, anyway? I knew it the day she left, and I still know it now.

All she's good for is keeping me from concentrating on important things — and apparently fucking up my dating/sex life. Not saying the candidates were stellar before, just saying that even if they weren't, at least I was still having sex. Now I'm like a freshly minted monk. Struggling with the call of old habits, but knowing that they're pointless because there is only one thing that can actually fulfill me.

Lost deep in thought, I fold my arms behind my head. None

of these things I feel fucking matter.

I didn't get the job in LA and she doesn't live here. It's a fool's errand chasing after that woman. Besides, she's probably already on to the next man that's willing to move heaven and Earth just to be with her. Hell, I almost uprooted my life halfway across the world just for a chance.

But it's time to be real with myself. I need to stop acting like some barmy love sick puppy and move the fuck *on*.

Moving.

Damnit, that's right.

I roll onto my side, grabbing my phone. I forgot to transfer the money into my account for my half of the deposit.

Alex and I have found the perfect flat. It's on the other side of Wimbledon, closer to the shops. I couldn't imagine living in any other neighborhood, when this one just feels so much like home. We meet the agent on Sunday to sign the papers and move in on the fifteenth.

Christ. That's in three weeks.

Pulling up Google calendar, I make a note for the moving day followed by ten reminders leading up to the actual move. Because let's face it, my ex-stoner brain is absolute shit at remembering.

I am finishing up a few other notes for Alex when my phone rings with a message from Nayelli.

So I have some news…

10:01 p.m.

She's pregnant with my child, isn't she?

The phone drops on my face, crashing into my mouth, and busting my lip.

Son of a fucking bitch.

I race to the bathroom and grab a cold towel. As I return back to bed, my terrible maths catches up to me and I realize once again that I am mental. She hasn't been here in over four months. Furthermore, she was just on Snapchat taking a shot with her mom at some family birthday party.

Why does my mind keep going there?

Oh yeah, because I am an idiot. No, more than that. I am an idiot sandwich. Gordon Ramsey would be disgusted.

Holding the compress to my busted lip, I sit up — one leg on the floor — staring at her message. I should ignore it. I have to ignore it. I *will* ignore it.

What's the news?
10:10 p.m.
I hate myself.
At the beginning of the month
I applied to study abroad for the summer.
10:12 p.m.
I received my letter this
Morning saying that I was approved.
10:13 p.m.
Well done, you. Congrats
Nemo. Very proud.
10:15 p.m.
Where abouts?
10:16 p.m.
Sussex
10:19 p.m.

My throat dries up and constricts. The phone slips out my hands, this time colliding with my big toe on the floor. I barely register the needles of pain stabbing my toe. I don't even bend to pick it back up.

What does this mean?

251

I stand and pace, slightly limping from my recent injury.

Did she apply because of me? I hope not. I'm no one special. But then why here? Shouldn't she go somewhere she hasn't been?

Excitement surges through me, knocking me off my feet and into my computer chair. None of that really matters, does it?

I get to be with Nayelli again.

The next morning, I am happy to the point of disgusting Alex at the breakfast table. Dad had to run out for work, but Mum has been extra attentive lately making breakfast and dinner for us almost every day since we move out in a few weeks. This morning it's Alex's favorite: French toast, eggs, and bacon.

"Mum, make him stop," Alex complains over his coffee.

She sets down her tea and gives me a soft glance. "And what is it you need him to stop, sweetheart?"

"I don't know, his face. Make him stop his face," Alex grumbles. "He's smiling at his toast. No one bloody does that."

"I'm just *happy* Alex. You should try it sometime, yeah?"

"Mm. Take it your date went well then," he smirks.

"Oh, that's exciting! You're taking my advice after all," my mum clasps her hands together, her face lighting up. "Tell me all about it." It's no surprise. I'm twenty-seven. She wants to see me settled soon. Especially since my older brother and his wife are expecting their first child. Which is probably the main motivation behind her whole "still be social" pep talk.

"Ahem." I take my time, clearing my throat and pretending my eggs are superbly interesting. "Nothing to tell. It was terrible."

"Louder, I can't hear you." Alex says.

"Mum, was Alex an accident?"

"Hey!"

"Boys, enough," Mum says, leveling her serious stare between the both of us. I resume picking at my eggs, Alex sips on his coffee.

"You notice she didn't answer," I mumble.

"James!" my mother chastises.

I hold my hands up in truce.

"Whatever happened to that one girl?" my mum asks, slight wrinkles gathering around her mouth in thought.

"Hmm?"

"You know, the one your dad and I met," she explains.

"I don't know who—"

"The one that looks *identical* to Emily," Alex supplies.

"And *how* exactly could you know that? You've never met her." It's my mother who I'm staring at.

"Oh, James calm down. Always so defensive," she fans at me with her hand. "Your father and I just thought she was a sweet girl. Quite stunning, too. She does favor Emily though, dear — if only a little."

"How so? Because she's black?" I arch my brow.

"Oh for the love of all that is holy, don't you go pulling the race card on Mum," Alex chastises.

"James, you *know* they look alike. No need to be rude about it because you're in denial," Mum shoots back.

"But why the need to talk about it behind my back? That's low Mum. I'd expect this betrayal from Alex, but you?" I shake my head.

"We are so glad you decided to pursue acting, dear. The drama suits you," she says.

"Oooohhhh, burned by your own mum. That's gotta hurt," Alex snarks.

"I don't need this." Standing from the table, I slide my chair backwards. Silently, I grab my things to clear my side of the table. They know I don't like talking about her. Do I have a type? Maybe. But who doesn't? Besides, the exterior of a person only goes so far and I would have never made the comparison between the two if they hadn't brought it up. Nayelli is *nothing* like Emily. At all.

Returning from the kitchen, my mother stands to stop me, placing her hand on my shoulder.

"We just care about you, that's all sweetheart. You haven't introduced anyone to us since you and Emily broke up. And you weren't my same James for a long, long time after that. I just don't want you seeing this girl solely because she reminds you of her. I've loved having you here again and your little light has grown so much since you moved back in, but I don't want to see you that sad and broken and having to start over again if it doesn't work out. Is that so bad?"

"No mum, it's not bad at all," I say, wrapping her in a big bear hug, her chestnut bob tickling my nose. "Thanks for being concerned about me, it's sweet. I'm okay though, it's not like that with Nayelli."

"Yes, *Nayelli*, that's her name. But are you absolutely positive it's not?" she asks, breaking the hug to look at me.

"Scout's honor," I promise.

"You were never a Boy Scout," Alex chimes in from the table.

I flip him the bird behind our mum's back. "Piss off and go ruin someone else's morning, Alex."

Nayelli

With each shuffle of the passport control line, my nerves sink deeper into the pit of my stomach. I scroll through different social media apps but run out of things to look at and people to talk to — it's four a.m. in Cali.

More than anything I wish I could call my mom, or even my sister, in the hopes of one of them telling me I'm crazy and should jump on the next plane home. What if I have a terrible time at this school too? What if now that I'm here he freaks out and doesn't want to see me? It could be my anxiety getting the best of me, but with James' mercurial treatment of our relationship, it could also be a reality. Still, I remind myself of what I said when I applied: I am here for the opportunity of a lifetime, not (solely) James. If school turns out to suck, it's not like things were great back home anyway. And if James freaks out and runs away from me, *again*, then so be it. It's his loss. For good this time.

The line shuffles a little more and the resolve from my mini pep talk dissipates. Damnit. Why am I so nervous? I don't remember feeling this way when we first met and that was a blind gamble on a stranger in his own home.

But that was before I got to know the other parts of him. The goofy, adorable, man who loves to sing sad music and tell jokes until I'm bursting at the seams with laughter.

Wow, there really isn't a single hope for me.

The bad with James was — is — heartbreaking, but the good... the good is so good that I've flown halfway across the world at the prospect of a chance. The way that James acts with me when he freaks out is not normal. It's clear that something — or someone — has really fucked him up in all things relationship related.

The memory of our last morning together drifts across my mind. Sitting in front of a train station after New Year's when the dawn was still tucked beneath a blanket of stars and the world refused to stir. All was quiet except for his even breaths that puffed into the cold air and then disappeared. I, on the other hand, felt like I couldn't breathe at all. In that moment, I felt so many things that I said nothing. And in return, he said, *Have a nice life Nayelli.*

Damn. There is literally no way to predict how this might go. The only thing I can do is hope that the pressure of all the maybes and uncertainties doesn't crumble us to ash.

The agent calls me up, halting my reveries. Passport in hand, I march forward not knowing but ever worrying what awaits me on the other side of the border.

*

After a relatively painless airport shuffle, I reach my hotel in the neighborhood of Chelsea and throw my suitcase open to unpack my things into the small closet. School didn't start for another week so I figured I could kill time in London before heading to Sussex. Not even ten minutes in, my phone chimes.

Have you landed?
2:35 p.m.
Yes
2:36 p.m.
What are you doing?

2:36 p.m.
Unpacking.
2:39 p.m.

My phone rings and it takes everything to not throw the phone down and pretend like I didn't see the call.

"Hello?" I answer, my heart pounding in my throat.

"Heeeeyyy you! Welcome back to London!" James says, excitement oozing out of his voice.

"Thanks." His cheerful welcome eases my lips into a smile.

"So, what are you doing?" he asks.

"I just told you," I chuckle, "unpacking."

"Wanna help me move?" he asks casually.

"Umm... what?" I blink, not quite sure if I heard him correctly. Did he mention before that he was moving? I struggle to remember him saying anything about it in our previous calls.

"I've gotten most of it moved to the new flat already. I'm at my parents' now grabbing the last of my things. Would you like to come help?"

"Now?" I ask.

"Yes, now," he laughs.

"Uh, sure. Just message me your parents' address."

"Will do, see you soon Nemo!" he replies and then hangs up.

I sit down on the tiny twin bed to call my Uber. Staring at my jacket draped across the foot of the bed I think about what else I should take with me. My mind draws a blank. I wasn't planning on seeing him just yet, let alone helping him move.

I look down at my skirt and crop top that I traveled in. Dear god, I look like I'm trying too hard. I opt for my old, faded jeans with the hole on the left knee and a white T-shirt. *Better.*

A few minutes later, Uber notifies me that my driver has arrived. I grab my purse and jacket and dash outside, not even bothering to tell the man behind the tiny front desk window hello.

Walking up to the silver Prius with the flashing lights, I say a quick prayer, and for the love of god I hope it gets answered. *Please, just once. Let his parents be gone out of the house this time.*

James

When it comes to certain things, I tend to be a bit obsessive. But Nayelli doesn't know that side of me and I don't feel like explaining, so when she asks why I have to unpack my entire room tonight I pretend I don't hear her. Clutter makes me fucking mental. And now that I think about it, uncleanliness in general. So much so, I am organizing my handmade clay figurines on the built-in shelf instead of spending time with the girl of my dreams.

By the time my electric applause sign is mounted above my computer desk, my clothes stored in the closet, and my instruments and their stands erected in the corner, Nayelli is fast asleep atop the duvet. I finish with my last bit of rubbish and small box of knick-knacks before sitting at the foot of the bed.

Dodginess aside, I feel compelled to watch her for a bit. Her chest rises and falls in the same rhythmic way it did in my arms all those months ago. She kicked off her shoes when she arrived but is still fully dressed in jeans, and jacket, the jet lag from the eleven-hour flight catching up with her. I want to ask her why she's here, why she *really* came back because it wasn't just for school, was it? My mouth moves to form the words but they choke and sputter to a stop in my throat.

What if I don't like her answer?

This moment — her here in my room, warm-bodied and as sleepy as always — is something that I have dreamed about since she left. Am I willing to burst our happy bubble over asking a question that doesn't matter?

I truly thought I would never see her again. Yet, here she is, curled up in my bed like she belongs here and as beautiful as the night I first laid eyes on her.

The applause sign lights up with intermittent colors, casting Nayelli's face in first blue, then green, and now red. My fingers move to stroke the dark curls back from her face. Her lips are slightly parted as she breathes softly, her eyes — that I have come to adore because of the life that lives behind them — closed and framed by dark lashes. Nayelli's eyes have a mind of their own and tell me everything that she is too afraid to, and it is sometimes them that I look to for answers, not her words.

It's painfully obvious that she edits so much of herself when we talk. I've lost count how many times she's started to say something but abruptly cut it off with a 'never mind'. Hasn't she realized by now that there's nothing she could do or say to make me not like her? Trust me, I've tried and have failed so many times that I have given up indefinitely. As much as I pretend it's doable, being without her presence just feels bloody fucking miserable.

My hand resumes its exploration of her face and finds a home in the cradle of her neck. My thumb strokes tenderly across her smooth cheek, and I call her name in hopes of waking her up.

"Nayelli? Nayelli, wake up."

I have said this many times and I will say it again: I hate affection. I really do. It usually turns my stomach into knots and I break out in a sweat and need to throw up. I become violently ill, I swear it. But when I say I cannot control the urge to melt into this woman and give her all of the disgusting adoration that I abhor so much, please believe that I am telling the truth. I do not know who I am with her, but it is clear that I am someone else because normal James would never *ever* behave in such a traitorous manner.

Her eyelids flutter open and upon recognizing my face, she leans her face further into my palm and gives a slow, sleepy grin. "Hey you," she says.

"There she is," I answer and smile back. "You were snoring so loud I thought I was going to have to call for help. You should really get that checked out."

"I do not snore!" she protests grumpily and moves my hand from her face.

"Nemo, I hate to be the one to break it to you, but yes you do."

She squints her eyes down to slits but says nothing more. Sitting up, she rubs her eyes and stretches her arms. "How long have I been out?"

"I'm not sure. It's well after midnight though, I believe."

"Jeez! I'm sorry," she says, pouting like she's disappointed in herself for falling asleep.

"I forgive you," I chuckle and shake my head and she laughs too. "Can I get you anything? Food? Water? Nose strips?"

Nayelli rolls her eyes at the last part. "No, thank you."

"Well, then," I begin. Feeling the need to be closer to her, I trail my fingertips lightly down her forearm. "What do you want to do?"

"The same thing you want to," she replies softly.

Even with the lights dimmed and the colors of the applause sign pulsing, her eyes visibly melt into chocolate pools of desire and I am a young lad again who can't control his stiffies. *Christ.*

Nayelli divests of her jacket and tee shirt and I follow suit with disrobing my own clothes. She fumbles with the button of her jeans, but I brush her hand away.

Gently, I pull her body to the center of the bed then tug off her jeans. She's wearing matching black lace undies again — like the first night. I sit back on my heels and take a moment to look at her.

"What?" she asks, knitting her eyebrows in confusion.

"It's umm — you are so beautiful Nayelli. It's seriously ridiculous." I shake my head in disbelief. Will it always feel this way? Will I always be sucked in like a magnet at the merest glimpse of her? Whatever drug she is to my veins, whatever hold it is that she has over me, I hope it never leaves.

"So are you," she says, reaching up to stroke my chest.

My eyes close at the sensation and I pull her palm to my lips for a kiss before entrapping her wrists and placing her hands on the bed above her head. Her mouth pops into an "O" and her back arches, her breast pushing into my chest. With one hand I hold her enclosed wrists, with the other I undo her bra with the flick of my fingers. Her brow arches at me, her eyes cast in a knowing gleam. It's not the first time I've impressed her with that move.

After sliding off her bra, I resume holding her wrists and crane my neck down to taste her gorgeous nipples. First the right, then the left. Faint notes of sweet citrus zings on my tongue, just how I remember. I take my time kissing my way down her body. Her breath speeds up in time with my hands and mouth sinking lower. When my lips reach the edge of her panties, I draw back onto my heels to look at her once more.

"You—" I start, but can't seem to find the words to finish. I distracted myself with unpacking so I wouldn't have to face the feelings that have been zipping through me and threatening to make me burst from the inside out. She's patiently quiet while I struggle to find the words to coherently express what these feelings even are. But I want — no, *need* — her to know that she affects the bloody hell out of me. Nayelli's curls frame her head in a halo, her eyes — appearing even more sultry under the red light — wait patiently for me to speak. Her body, when laying down like this, looks like a sculpted vision. I want to take all fucking night; I want to immortalize this, her; I want to never know what it's like for her to leave me again. "You are like my own fantasy come to life," I say, my face hovering above her thighs. "If someone asked me what my dreams are made of — I'd tell them you."

In one clean swoop, I slide her panties to the side and taste the fucking delicious woman that is Nayelli. Surprise pleasure erupts from her mouth in a moan, "Mmmm, damn you James," she chastises, grabbing my hair and pulling me in closer. She tastes so good, but then again she always does. My tongue slides higher and I replace its old position with my finger, dancing at the entrance of her. "Please," she whimpers.

"Open your eyes," I ask, and she obliges. Holding her gaze, I lick my middle finger then slip it slowly inside of her while continuing the swirling dance of my tongue on her clit. As I reach the end of my knuckle she makes the most erotic sound I have ever heard.

A second finger joins the first and I stroke her delicately, but firmly, wanting her just at the edge but not completely falling. Nayelli's breaths come fast in pants, her fingers clawing at the sheets, her core squeezing my fingers tighter and I know she's close.

"I think I'm going to... mmm... Inside me... please... I need to feel you." Her words come out as a broken plea.

I release my mouth and hand to hover above her. Already hard as a fucking rock, I stroke myself with her wetness before teasing it in circles at her entrance. "Grab a condom from that nightstand drawer," I say, tilting my chin to the bedside table.

This way, I can put my self-induced pregnancy scares to rest.

She curves her body and grabs the first one her hand touches, then hands it to me, a reproachful look on her face. "If we're going to be using condoms now, it kinda defeats the purpose if you rub your dick all over me and *then* put it on."

"Hmm," I muse, rolling the condom on and tossing the wrapper to the floor. She's right. I have to be better about that.

As I lean down over Nayelli again, she reaches between us to stroke me. The pressure from her little squeezes at the base of me makes my eyes roll. Her other hand reaches up to tangle in my hair and pull me down for a kiss. We bite and kiss and taste each other as if within our touch lies a cure for our addiction.

She doesn't miss a beat, never breaking our kiss while guiding me with her hand to where we need each other most.

The second that I am finally inside her is something divine.

A grunt that I have been holding back escapes at the same time she gasps from the new fullness. I slide deeper and her hands still my movements, her eyes popping open wide.

"Are you okay?"

"Yes," she whispers, "I just... the first time you enter me is always so *good*. I want to savor it, you know?" she smiles.

"Yeah," I chuckle, "I do." Granting the request, I withdraw painstakingly slowly before sliding in as deep as she'll allow me to. Then repeat my movements again and again. "How's that?" I ask, my voice drawn tight with barely contained self-control.

"You're going to kill me," she answers, her brows drawn together. She pushes against me and in an act of witchcraft switches her position. How Nayelli is now on her hands and knees without ever letting me slip out of her, I haven't a clue. With a devilish grin and matching gleam to her eyes, she throws a knowing look over her shoulder as she begins working me over from her new position. I grab hold of her hips for dear life, while she reaches between her legs and plays with herself.

Our tempo picks up to a rhythm that I know I won't be able to sustain.

"Don't stop. Please... I'm so close." She leans forward into the pillows, her eyes screw shut, her breath grows even choppier, and she tightens around me, squeezing me like a bloody grape.

"Fuck you are so sexy." I grab Nayelli's hair and tilt her head so that I know she hears me. "Let go," I whisper, then release her. "I'm right behind you."

And she does.

She cries out into the pillow as waves pulse through her and force my own climax out of me. An all-consuming pleasure racks through me so viciously that I have to wrap my arms around her waist to keep from collapsing.

"Holy *fuck*," I say, my cheek resting atop her lower back. "That was..."

"I know," she answers.

We untangle and I tidy up by the bin while she goes to the toilet. Upon her return, I open the blankets with a grand sweeping gesture. "Get in here Nemo," I say, a big dumb grin on my face.

At my goofy proposal, a wide grin splits her face and she jumps into bed, snuggling up to me with enthusiasm. "I wanna do that again," she murmurs into my chest.

"Right *now*?" I almost choke on my own spit. "I mean I'm not sure if it's biologically possible but I could always try..."

"Nooo, crazy. Not right now," she giggles. "But... definitely later. We have some time to make up for," She kisses my chest and cuddles deeper.

"I suppose you're right." There is no denying that I have a craving for her that cannot be satiated with one mere shag.

We grow quiet in the dark, the soft music from my computer now loud enough to fill the space.

Nayelli shifts her leg in between mine and the movement wraps me even more in her warmth. My fingers stroke through her soft hair as I listen to her breaths dive deeper into sleep, leaving me alone with my own musings.

I never thought I'd have this again. It's why I struggled so hard in her absence. No amount of FaceTime calls or texts could bring this feeling back. I especially gave up the hope of seeing her after she told me she canceled her flight here for spring break. I really thought I'd never physically see her again. That we would never be here, skin to skin, again.

And this time not only is she back but she's back for uni. Meaning she isn't leaving anywhere for a while.

I could show her my favorite market in Brixton, or my parent's beach home up the way, or the best chicken and chips shop in town or…

Ticking off a list makes me realize that the more things I want to do with Nayelli, the more it's starting to sound an awful lot like a relationship.

Ice cold fear constricts in my chest, making it hard to breathe. My arms twitch in reflex, grabbing her tighter but she stays asleep.

Am I the man in the flood? Waiting for some kind of divine intervention and all the while letting a boat pass me by?

Nayelli is everything I've ever wanted. *Everything.* And that thought alone scares me positively shitless.